*The Turkish Gambit*

# BORIS AKUNIN

Translated by Andrew Bromfield

RANDOM HOUSE
LARGE PRINT

*The*

# TURKISH
# GAMBIT

*A Novel*

Translation copyright © 2005 by Random House, Inc.

This work was originally published in Russian in 1998. Copyright © 1998 by Boris Akunin.

All rights reserved.
Published in the United States of America
by Random House Large Print in association
with Random House, New York.
Distributed by Random House, Inc., New York.

**The Library of Congress has established a Cataloging-in-Publication record for this title.**

0-375-43466-6

www.randomlargeprint.com

FIRST LARGE PRINT EDITION

10  9  8  7  6  5  4  3  2  1

This Large Print edition published in accord with the standards of the N.A.V.H.

*The Turkish Gambit*

# CHAPTER ONE

—ɯ—

## In which a progressive woman finds herself in a quite desperate situation

## LA REVUE PARISIENNE (Paris) 14 (2) July 1877

Our correspondent, now already in his second week with the Russian Army of the Danube, informs us that in his order of the day for yesterday, 1st July (13th July in the European style), the Emperor Alexander thanks his victorious troops, who have succeeded in forcing a crossing of the Danube and breaching the borders of the Ottoman state. His Imperial Majesty's order affirms that the enemy has been utterly crushed and in no more than two weeks' time at the very most the Orthodox cross will be raised over Saint Sophia in Constantinople. The advancing army is encountering almost no resistance, unless one takes into account the mosquito bites inflicted on the Russian lines of communication by flying detachments of the so-called Bashi-Bazouks ("mad-heads"), a species of half-bandit and half-partisan, famed for their savage disposition and blood-thirsty ferocity.

ACCORDING TO ST. AUGUSTINE, woman is a frail and fickle creature, and the great obscurantist and misogynist was right a thousand times over—at least with regard to a certain individual by the name of Varvara Suvorova.

It had all started out as such a jolly adventure, but now it had come to this. She only had her own stupid self to blame—Mama had told Varya time and again that sooner or later she would land herself in a fix, and now she had. In the course of one of their many tempestuous altercations, her father, a man of great wisdom and endowed with the patience of a saint, had divided his daughter's life into three periods: the imp in a skirt; the perfect nuisance; the loony nihilist. To this day Varya prided herself on this characterization, declaring that she had no intention of resting on her laurels as yet, but this time her self-confidence had landed her in a world of trouble.

Why on earth had she agreed to make a halt at the tavern—this **korchma,** or whatever it was they called the abominable dive? Her driver, that dastardly thief Mitko, had started whining, using those peculiar Bulgarian endings: "Let's water the hossesta, let's water the hossesta." So they had stopped to water the horses. Oh, God, what was she going to do now?

Varya was sitting in the corner of a dingy and utterly filthy shed at a table of rough-hewn planks, frightened to death. Only once before had she ever experienced such grim, hopeless terror: when at the age of six she broke her grandmother's favorite teacup and hid under the divan to await the inevitable retribution.

If she could only pray—but progressive women didn't pray. And, meanwhile, the situation looked absolutely desperate.

So . . . the St. Petersburg–Bucharest leg of her route had been traversed rapidly enough, even comfortably: The express train (two passenger coaches and ten flatcars carrying artillery pieces) had rushed Varya to the capital of the principality of Romania in three days. The brown eyes of the lady with the cropped hair, who smoked **papyrosa**s and refused on principle to allow her hand to be kissed, had very nearly set the army officers and staff functionaries bound for the theater of military operations at one another's throats. At every halt Varya was presented with bouquets of flowers and baskets of strawberries. She threw the bouquets out the window, because they were vulgar, and soon she was obliged to forswear the strawberries as well, because they brought her out in a rash. It had turned out to be a rather amusing and pleasant journey, although, from an intellectual and ideological perspective, of course, all her suitors were complete worms. There was, to be sure, one cornet who was reading Lamartine and had even heard of Schopenhauer, and he had been more subtle in paying court to her than the others, but Varya had explained to him—as one comrade to another—that she was traveling to join her fiancé, after which the cornet's behavior had been quite irreproachable. He had not been at all bad-looking, either, rather like Lermontov. Oh, to hell with the cornet.

The second stage of her journey had also gone off without a hitch. There was a stagecoach that ran from Bucharest to Turnu-Magurele. She had been obliged to swallow a little dust as she bounced and jolted along, but it had brought her within arm's reach of her goal—for rumor had it that the general headquarters of the Army of the Danube was located on the far side of the river, in Tsarevitsy.

This was the point at which she had to put

into effect the final and most crucial part of The Plan that she had worked out back in St. Petersburg (that was what Varya called it to herself—"The Plan," with capital letters). Yesterday evening, under cover of darkness, she had crossed the Danube in a boat a little above Zimnitsa, where two weeks previously the heroic Fourteenth Division under General Dragomirov had completed a forced crossing of that formidable water barrier. This was the beginning of Turkish territory, the zone of military operations, and it would certainly be only too easy to slip up here. There were Cossack patrols roaming the roads, and if she ever let her guard down she was as good as done for—she would be packed off back to Bucharest in the blink of an eye. But Varya was a resourceful girl, so she had anticipated this and taken appropriate measures.

The discovery of a coaching inn in the Bulgarian village on the south bank of the Danube had been a really great stroke of luck, and after that things had gone from good to better; the landlord understood Russian and had promised to give her a reliable **vodach**—a guide—for only five rubles. Varya had bought wide trousers much like Turkish **chalvars**, a shirt, boots, a sleeveless jacket, and an idiotic cloth cap, and the change of clothes had instantly transformed her from a European lady into a skinny Bulgarian youth who would not arouse the slightest suspicion from any patrol. She had deliberately commissioned a round-about route, avoiding the marching columns, in order to enter Tsarevitsy not from the north, but from the south. And there, in the general army headquarters, was Pyotr Yablokov, Varya's . . . Well, actually, it is not quite clear who he is. Her fiancé? Her comrade? Her husband? Let us call him her former husband and future fiancé. And also—naturally—her comrade.

They had set out while it was still dark on a creaky, ramshackle **carutza,** a Romanian-style cart. Her **vodach,** Mitko, tight-lipped with a gray mustache, chewed tobacco all the while, constantly ejecting long streams of brown spittle onto the road. (Varya winced every time he did it.) At first he had crooned some exotic Balkan melody; then he had fallen silent and sunk into a reverie—it was clear enough now what ideas he had been entertaining.

He could have killed me, Varya thought with a shudder. Or even worse. And without the slightest problem—who would bother investigating in these parts? They would just blame those, what's-their-names, Bashi-Bazouks.

But though things may have stopped short of murder, they had turned out quite badly enough. That traitor Mitko had led his female traveling companion to a tavern that more than anything else resembled a bandit's den. He had seated her at a table and ordered some cheese and a jug of wine to be brought, while he himself turned back toward the door, gesturing as much as to say: I'll be back in a moment. Varya had dashed after him, not wishing to be left alone in this dim, dirty, and distinctly malodorous sink of iniquity, but Mitko had said he needed to step outside—not to put too fine an edge on it—in order to satisfy a call of nature. When Varya did not understand, he had explained his meaning with a gesture and she had returned to her seat, covered in confusion.

The duration of the call of nature had exceeded all conceivable limits. Varya ate a little of the salty, unappetizing cheese, took a sip of the sour wine, and then, unable any longer to endure the curiosity that the fearsome denizens of the public house had begun to evince toward her person, she went out into the yard.

Outside the door, she froze in horror.

There was not a trace of the **carutza** or of the trunk with all her things that it contained. Her traveling medicine chest was in the trunk, and in the medicine chest, between the lint and the bandages, lay her passport and absolutely all her money.

Varya was just about to run out onto the road when the landlord, with a bright crimson nose and warts on his cheek, had come darting out of the **korchma** in his red shirt. He shouted angrily and gestured: Pay up first, and then you can leave. Varya went back inside because the landlord had frightened her and she had nothing with which to pay him. She sat down quietly in the corner and tried to think of what had happened as an adventure. But she failed miserably.

There was not a single woman in the tavern. The dirty, loud-mouthed yokels behaved quite unlike Russian peasants, who are quiet and inoffensive and talk among themselves in low voices until they get drunk, while these louts were bawling raucously as they downed red wine by the tankard, constantly erupting into loud and predatory (or so it seemed to Varya) laughter. At a long table on the far side of the room they were playing dice, breaking into uproarious disputes at every throw. On one occasion when they fell to quarrelling more loudly than usual, a small man who was extremely drunk was struck over the head with a clay tankard. He lay there sprawled under the table and nobody paid the slightest attention to him.

The landlord nodded in Varya's direction and

made some crude remark, at which the men sitting at nearby tables turned in her direction and roared with malevolent laughter. Varya squirmed and tugged her cap down over her eyes. Nobody else in the tavern was wearing a cap, but she couldn't take it off or her hair would come tumbling down. Not that it was really long—Varya wore her hair short, as befitted a modern woman—but even so it would betray her as a member of the weaker sex. That disgusting designation invented by men—"the weaker sex." But, alas, it was only too true.

Now their eyes were boring into Varya from every side, and their glances were oily and repulsive. The only ones who seemed to have no time for her were the dice players and a dejected-looking type seated two tables away with his back to her, his nose buried in a tankard of wine. All she could see of him was a head of short-trimmed black hair, graying at the temples.

Varya began to feel really terrified. Stop sniveling, she said to herself. You're a strong, grown-up woman, not some prim young lady. You have to tell them you're Russian and you're traveling to join your fiancé in the army. We are the liberators of Bulgaria; everyone here is glad to see us. And then, speaking Bulgarian is so easy, you just have to add "ta" to everything.

Russian armyta. Fiancéta. Fiancéta of Russian soldierta. Or something of the sort.

She turned toward the window—maybe Mitko would suddenly turn up. Maybe he had taken the horses to the watering place and now he was on his way back. But, alas, there was no sign of Mitko or any **carutza** out on the dusty street. Varya did, however, notice something that had failed to catch her attention earlier: Protruding above the houses was a low minaret covered in chipped and peeling paint. Oh! Could the village possibly be Muslim? But the Bulgarians were Christians, Orthodox, everybody knew that. What's more, they were drinking wine, and that was forbidden to Muslims by the Koran. But if the village was Christian, then what on earth did the minaret mean? And if it was Muslim, then whose side were they on, ours or the Turks'? Hardly ours. It looked as though the "armyta" might not be much help after all.

Oh, Lord, what was she to do?

At the age of fourteen, in a Holy Scripture class, little Varya Suvorova had been struck by an idea so unimpeachable in its very obviousness that it was hard to believe nobody had ever thought of it before. If God created Adam first and Eve afterward, far from demonstrating that men were more important, it showed that women were more perfect. Man was the experimental prototype of the human being, the rough draft, while woman was the final, approved version, as revised and amended. Why, it was as clear as day! But for some reason the real and interesting side of life belonged exclusively to the men, and all the women did was have children and do embroidery, then have more children and do more embroidery. Why was there such injustice in the world? Because men were stronger. And that meant she had to be strong.

And so little Varya had decided she was going to live her life differently. The United States already had the first woman doctor in Mary Jacobi and the first woman minister in Antoinette Blackwell, while life in Russia was still riddled with dodoism and patriarchical discipline. But never mind—just give her time.

On graduating from girls' high school, Varya had emulated the United States in waging a victorious war of independence (her papa, the solicitor Suvorov, proved to be a spineless weakling) and started training to be a midwife—thereby making the transition from "perfect nuisance" to "loony nihilist."

The training did not work out well. Varya mastered the theoretical part with no difficulty, although she found many aspects of the process of creating a human being astonishing, even incredible, but when her turn came to assist at an actual birth, it had proved very embarrassing. Unable to bear the heart-rending howls of the woman giving birth and the terrible sight of the flattened head of the infant as it emerged from the tormented and bloody flesh, Varya had disgraced herself by slumping to the floor in a dead faint, after which the only course left open to her had been to study to be a telegraphist. It had been flattering at first to become one of the first female telegraphists in Russia—they had even written about Varya in the **St. Petersburg Gazette** (an article entitled "Long Overdue" in the issue of 28 November 1875), but the job had proved to be boring beyond all endurance and without any prospects of advancement whatsoever.

And so Varvara, to her parents' relief, had taken herself off to their Tambov estate—not to idle her time away, but to nurture and educate the local peasant children. It was there, in a brand-new school building still exuding the scent of fresh pinewood sawdust, that she had met the St. Petersburg student Pyotr Yablokov, her Petya. Pyotr taught arithmetic, geography, and basic natural science, while Varvara taught all the other subjects. Quite soon, however, the peasants had realized that there were neither wages nor any other form of recompense to be earned by attending school, and they had taken their children back home—enough of that loafing about, there's work to be done! But by that time Varya and Petya had already mapped out the course of their future life: free, modern, founded on mutual respect and a rational division of responsibilities.

She had put an end to humiliating dependence on her parents' handouts and they had returned to St. Petersburg and rented an apartment on the Vyborg side of the river—with mice, but also with three whole rooms—in order to be able to live like Vera Pavlovna and Lopukhov in Chernyshevski's **What Is to Be Done?** They each had their own territory and the third room was reserved for one-to-one discussions and receiving guests. To the landlords they had called themselves husband and wife, but their cohabitation was exclusively comradely in nature: In the evening they would read, drink tea, and converse in the communal living room, then they wished each other good night and went to their separate rooms. They had lived in this way for almost a year, and lived very well, in perfect harmony, without any vulgarity or filth. Pyotr studied at the university and gave lessons and Varvara qualified as a stenographer and earned as much as a hundred rubles a month. She kept the records of court proceedings and took down the memoirs of a crazy old general, the conqueror of Warsaw, and then on the recommendation of friends she had found herself taking the dictation of a novel for a Great Writer (we shall dispense with names, since the arrangement ended unpleasantly). Varya regarded the Great Writer with veneration and had absolutely refused to accept any payment, feeling that she was quite fortunate enough to be doing such work at all, but the intellectual luminary had misinterpreted her refusal. He was terribly old, over fifty, burdened with a large family, and not at all good-looking, but there was no denying that he spoke eloquently and convincingly: Virginity really was a ridiculous prejudice, bourgeois morality was repulsive, and there was nothing shameful about human nature. Varya had listened and then consulted for hours on end with her Petya about what she ought to do. Petya agreed that chastity and hypocritical piety were shackles imposed on women, but he resolutely counseled her against entering into physiological relations with the Great Writer. He grew heated and attempted to demonstrate that the Writer was not so very Great after all, even though he did have past services to his credit—that many progressive people actually regarded him as a reactionary. It all ended, as previously mentioned, unpleasantly. One day the Great Writer, breaking off the dictation of a scene of exceptional power (Varya was writing with tears in her eyes), began breathing noisily, then he gave a loud snort, embraced his brown-haired stenographer clumsily around the shoulders, and dragged her over to the divan. For a while she endured his unintelligible whisperings and the touch of his trembling fingers, which had become hopelessly entangled in her hooks and buttons, until suddenly she realized quite clearly—she did not, in fact, understand it so much as sense it—that this was all wrong and simply could not happen. She shoved the Great Writer away, ran out of the room, and never went back.

This story produced a negative effect on Pyotr. It was March, spring had come early, the breeze blowing from the Neva was redolent of open spaces and drifting ice, and he had given her an ultimatum. Things could not go on as they were—they were made for each other, their relations had stood the test of time. They were both flesh and blood and they had no business attempting to defy the laws of nature. Of course, he would settle for carnal love without a wedding ceremony, but it would be better to get married properly, since that would spare them numerous complications. And somehow he had managed to put things so cleverly that afterward only one thing was discussed—what kind of wedding they should have, civil or church. The arguments continued until April, but in April the long-expected war for the liberation of the Russian people's Slavic brethren had broken out, and as a man of honor Pyotr Yablokov had signed up as a volunteer. Before his departure, Varya had promised him two things: that she would soon give him her definitive answer and that they would assuredly fight together side by side—somehow she would think of a way.

And so she had. Not immediately, but she had thought of a way. She had failed to get a job as a nurse in a temporary military infirmary or a field hospital—they refused to take her incomplete midwifery studies into consideration. Nor were female telegraphists being taken on for active army service. Varya had been on the point of succumbing to despair when a letter arrived from Romania: Petya complained that he had not been allowed to join the infantry because of his flat feet and had been retained at headquarters on the staff of the commander-in-chief, the grand duke Nikolai Nikolaievich—because volunteer Yablokov was a mathematician and the army was desperately short of cryptographers.

It would not be too difficult to find some kind of work at general headquarters, Varya had decided, or, if worst came to worst, simply to lose herself in the hurly-burly at the rear, and she had immediately formulated The Plan, of which the first two stages had worked so wonderfully, but the third had culminated in disaster.

Meanwhile, events were moving to a conclusion. The crimson-nosed landlord mumbled something menacing and began waddling toward Varya, wiping his hands on a gray towel and looking, in his red shirt, much like an executioner approaching the block. Her mouth went dry and she felt sick. Perhaps she should pretend to be deaf and dumb?

The dejected type sitting with his back to her rose unhurriedly to his feet, walked over to Varya's table, and sat down across from her without a word. She saw a pale face, almost boyish despite the graying temples, with cold blue eyes, a thin mustache, and an unsmiling mouth. It was a strange face, quite unlike the faces of the other peasants, although the stranger was dressed in the same way they were—except that his jacket was a little newer and his shirt cleaner.

The blue-eyed stranger did not even glance round at the landlord; he merely waved his hand dismissively and the menacing executioner immediately withdrew behind his counter. Varya, however, felt none the calmer for it. On the contrary, indeed, the most terrifying part was only just about to begin.

She wrinkled her forehead, readying herself for the sound of foreign speech. Better if she didn't talk but merely nodded or shook her head. Only she mustn't forget that the Bulgarians did everything in reverse: When you nodded it meant "no," when you shook your head it meant "yes."

The blue-eyed man, however, did not ask her any questions. He sighed dejectedly and spoke to her with a slight stammer in perfect Russian: "Ah, m-mademoiselle, you would have done better to wait for your fiancé at home. This is not a novel by Mayne Reid. Things could have t-turned out very badly."

# CHAPTER TWO

—ɯ—

## In which many interesting men appear

## THE RUSSIAN INVALID
### (St. Petersburg)
### 2 (14) July 1877

Following the conclusion of an armistice between the Sublime Porte and Serbia, many patriots of the Slavic cause, valiant knights of the Russian land who served as volunteers under the leadership of the courageous General Chernyaev, have hearkened to the call of the Tsar-Liberator and at the risk of their lives are making their way over wild mountains and through dark forests to the land of Bulgaria, in order to be re-united with the Orthodox Christian forces and crown their sacred feat of arms with the long-awaited victory.

VARYA DID NOT IMMEDIATELY grasp the meaning of what had been said. Out of inertia she first nodded, then shook her head, and only after that did she open her mouth wide in amazement.

"Don't be surprised," the strange peasant said in a dull voice. "The fact that you are a g-girl is immediately obvious—a strand of your hair has crept out from under your cap on that side. That is one." (Varya furtively tucked the mutinous curl back into place.) "The fact that you are Russian is also obvious: the snub nose, the Great Russian line of the cheekbones, the light brown hair, and most important—the absence of any suntan. That is two. As for your fiancé, that is equally simple: You are p-proceeding on your way surreptitiously, so you must be on private business. And what private business could a young woman of your age possibly have with an army in the field? Only romance. That makes three. Now for number f-four: That mustachioed fellow who brought you in here and then disappeared was your guide? And, of course, your money was hidden among your things? F-foolish. You should keep everything of importance about your p-person. What is your name?"

"Varya Suvorova, Varvara Andreevna Suvorova," Varya whispered, frightened. "Who are you? Where are you from?"

"Erast Petrovich Fandorin. A Serbian volunteer. I am making my way home from Turkish captivity."

Thank God! Varya had already decided he must be a hallucination. A Serbian volunteer! From Turkish captivity! Glancing reverentially at his gray temples, she was unable to refrain from asking, and even pointing impolitely with her finger: "Is that because they tortured you there? I've read about the horrors of Turkish captivity. And I suppose that's what caused your stammer, too?"

Erast Fandorin frowned and replied reluctantly. "Nobody tor-tured me. They plied me with coffee from morning till night and conversed exclusively in French. I lived as a guest with the k-kaimakam of Vidin."

"With whom?"

"Vidin is a town on the Romanian border. And a kaimakam is a governor. As for the stammer, that is a c-consequence of an old concussion."

"So you escaped?" she asked enviously. "And you're on your way to the active army to continue the fight?"

"No, I have done quite enough fighting already."

Varya's face must have expressed extreme bewilderment. In any event, the volunteer felt it necessary to elucidate.

"War, Varvara Andreevna, is abominable and disgusting. In war no one is right and no one is wrong. And there are good men and bad on both sides. Only the good are usually k-killed first."

"Then why did you go to Serbia as a volunteer?" she asked heatedly. "Nobody forced you to, I suppose?"

"Out of egotistical considerations. I was unwell and in need of treatment."

Varya was astonished.

"Can people be healed by war?"

"Yes. The sight of others' p-pain makes it easier to bear one's own. I found myself at the front two weeks before Chernyaev's army was routed. After that I had more than my fill of wandering through the mountains and shooting. Thank God, I don't th-think I hit anybody."

He's either trying to strike a pose or he's just a cynic, Varya thought, rather annoyed, and she remarked caustically: "You should have stayed with your kaimakam until the war was over. What point was there in escaping?"

"I did not escape. Yusuf Pasha let me go."

"Then what on earth brought you to Bulgaria?"

"A certain matter," Fandorin replied curtly. "Where were you heading yourself?"

"To Tsarevitsy, to the commander in chief's headquarters. And you?"

"To Bela. Rumor has it that His Majesty's staff is located there." The volunteer paused, knitted his narrow eyebrows briefly in displeasure, and sighed. "But I could go to the commander in chief."

"Really?" Varya exclaimed in delight. "Oh, let's go together, shall we? I really don't know what I would have done if I hadn't met you."

"There is really nothing t-to it. You would have ordered the landlord to deliver you into the custody of the nearest Russian unit, and that would have been the end of the matter."

"Ordered? The landlord of a **korchma**?" Varya asked fearfully.

"This is not a **korchma,** but a **mehana.**"

"Very well, a **mehana.** But the village is Muslim, surely?"

"It is."

"Then they would have handed me over to the Turks."

"I have no wish to offend you, Varvara Andreevna, but you are not of the slightest interest to the Turks, and this way the landlord would m-most certainly have received a reward from your fiancé."

"I would much rather go with you," Varya implored him. "Oh, please!"

"I have one old nag, on its last legs. It cannot take two of us. And all the money I have is three

**kurus**. Enough to pay for the wine and cheese, but no more. . . . We need another horse, or at least a mule. And that will require at least a hundred."

Varya's new acquaintance paused while he pondered something. He glanced across at the dice players and sighed heavily once again.

"Stay here. I shall be back in a moment."

He walked slowly over to the gamblers and stood beside their table for five minutes, observing. Then he said something (Varya could not hear it) that made all of them instantly stop throwing the dice and turn toward him. Fandorin pointed to Varya, who squirmed on her chair under the stares directed at her. Then there was a burst of general laughter—quite obviously lewd and insulting to Varya, but it clearly never even entered Fandorin's head to defend a lady's honor. Instead he shook the hand of one fat man with a mustache and sat down on the bench. The others made room for him and a knot of curious observers rapidly gathered round the table.

It seemed that the volunteer had ventured a bet. But with what money? Three **kurus**? He would have to play for a long time to win a horse. Varya began to worry, realizing she had put her trust in a man she didn't know at all. He looked strange, spoke strangely, acted strangely—but, on the other hand, what choice did she really have?

There was a murmur in the crowd of idle onlookers—the fat man had thrown the dice. Then they clattered once again and the walls shook as the crowd howled in unison.

"T-twelve," Fandorin announced calmly in Bulgarian and stood up. "Where are my winnings?"

The fat man also leapt to his feet, seized the volunteer by his sleeve, and started speaking rapidly, his eyes bulging wildly.

He kept repeating: "Another round, another round!"

Fandorin waited for him to finish before nodding decisively, but his acquiescence apparently failed to satisfy the loser, who began yelling more loudly than before and waving his arms around. Fandorin nodded again, even more decisively, and then Varya recalled the Bulgarian paradox in which a nod meant "no."

At this point the loser decided to move from words to actions—he drew his arm well back and all the idle onlookers shied away, but Erast Fandorin didn't budge, except that his right hand, seemingly inadvertently, slipped rapidly into his pocket. The gesture was almost imperceptible, but its effect on the fat man was magical. He wilted instantly, sobbed, and muttered some plaintive appeal. This time Fandorin shook his head, tossed a couple of coins to the landlord, who had appeared beside him, and set off toward the door. He did not even glance at Varya, but she had no need of an invitation—she was up from her seat and at her rescuer's side in an instant.

"The second l-last," said Erast Fandorin, squinting in concentration as he halted on the porch.

Varya followed the direction of his gaze and saw a long row of horses, mules, and donkeys standing along the hitching rail, calmly munching hay.

"There he is, your B-Bucephalus," said the volunteer, pointing at a small brown donkey. "Not much to look at, but then there's not so far to fall."

"You mean you won it?" Varya asked in sudden realization.

Fandorin nodded without speaking as he unhitched a mangy gray mare.

He helped his traveling companion into the wooden saddle of the donkey, leapt up on to his own gray with considerable agility, and they rode out onto a country road brightly illuminated by the midday sun.

"Is it far to Tsarevitsy?" Varya asked, jolting

in time to the short steps of her fluffy-eared mount.

"If we do not g-go astray, we shall reach it by nightfall," the horseman replied grandly from above her.

He had become totally Turkified in captivity, Varya thought angrily. He could at least have seated the lady on the horse. Typical male narcissism! A preening peacock! A vain drake, interested in nothing but flaunting himself before the dull gray duck. I already look like God only knows what, and now I have to play Sancho Panza to the Knight of the Mournful Visage.

"What have you got in your pocket?" she asked, remembering. "A pistol, is it?"

Fandorin was surprised.

"In what pocket? Ah, in my p-pocket. Nothing, unfortunately."

"I see, and what if he had not been frightened?"

"I would not have sat down to play with someone who would not be frightened."

"But how could you win a donkey with a single throw?" Varya asked inquisitively. "Surely that man didn't bet his donkey against three **kurus**?"

"Of course not."

"Then what did you bet?"

"You," Fandorin replied imperturbably. "A girl for a donkey—now that is a worthwhile wager. I beg your gracious forgiveness, Varvara Andreevna, but there was no alternative."

"Forgiveness!" Varya swayed so wildly in the saddle that she almost slipped over to one side. "What if you had lost?"

"Varvara Andreevna, I happen to possess one unusual quality. I absolutely detest games of chance, but whenever I do happen to play, I am sure to win without fail. **Les caprices de la f-fortune!** I even won my freedom from the pasha of Vidin at backgammon."

Not knowing what reply to make to such a flippant declaration, Varya chose to be mortally offended, and therefore they rode on in silence. The barbarous saddle, a veritable instrument of torture, caused her a host of discomforts, but she endured them all, from time to time shifting her center of gravity.

"Is it too hard?" Fandorin asked. "Would you like to place my jacket under you?"

Varya did not reply because, in the first place, his suggestion seemed to her not entirely proper and, in the second place, it was a point of principle.

The road wound on for a long time between low wooded hills, then descended to a plain. In all this time the travelers encountered no one, and Varya was beginning to feel alarmed. Several times she stole a sideways glance at Fandorin, but the oaf remained absolutely imperturbable and made no further attempt to strike up a conversation.

Wouldn't she cut a fine figure, though, appearing in Tsarevitsy in an outfit like this? It wouldn't matter to Petya, she supposed—she could dress in sack cloth as far as he was concerned. He wouldn't notice, but there would be the headquarters staff, society people. If she turned up looking like a scarecrow. . . . Varya tore her cap off her head, ran her hand through her hair, and felt really depressed. Not that her hair was anything special in any case—it was that dull, mousy color called light brown, and her disguise had left it all tangled and matted. It had last been washed over two days ago in Bucharest. No, she had better wear the cap. A Bulgarian peasant's outfit wasn't so bad after all; it was practical and even striking in its own way. The **chalvars** were actually rather like the famous bloomers English suffragettes used to wear in their rebellion against those absurd and humiliating drawers and petticoats. If only she could draw them in round the waist with a broad scarlet sash, like in Mozart's **Die Entführung aus**

**dem Serail** (she and Petya had seen it last autumn at the Mariinsky Theater), they'd actually be rather picturesque.

Suddenly Varvara Suvorova's musings were interrupted in a most unceremonious fashion. The volunteer leaned over and seized the donkey's bridle, the dumb animal came to an abrupt halt, and Varya was almost sent flying over its long-eared head.

"What's wrong with you, have you gone mad?"

"Whatever happens now, do not say a word," Fandorin said in a quiet and very serious voice, gazing forward along the road.

Varya raised her head and saw an amorphous throng galloping toward them, enveloped in a cloud of dust—a group of riders, probably about twenty men. She could see their shaggy caps and the bright spots of sunlight glinting on their cartridge belts, harnesses, and weapons. One of the horsemen was riding ahead of the rest and Varya could make out a scrap of green cloth wound around his tall fur hat.

"Who are they, Bashi-Bazouks?" Varya asked in a low, tremulous voice. "What will happen now? Are we done for? Will they kill us?"

"I doubt it, as long as you keep quiet," Fandorin replied, somehow not sounding very confident. "Your sudden talkativeness is rather untimely."

He had completely stopped stammering, which alarmed Varya greatly.

Erast Fandorin took the donkey by the bridle once again and moved over to the edge of the road, then he tugged Varya's hat right down over her eyes and whispered: "Keep your eyes on the ground and don't make a sound."

However, she was unable to resist darting a furtive glance at these famous cutthroats about whom all the newspapers had been writing for more than a year.

The one riding ahead (probably the **bek**), with the ginger beard, was wearing a tattered and dirty quilted **beshmet,** but his weapons were silver. He rode past without so much as a glance at the wretched pair of peasants, but his gang proved less standoffish. Several of the riders halted beside Varya and Fandorin, talking among themselves in guttural voices. The Bashi-Bazouks wore expressions that made Varvara Andreevna want to squeeze her eyes tightly shut—she had never suspected that people could have such horrible masks for faces. Then, suddenly, in among these nightmarish visages she caught a glimpse of an entirely normal human face. It was pale, with one eye swollen and bruised, but the second brown eye was staring directly at her with an expression of mortal anguish.

Among the bandits, seated facing backward in the saddle, was a Russian officer in a dusty, tattered uniform. His arms were twisted behind his back, an empty saber scabbard hung round his neck, and there was caked blood at the corner of his mouth. Varya bit her lip in order not to cry out. Unable to bear the hopeless despair that she read in the prisoner's gaze, she lowered her eyes. But even so terror forced a cry, or rather a hysterical sob, from her dry throat, for strapped to the pommel of one of the partisans' saddles was a light-haired human head with a long mustache. Fandorin squeezed Varya's elbow hard and said a few short words in Turkish—she could distinguish the words "Yusuf Pasha" and "kaimakam"—but they made no impression on the bandits. One of them, with a pointed beard and an immense crooked nose, pulled back the upper lip of Fandorin's horse, baring the long, rotten teeth. He spat contemptuously and said something that made the others laugh. Then he lashed the nag on its crupper with his whip and the startled beast shied off, immediately breaking into an uneven trot. Varya struck at the donkey's bloated sides with her heels and trudged after Fandorin's horse, afraid to believe the danger was past. The world was swirling around her; that nightmarish head with its eyes closed in suffering and the blood caked in the corners of its mouth tormented her. Cutthroats are people who cut throats—the absurd, delirious phrase kept running round and round in her head.

"No fainting, if you please," Fandorin said quietly. "They could come back."

It was tempting fate. A moment later they heard the drumming of hooves approaching from behind.

Erast Fandorin glanced round and whispered: "Do not turn around. F-forward."

Varya, however, did turn around, although it would have been better if she had not. They had ridden about two hundred paces away from the Bashi-Bazouks, but one of the horsemen—the one with the severed head—was galloping back again and rapidly overtaking them, with that terrible trophy bouncing merrily against the flank of his steed.

Varya glanced despairingly at her companion, but his customary presence of mind seemed to have deserted him. He had thrown back his head and was nervously quaffing water from a large copper canteen.

The accursed donkey plodded along in a melancholy fashion, absolutely refusing to walk any faster. A few moments later, the impetuous horseman drew level with the unarmed travelers and reared up his bay. Leaning down, the Bashi-Bazouk grabbed Varya's cap from her head and burst into rapacious laughter when her light-brown hair came tumbling down.

"Kadin!" he cried with a gleam of white teeth.

In one swift movement the gloomily preoccupied Erast Fandorin snatched off the bandit's tall, shaggy hat and swung the heavy canteen hard against back of his shaven head. There was a sickeningly moist thud, the flask glugged, and the Bashi-Bazouk went tumbling into the dust.

"To hell with the donkey! Give me your hand. Into the saddle. Ride for all you're worth. Don't look back!" Fandorin rattled out in staccato fashion, once again without any stammer.

He helped the numbed Varya up onto the bay, pulled the rifle out of its saddle holster, and they set off at a gallop.

The bandit's horse went hurtling forward and Varya pulled her head down into her shoulders, afraid that she wouldn't be able to keep her seat. The wind whistled in her ears, her left leg slipped out of the overlong stirrup at just the wrong moment, shots rang out behind her, and something heavy thumped painfully against her right hip.

Varya glanced down briefly, saw the mottled, blotchy skin of the severed head jostling up and down, and gave a strangled cry, letting go of the reins, which she should not have done under any circumstance.

The next moment she went flying out of the saddle, describing an arc through the air and landing heavily in something green, yielding, and rustling—a bush at the side of the road.

This was just the right moment for her to slip into unconsciousness, but somehow it didn't happen. Varya sat there on the grass, holding her scratched cheek, with broken branches swaying around her.

Meanwhile, events were proceeding on the road. Fandorin was lashing the unfortunate nag with the rifle butt and it was giving its all, desperately flinging its large-boned legs forward. It had already almost reached the bush where Varya was sitting, still stunned from her fall, but galloping along in pursuit, in a thunderous hail of rifle fire at a distance of about a hundred paces, was a posse of horsemen, ten of them at least. Suddenly the gray mare faltered, flailing its head piteously to the left and the right, and staggered sideways a little, then a little further, finally collapsing smoothly to the ground and pinning down its rider's leg. Varya gasped out loud. Fandorin somehow managed to extricate himself from under the horse as it struggled to get to its feet and drew himself erect. He glanced around at Varya, shouldered the rifle, and took aim at the Bashi-Bazouks.

He took his time before firing, taking careful aim, and his pose was so impressive that none of the bandits chose to be the first in line for a bullet—the partisan detachment spilled off the road and scattered across the meadow, forming a semicircle around the fugitives. The shooting subsided, and Varya guessed that the bandits wanted to take them alive.

Fandorin backed along the road, aiming the rifle first at one horseman, then another. Little by little the distance between them was shortening. When the volunteer was almost level with the bush Varya shouted: "Shoot, why don't you!"

Without turning his head, Erast Fandorin hissed: "This particular partisan's rifle isn't loaded."

Varya looked to her left (the Bashi-Bazouks were there), then to her right (horsemen in tall fur hats loomed into view on that side as well), then she glanced behind her—and through the sparse brush she saw a truly remarkable sight.

There were horsemen galloping across the meadow. At the front, racing along—or rather flying through the air—on a powerful black stallion, his elbows held out jockey-style, was an individual in a wide-brimmed American hat; ambling along in pursuit came a white uniform with gold-trimmed shoulders; then came a tight pack of a dozen or so Kuban Cossacks scurrying along at a fast trot; and bringing up the rear at a considerable distance, bouncing up and down in the saddle, was a perfectly absurd gentleman in a bowler hat and a long redingote.

As Varya gazed, mesmerized, at this bizarre cavalcade, the Cossacks started whistling and hallooing wildly. The Bashi-Bashouks also began making a fearsome din and bunched together into a tight group—the remainder of their number were hurrying to their rescue, led by the ginger-bearded **bek.** Varya and Fandorin were forgotten now; the terrible men had lost interest in them.

Bloody slaughter was imminent, but Varya forgot all about the danger as she turned her head first one way and then the other to observe the fearsome beauty of the spectacle.

The battle, however, was over before it had even begun. The horseman in the American hat (he was very close now, and Varya could make out his sunburnt face and little tuft of beard à la Louis-Napoleon and his light mustache with the ends curled up) pulled hard on his reins, coming to a total standstill, and out of nowhere a long-barreled pistol appeared in his hand. Bang! Bang! The pistol spewed out two angry little clouds of smoke and the **bek** in the tattered **beshmet** swayed in his saddle as if he were drunk and began slumping over to one side. One of the Bashi-Bazouks grabbed hold of him and threw him across the withers of his steed; instead of joining battle, the entire horde galloped away in retreat.

The pursuers streaked past Varya, past the weary Fandorin leaning on his rifle—the magical marksman, the horseman in the snow-white uniform (one general's gold shoulder-strap glinted brightly), and the Cossacks with their lances bristling.

"They have a Russian officer!" the volunteer shouted after them.

In the meantime the last member of the miraculous cavalcade, the civilian gentleman, had ridden up and halted—he did not appear to be interested in the pursuit.

His bright round eyes peered sympathetically at the rescued couple over the top of his spectacles.

"**Chetnik**s?" the civilian gentleman asked in a strong English accent.

"No, sir," Fandorin replied in English, adding something else in the same language that Varya did not understand, since in her high school she had studied French and German.

She tugged impatiently at the volunteer's sleeve, and he explained apologetically: "I s-said that we are not **chetnik**s, but Russians on our way to join our own people."

"What are **chetnik**s?"

"Bulgarian rebels."

"Oh, yoor a laydee?" The Englishman's fleshy, good-natured face mirrored his astonishment. "My, my, what a masquaraid! I didn't know Russians uses wimmin for aspionage. Yoor a haroin, medam. What is yoor name? This will be veree intrestin for my reedas."

He pulled a notepad out of his saddlebag, and it was only then that Varya spotted the three-colored armband on his sleeve bearing the number 48 and the word "Correspondent."

"I am Varvara Andreevna Suvorova, and I am not involved in any kind of espionage. My fiancé is at the general headquarters," she said with dignity. "And this is my traveling companion, the Serbian volunteer Erast Petrovich Fandorin."

The correspondent hastily doffed his hat in embarrassment and switched into French.

"I beg your pardon, mademoiselle. Seamus McLaughlin, correspondent of the London newspaper **The Daily Post**."

"The same Englishman who wrote about the

Turkish atrocities in Bulgaria?" asked Varya, removing her cap and straightening her hair as best she could.

"Irishman," McLaughlin corrected her sternly. "It's not the same thing at all."

"And who are they?" asked Varya with nod in the direction of the swirling dust and rattling gunfire. "Who is the man in the hat?"

"That peerless cowboy is none other than monsieur Paladin, a brilliant stylist, the darling of the French reading public, and the leading light of the **Revue Parisienne.**"

"The **Revue Parisienne**?"

"Yes, one of the Paris dailies. With a circulation of a hundred and fifty thousand, which is a quite remarkable figure for France," the correspondent explained rather offhandedly. "But my **Daily Post** sells two hundred and forty thousand copies every day. How about that?"

Varya swung her head to and fro to shake her hair into place and began wiping the dust off. her face with her sleeve.

"Ah, monsieur, you arrived in the nick of time. Providence itself must have sent you."

"It was Michel who dragged us out this way," the Briton, or rather Irishman, said with a shrug. "He has nothing to do here, attached to general HQ, and the idleness drives him wild.

This morning the Bashi-Bazouks were getting up to a little mischief in the Russian rear, so Michel set off in pursuit of them himself. Paladin and myself are like his lap dogs—wherever he goes, we go. In the first place, we're old friends from back in Turkestan, and in the second place, wherever Michel is, there's always bound to be a good story for an article. . . . Ah, look, they're coming back. Empty-handed, of course."

"Why 'of course'?" Varya asked.

The correspondent smiled condescendingly but said nothing, and Fandorin, who so far had taken almost no part in the conversation, answered for him.

"You must have seen, mademoiselle, that the Bashi-Bazouks' mounts were fresh, but the pursuers' horses were exhausted."

"Precisely so," McLaughlin agreed with a nod.

Varya gave them both a cross look for conspiring so outrageously to make a woman look like a fool. However, Fandorin immediately earned her forgiveness by taking an amazingly clean handkerchief out of his pocket and applying it to her cheek. Oh, she had forgotten all about the scratch!

The correspondent had been mistaken when he declared that the pursuers were coming back "empty-handed"—Varya was delighted to see that they had managed to recover the captive officer after all: Two Cossacks were carrying the limp body in the black uniform by its arms and legs. But had he—God forbid—been killed?

This time the dandy whom the Briton had called Michel was riding in front. He was a young general with smiling blue eyes and a rather distinctive beard—bushy, carefully tended, and combed over on both sides like a pair of wings.

"They got away, the scoundrels!" he shouted from a distance, and added an expression that Varya did not entirely understand.

"There's a lady present," said McLaughlin, wagging his finger. He removed his bowler hat and ran a hand over his pink bald patch.

The general drew himself erect and glanced at Varya, but immediately lost interest, which was natural enough, considering her unwashed hair, scratched face, and absurd costume.

"Major General Sobolev the Second of His Imperial Highness's retinue," Michel introduced himself and glanced inquiringly at Fandorin.

But Varya, thoroughly vexed by the general's indifference, asked: "The second? And who is the first?"

Sobolev was astonished.

"What do you mean? My father, Lieutenant General Dmitry Ivanovich Sobolev, commander of the Caucasian Cossack Division. Surely you must have heard of him?"

"No. Neither of him nor of you," Varya snapped, but she was lying, because the whole of Russia had heard of Sobolev the Second, the hero of Turkestan, the conqueror of Khiva and Makhram.

People said various things about the general. Some idolized him as a warrior of matchless bravery, a knight without fear or reproach, calling him the next Suvorov or even Bonaparte, while others derided him as an ambitious poseur. The newspapers wrote of how Sobolev had single-handedly beaten off an entire horde of Turkomans, standing his ground even though he was wounded seven times; how he had crossed the lifeless desert with a small detachment of men and crushed the forces of the fearsome Abdurahman-bek, who had a tenfold advantage in numbers; but one of Varya's acquaintances had relayed rumors of a very different kind—claims that hostages had been executed and the treasury of Kokand had been plundered.

Gazing into the handsome general's clear blue eyes, Varya could see immediately that the stories about the seven wounds and

Abdurahman-bek were perfectly true, but the tales of hostages and the khan's treasury were obviously absolute nonsense, the inventions of envious slanderers: Especially since Sobolev had now begun paying attention to Varya again, and this time he seemed to have noticed something interesting about her.

"But how on earth, madam, did you come to be here, where the blood flows in streams? And dressed like this? I am intrigued."

Varya introduced herself and gave a brief account of her adventures, an infallible instinct telling her that Sobolev would not betray her secret and have her despatched to Bucharest under armed escort.

"I envy your fiancé, Varvara Andreevna," said the general, caressing Varya with his eyes. "You are an extraordinary young woman. However, allow me to introduce my comrades. I believe you have already made the acquaintance of Mr. McLaughlin, and this is my orderly, Sergei Bereshchagin, the brother of the other Bereshchagin, the artist." (A slender, good-looking youth in a long-waisted Cossack coat bowed awkwardly to Varya.) "By the way, he is an excellent draftsman himself. During a reconnaissance mission on the Danube, he drew a picture of the Turkish positions—it was quite lovely. But where has Paladin got to? Hey, Paladin, come over here, let me introduce you to an interesting lady."

Varya peered curiously at the Frenchman, who had ridden up last. The Frenchman (the armband on his sleeve said "Correspondent No. 32") was impressively handsome, no worse in his own way than Sobolev: a slim, aquiline nose, a sandy mustache with the ends curled up, a little imperial beard, intelligent gray eyes. But the expression in those eyes was angry.

"Those villains are a disgrace to the Turkish army!" the journalist exclaimed passionately in French. "They're good for nothing but slaughtering peaceful civilians, but as soon as they even smell a battle—they're off into the bushes. If I were Kerim Pasha I'd disarm every one of them and have them hanged."

"Calm down, my bold **chevalier,** there's a lady present," McLaughlin interrupted him jovially. "You're in luck; you have made your entrance in the guise of a romantic hero, so make the most of it. See the way she is looking at you."

Varya blushed and hurled a furious glance at the Irishman, but McLaughlin simply burst into good-natured laughter. Paladin, however, behaved as a genuine Frenchman should: He dismounted and bowed.

"Charles Paladin at your service, mademoiselle."

"Varvara Suvorova," she said amiably. "Pleased to make your acquaintance. And thank you all, gentlemen. Your appearance was most timely."

"And may I know your name?" Paladin asked with an inquisitive glance at Fandorin.

"Erast Fandorin," replied the volunteer, although he was looking at Sobolev, not the Frenchman. "I have been fighting in Serbia and am now on my way to general headquarters with an important message."

The general looked Fandorin over from head to toe. He inquired deferentially: "I expect you've seen your share of grief? What did you do before Serbia?"

"I was at the Ministry of Foreign Affairs. A titular counselor."

This was a surprise. A diplomat? To be quite honest, all these new impressions had rather undermined the immense (why pretend otherwise?) impact produced on Varya by her taciturn companion, but now she looked at him with newly admiring eyes. A diplomat going off to war as a volunteer—that certainly didn't happen very often. Yes indeed, all three of them were quite remarkably handsome, each in his own way: Fandorin, Sobolev, and Paladin.

"What message?" Sobolev asked with a frown.

Fandorin hesitated, evidently unwilling to say.

"Come on now, don't go making a Spanish court secret out of it!" the general shouted at him. "After all's said and done, that's simply being impolite to your rescuers."

The volunteer replied in a low voice that made the correspondents prick up their ears, "I am making my way from Vidin, g-general. Three days ago, Osman Pasha set out for P-Plevna with an army corps."

"Who is this Osman? And where in the blazes is Plevna?"

"Osman Nuri Pasha is the finest commander in the Turkish army, the conqueror of the Serbs. At the age of only forty-five, he is already a **m-mushir,** that is, a field marshal. And his soldiers are beyond all com-parison with those who were stationed on the Danube. Plevna is a little town thirty versts to the west of here. It controls the road to Sofia. We must reach that strategically vital point before the pasha and occupy it."

Sobolev slapped a hand against his knee and his horse shifted its feet nervously.

"Ah, if I only had at least a regiment! But I am not involved in the action, Fandorin. You need to go to headquarters, to the commander in chief. I have to complete my reconnaissance, but I'll provide you with an escort to Tsarevitsy.

Perhaps you will be my guest this evening, Varvara Andreevna? It can be quite jolly at times in the war correspondents' marquee."

"With pleasure," said Varya, casting a nervous glance toward the spot where the freed prisoner had been laid on the grass. Two Cossacks were squatting on their haunches beside the officer and doing something to him.

"That officer is dead, isn't he?"

"Alive and kicking," replied the general. "The lucky devil, he'll live for a hundred years now. When we started chasing the Bashi-Bazouks, they shot him in the head and hightailed it. But everyone knows you can't trust a bullet. It shot off at a tangent and only tore off a little scrap of skin. Well, then, my lads, have you bandaged up the captain?" he shouted loudly to the Cossacks.

The Cossacks helped the officer get up. He swayed, but remained on his feet and stubbornly pushed away the Cossacks, who were trying to support him by the elbows. He took several jerky, faltering steps on legs that seemed about to buckle under him at any moment, stood to attention, and wheezed in a hoarse voice: "Captain of general headquarters Eremei Perepyolkin, your excellency. I was proceeding from Zimnitsa to my posting at the headquarters of the Western Division, where I had been appointed to Lieutenant General Kriedener's operations section. On the way I was attacked by a unit of hostile irregular cavalry and taken prisoner. It was my own fault . . . I simply did not expect anything of the kind in our rear . . . I did not even have a pistol with me, only my sword."

Varya was able to get a better look at the poor victim now. He was short and sinewy, with disheveled chestnut hair, a narrow mouth with almost no lips, and stern brown eyes. Or rather, one brown eye, because the second one was still not visible, but at least the captain's gaze was no longer full of anguish or despair.

"You're alive, and that's splendid," Sobolev said magnanimously. "But an officer must always carry a pistol, even a staff officer. Otherwise it's like a lady going out into the street without a hat—she'll be taken for a loose woman." He laughed, then caught Varya's angry look and hemmed as if he were clearing his throat. "Pardon, mademoiselle."

A dashing Cossack sergeant approached the general and jabbed with his finger, pointing to something.

"Look, your excellency, I think it's Semyonov!"

Varya turned to look and suddenly felt sick: The bandit's bay on which she had made her recent inauspicious gallop had reappeared beside the bush. The horse was nibbling on the grass as if nothing had happened, with the loathsome trophy still suspended, swaying, on its flank.

Sobolev jumped down and walked over to the horse with his eyes screwed up skeptically and turned the nightmarish sphere this way and that.

"That's not Semyonov, surely?" he said doubtfully. "You're talking nonsense, Nechitailo. Semyonov's face is quite different."

"It certainly is Semyonov, Mikhail Dmitrich," the sergeant said heatedly. "See, there's his torn ear, and look here." He parted the dead head's purple lips. "The front tooth's missing as well. It's Semyonov, all right!"

"I suppose so," said the general, nodding thoughtfully. "He must have had a pretty rough time of it. Varvara Andreevna," he said, turning to Varya to explain, "this is a Cossack from the second cavalry squadron who was abducted by Daud-bek's Meskhetians this morning."

But Varya was no longer listening—the earth and the sky somersaulted, exchanging places, and Paladin and Fandorin were only just in time to catch the suddenly limp young lady as she fell.

# CHAPTER THREE

—ɷ—

## Which is devoted almost entirely to oriental guile

## LA REVUE PARISIENNE (Paris) 15 (3) July 1877

The double-headed eagle that serves the Russian Empire as its crest illustrates quite magnificently the entire system of government of that country, where any matter of even the slightest importance is not entrusted to a single authority but at least two, and these authorities hamper each other's efforts while taking no ultimate responsibility for anything. The same thing is happening now in the Russian army in the field. Formally speaking, the commander in chief is the Grand Prince Nikolai Nikolaievich, who is currently based in the village of Tsarevitsy. However, located in the small town of Bela, in the immediate vicinity of Nikolai's headquarters, is the staff of Emperor Alexander II, to which are attached the Chancellor, the Minister of War, the Chief of Gendarmes, and other dignitaries of the highest rank. Taking into account the fact that the allied Romanian army possesses its own commander in the person of Prince Karl Hohenzollern-Siegmaringen, one is reminded less of the double-headed king of the feathered tribe than of the droll humor of the Russian fable in which a swan, a crayfish, and a pike are harnessed to the same carriage . . .

"WELL, THEN, HOW AM I TO address you—as 'madame' or 'mademoiselle'?" asked the beetle-black lieutenant colonel of gendarmes, twisting his lips revoltingly. "This is not a ballroom, but army headquarters, and I am not paying you compliments, but conducting an interro-gation, so I would be obliged if you would stop beating about the bush!"

The lieutenant colonel was called Ivan Kharitonovich Kazanzaki, and since he was resolutely determined not to see Varya's side of things, the most likely outcome in prospect for her was clearly compulsory deportation to Russia.

When they had finally reached Tsarevitsy the day before, it was almost night. Fandorin had immediately set out for the headquarters staff building and Varya, by this time so tired that she could barely stand, had set about doing what had to be done. The charitable nurses from Baroness Vreiskaya's medical unit had given her some clothes and heated some water for her, and after she had tidied herself up, Varya had collapsed onto a field-hospital bed— fortunately, the wards were almost completely empty of wounded. Her meeting with Petya had been postponed until the following day, for she would require full command of all her faculties during the important discussion that lay ahead.

In the morning, however, Varya had not been not allowed to catch up on her sleep. Two gendarmes wearing hard helmets and carrying carbines had turned up and escorted "the individual styling herself 'Miss Suvorova' " directly to the special unit of the Western Division, without even allowing her to arrange her hair properly.

And now she had been attempting for hours to explain to this clean-shaven, bushy-browed monster in the blue uniform the precise nature of the relationship that bound her to the cryptographer Pyotr Yablokov.

"Why on earth don't you call Pyotr Afanasievich and he will confirm everything himself," Varya kept repeating, but the lieutenant colonel's reply was always the same.

"All in good time."

Kazanzaki was particularly interested in the details of her encounter with "the individual styling himself 'Titular Counselor Fandorin.'" The lieutenant colonel noted down all about Yusuf Pasha and Vidin, and the coffee with conversation in French, and freedom won in a game of backgammon. But his professional curiosity was galvanized most powerfully by the discovery that the volunteer had spoken to the Bashi-Bazouks in Turkish, and he demanded to know exactly how he had spoken—with a stammer or without. Simply clarifying all that nonsense about the stammer must have taken at least half an hour.

And then, when Varya was already on the verge of dry, tearless hysterics, the door of the mud-walled peasant hut that housed the special section had suddenly swung open and in had walked, or rather run, an extremely important-looking general with imperiously bulging eyes and luxuriant whiskers.

"Adjutant General Mizinov," he bellowed

from the doorway and glanced sternly at the lieutenant colonel. "Kazanzaki?"

Taken by surprise, the gendarme stood sharply to attention and began twitching his lips, while Varya stared wide-eyed at the oriental despot and butcher whom the progressive youth of Russia believed the head of the Third Section and chief of gendarmes, Lavrenty Arkadievich Mizinov, to be.

"Yes, sir, your excellency!" Varya's tormentor wheezed hoarsely. "Lieutenant Colonel of the Gendarmes Corps Kazanzaki. Previously serving in the Kishinev office, now appointed to head the special section, Western Division Headquarters. Conducting the interrogation of a prisoner."

"Who is she?" asked the general, raising an eyebrow and giving Varya a disapproving glance.

"Varvara Suvorova. Claims to have traveled here in a private capacity in order to see her fiancé, operations section cryptographer Yablokov."

"Suvorova?" Mizinov mused, intrigued. "Could we perhaps be related? My great-grandfather on my mother's side was Alexander Vasilievich Suvorov-Rymniksky."

"I very much hope not," Varya snapped.

The satrap gave a wry smile and paid no more attention to the prisoner.

"Now then, Kazanzaki, don't you go trying to pull the wool over my eyes. Where's Fandorin? It says in the report that you have him."

"Yes, sir, he is being held in custody," the lieutenant colonel reported smartly and added, lowering his voice, "I have reason to believe that **he** is our keenly anticipated visitor, Anwar-effendi. Everything fits perfectly, your excellency. That story about Osman Pasha and Plevna is blatant misinformation. But how skillfully he spun the—"

"Idiot!" roared Mizinov, so fiercely that the lieutenant colonel cringed and pulled his head down into his shoulders. "Bring him here immediately! And look lively about it!"

Kazanzaki dashed headlong out of the room and Varya shrank back into her chair, but the agitated general had forgotten all about her. He carried on wheezing loudly and drumming his fingers nervously on the table, only stopping when the lieutenant colonel returned with Fandorin.

The volunteer looked haggard and exhausted and dark circles had appeared under his eyes—he had obviously not slept the night before.

"G-good morning, Lavrenty Arkadievich," he said listlessly, and bowed briefly to Varya.

"My God, Fandorin, is it really you?" the

satrap gasped. "I would never have recognized you. You've aged a good ten years! Have a seat, my dear fellow—I'm delighted to see you."

The general sat Erast Petrovich on a chair and took a seat himself, so that Varya was behind him and Kazanzaki was left standing to attention, rooted to the spot outside the door.

"How are you now?" asked Mizinov. "I wanted to give you my most sincere—"

Fandorin interrupted politely but firmly. "I would rather not talk about that, your excellency. I am perfectly all right now. Tell me, rather, whether this g-gentleman" (he nodded dismissively toward the lieutenant colonel) "has told you about Plevna. Every hour is precious."

"Yes, yes. I have with me an order from the commander in chief, but first of all I wanted to make sure that it was really you. Here, listen." He took a sheet of paper out of his pocket, set a monocle in his eye, and read: "To the commander of the Western Division Lieutenant General Baron Kriedener. I order you to occupy Plevna and secure your position there with a force of at least one division. Nikolai."

Fandorin nodded.

"Lieutenant Colonel, have this encoded immediately and forwarded to Kriedener by telegraph," Mizinov ordered.

Kazanzaki respectfully took the sheet of paper and ran off to carry out the order, his spurs jangling.

"So perhaps you can come back to work now?" the general asked.

Erast Petrovich frowned.

"Lavrenty Arkadievich, I believe I have fulfilled my d-duty by reporting the Turkish flanking maneuver. But as for fighting against poor Turkey, which would have fallen apart quite happily without our heroic efforts—please spare me that."

"I shall not spare you, sir, I will not!" said Mizinov, growing angry. "If patriotism is merely an empty word to you, then permit me to remind you, mister titular counselor, that you are not in retirement, but only on indefinite leave, and although you may be listed as a member of the diplomatic corps, you are still on service with me, in the Third Section!"

Varya gave a feeble gasp of amazement. She had taken Fandorin for a decent man—but he was a police agent! And he had even made himself out to be some kind of romantic hero, like Lermontov's Pechorin. That intriguing pallor, that languid glance, that nobly graying hair. How could she trust anyone after this?

"Your excellency," Erast Petrovich said in a quiet voice, clearly not even suspecting that in

Varya's eyes he was now irrevocably damned, "it is not you that I serve, but Russia. And I do not wish to take any part in a war that is not only pointless, but actually ruinous for her."

"It is not your place, or mine, to draw conclusions concerning the war. His Majesty the Emperor decides such matters," Mizinov retorted curtly.

An awkward pause ensued. When the chief of gendarmes began speaking again, his voice sounded quite different.

"Erast Petrovich, my dear fellow," he began imploringly. "Hundreds of thousands of Russian people are risking their lives, the burden of war has almost brought the country to its knees . . . and I have a dark presentiment of disaster. Things are going far too smoothly altogether. I am afraid it will all end very badly."

When no reply was forthcoming, the general rubbed his eyes wearily and confessed: "It is hard, Fandorin, I am struggling, surrounded by chaos and incompetence. I am short of men, especially intelligent and capable ones, and I have no wish to burden you with dull routine. I have a little task in mind that is very far from simple, but just the very thing for you."

At that, Erast Petrovich inclined his head, intrigued, and the general continued ingratiatingly: "Do you recall Anwar-effendi? Sultan

Abdul-Hamid's secretary. You know, the Turk who surfaced briefly in the Azazel case?"

Erast gave the faintest of shudders, but he said nothing.

Mizinov hemmed ironically.

"You know, that idiot Kazanzaki took you to be him, I ask you! We have information that this interesting Turk is personally heading a secret operation against our forces. An audacious individual, with a flair for adventure. He could quite easily turn up at our positions in person—in fact, it would be just like him. Well, are you interested?"

"I am l-listening, Lavrenty Arkadievich," said Fandorin, with a sideways glance at Varya.

"Well, that's splendid," Mizinov said delightedly and shouted. "Novgorodtsev! The file!"

A middle-aged major with adjutant's aiguillettes walked quietly into the room, handed the general a folder bound in red calico, and immediately went out again. Varya spotted Lieutenant Colonel Kazanzaki's sweaty features through the doorway and gave him a gleeful, mocking grin—serves you right, you sadist, stand out there now and stew in your own juice.

"Right, then, this is what we have on Anwar," said the general, rustling the sheets of paper. "Would you like to take notes?"

"I shall remember it," replied Erast Petrovich.

"The facts about his early life are very scanty. He was born approxi-mately thirty-five years ago. According to some sources, in the Bosnian Muslim village of Hef-Rais. Who his parents are is unknown. He was raised somewhere in Europe, in one of Lady Astair's celebrated educational institutions. You remember her, of course, from the Azazel business."

It was the second time that Varya had heard that strange name, and the second time that Fandorin reacted strangely, jerking his chin as though his collar had suddenly become too tight for him.

"Anwar-effendi's name cropped up about ten years ago, when Europe first began hearing about the great Turkish reformer Midhat Pasha. Our Anwar, who at that time was still far from being any kind of effendi, worked as his secretary. Just lend a brief ear to this Midhat's service record." Mizinov took out a separate sheet of paper and coughed to clear his throat. "At that time he was the governor general of the Danubian Vilajet. Under his patronage Anwar established a stagecoach service in those parts, built railways, and even set up a network of **islahhan**s—charitable educational establishments for orphan children from both the Muslim and Christian confessions."

"Did he, indeed?" Fandorin remarked.

"Yes. A most praiseworthy initiative, is it not? Overall, the scale of Midhat Pasha's and Anwar's activities was so great that a genuine danger arose of Bulgaria escaping from the sphere of Russian influence. Our ambassador in Constantinople, Nikolai Pavlovich Gnatiev, used all his influence with Sultan Abdul-Aziz and eventually managed to have the excessively zealous governor recalled. After that, Midhat became chairman of the council of state and steered through a law introducing universal public education—a remarkable law, and also, by the way, one that we still do not have here in Russia. Can you guess who drafted the bill? Yes, of course: Anwar-effendi. This would all be very moving if not for the fact that in addition to his educational activities, at that time our opponent was also very actively involved in the intrigues at court, seeing that his patron had more than his share of enemies. Assassins were sent to kill Midhat, his coffee was poisoned—once, indeed, they even slipped him a concubine infected with leprosy. Anwar's duties included protecting the great man from all these delightful pranks. But in any case, the Russian party at court got the upper hand and the pasha was banished into remote exile as the governor general of poor and backward Mesopotamia. When Midhat tried to introduce his reforms there, an insurrection broke out in Baghdad. And do you know what he did? He summoned all the city elders and the clergy and made a brief speech as follows. I shall read it verbatim, since I find its power and style genuinely delightful: 'Venerable mullahs and elders, if the public disorders have not ceased by two hours from now, I shall order you all to be hanged and will put the four quarters of the glorious city of Baghdad to the torch. And afterward may the great padishah, Allah preserve him, also have me hanged for this heinous crime.' " Mizinov chuckled and shook his head. "So now he could proceed with his reforms. In less than three years of Midhat's governorship, his devoted deputy Anwar-effendi managed to build telegraph lines, introduce horse-drawn streetcars in Baghdad, set steamships sailing up and down the Euphrates, establish the first Iraqi newspaper, and enroll pupils in a school of commerce. Not bad, eh? I hardly even need mention a mere trifle such as the establishment of the Osman-Osman Shipping Line, whose boats sail as far as London via the Suez Canal. Then, by means of a certain cunning intrigue, Anwar managed to depose the grand vizier, Mahmoud Nedim, who was so intimate with the Russian ambassador that the Turks used to call him 'Nedimov.' Midhat became the head of the sultan's government, but only managed to hold on to this high office for two and a half months—our Gnatiev outwitted him yet again. Midhat's greatest failing—and one that is absolutely unforgivable in the eyes of the other pashas—is his incorruptibility. He launched a campaign against bribe-taking and was incautious enough to utter in the presence of European diplomats the phrase that was his undoing: 'The time has come to show Europe that not all Turks are despicable prostitutes.' For that word—'prostitutes'—he was thrown out of Istanbul and appointed governor of Salonika. The little Greek town immediately began to flourish, while the sultan's court settled back into luxurious indolence and sloth financed by the embezzlement of public funds."

"I see you are p-perfectly enamored of this man," Erast Petrovich said, interrupting the general.

"You mean Midhat? Absolutely," said Mizinov with a shrug. "And I would be more than glad to see him at the head of the Russian government. But he's not a Russian, he's a Turk. And, moreover, a Turk who looks first to England. Our aspirations are directly opposed, which makes Midhat our enemy, and an extremely dangerous enemy he is. Europe dislikes and fears us, but it lauds Midhat to the heavens, especially since he gave Turkey a constitution.

And now, Erast Petrovich, I must ask you to bear with me while I read you a long letter that Nikolai Pavlovich Gnatiev wrote to me last year. It will give you a clear picture of the enemy with whom we shall be dealing."

The chief of gendarmes drew out of the folder several sheets of paper covered in the fine, regular handwriting of a clerk and began reading.

> **Dear Lavrenty,**
> **Events here where Allah watches over us in Istanbul are unfolding so rapidly that even I am unable to keep up with them, although, setting aside all false modesty, your humble servant has had his finger on the pulse of the Sick Man of Europe for no small number of years. Due in some measure to my own zealous efforts, that pulse was gradually fading away and promised soon to come to a complete stop, but since the month of May . . .**

"He is talking about May of last year, 1876," Mizinov felt it necessary to explain.

> **. . . but since the month of May it has begun beating so frantically that any**

moment the Bosphorus could burst its banks and the walls of Constantinople could crumble, leaving you with nothing on which to hang your shield.

And all this due to the fact that in May Midhat Pasha made a triumphant return from exile to the capital of the mighty and in-comparable Sultan Abdul-Aziz, Shadow of the Most High and Defender of the Faith, bringing with him his "éminence grise," the wily Anwar-effendi.

On this occasion, Anwar was wiser and he took no risks, acting like both a European and an Oriental. He began in the European style: his agents started to frequent the dockyards, the arsenal, and the mint—and the workers, who had not been paid their wages for a very long time, poured out into the streets. That was followed by a purely Eastern ruse. On the 25th of May, Midhat Pasha announced that the Prophet had visited him in a dream (verify that if you can!) and instructed His servant to save Turkey from ruin.

Meanwhile, my dear friend Abdul-Aziz, as usual, was sitting in his harem, delighting in the company of his favorite wife, the charming Mihri-khanum, who was due to give birth soon and was therefore acting very capriciously, demanding that her lord and master be constantly at her side. In addition to her celestial beauty, this golden-haired, blue-eyed Circassian woman is also famed for having drained the sultan's treasury absolutely dry. During the last year alone, she left more than ten million rubles in the French shops on Pera Avenue, and it is quite understandable that the people of Constantinople were, as the English would say, with their penchant for understatement, far from fond of her.

Believe me, Lavrenty, there was nothing I could do to alter matters. I entreated, I threatened, I intrigued like a eunuch in the harem, but Abdul-Aziz was deaf and dumb. On the 29th of May there was a crowd of many thousands buzzing round the Dolmabahçe Palace (an extremely ugly building in an eclectic European-Oriental style), but the padishah did not even attempt to reassure his subjects—he locked himself into the female quarters of his residence, access to which is barred to me, and listened to Mihri-khanum playing Viennese waltzes on the fortepiano.

Meanwhile, Anwar was ensconced in the offices of the Minister of War, where he was inclining that cautious and prudent gentleman to a change in political orientation. According to a report from one of my agents, who worked for the pasha as a cook (hence the specific tone of the report), the course of the epoch-making negotiations ran as follows. Anwar came to see the minister at precisely midday, and coffee and bread rolls were ordered. A quarter of an hour later, His Excellency the minister was heard bellowing in indignation and his adjutants led Anwar out of his office and away to the guardroom. Then the pasha strode about his office on his own for half an hour and ate two plates of halva, of which he was extremely fond. After that he decided to interrogate the traitor in person and set out for the guardroom himself. At half past two, the order was given to bring fruits and sweets. At a quarter to four, it was cognac and champagne. Some time between four and five, after taking coffee, the pasha and his guest left to see

Midhat. According to the rumors, for his involvement in the conspiracy the minister was promised the position of Grand Vizier and a million pounds sterling from English patrons.

Before the end of the day, the two main conspirators had reached a close understanding and the coup d'état took place that very night. The fleet blockaded the palace from the seaward side, the commander of the metropolitan garrison replaced the guard with his own men, and the sultan, his mother, and the pregnant Mihri-khanum were transported to the Feriie Palace by boat.

Four days later, the sultan attempted to trim his beard with a pair of nail scissors, but he was so clumsy that he cut the veins on both of his wrists and expired forthwith. The doctors from the European embassies, who were summoned to examine the body, unanimously declared that it was a case of suicide, since absolutely no signs of a struggle had been discovered about the dead man. In short, it was all played out as simply and elegantly as a good game of chess. Such is the style of Anwar-effendi.

But that was merely the opening: next came the midgame.

Once he had played his part, the Minister of War became a serious hindrance, for he had not the slightest inclination to introduce reforms and a constitution, and the only question that really interested him was when he would receive the million pounds he had been promised by Anwar. In fact, the Minister of War began behaving as if he were the most important member of the government and never wearied of reminding people that it was he, and not Midhat, who had overthrown Abdul-Aziz.

Anwar endeavored to convince a certain gallant officer, who had served as the deceased sultan's adjutant, that the minister's claim was true. The officer in question was called Hasan-bei; he was the brother of the beautiful Mihri-khanum. He enjoyed quite remarkable popularity among the sultry temptresses at court, since he was very handsome and dashing and he performed Italian arias with superlative flair. Everybody referred to Hasan-bei simply as "the Circassian."

Several days after Abdul-Aziz trimmed his beard in such a clumsy fashion, the inconsolable Mihri-khanum delivered a stillborn child and herself died in great torment. And that was the precise moment at which Anwar and the Circassian became bosom friends. On one occasion when Hasan-bei entered Anwar's residence to pay him a visit, his friend was not at home, but the ministers had gathered at the pasha's house for a meeting. The Circassian was a familiar face in the house and nobody questioned his presence. He drank coffee with the adjutants, had a smoke, and chatted about this and that. Then he strolled slowly down the corridor and suddenly burst into the hall where the meeting was taking place. Hasan-bei did not touch Midhat and the other dignitaries, but he fired two bullets from his revolver into the chest of the Minister of War, and then finished the old man off with his yataghan. The more judicious ministers took to their heels, and only two decided to be heroic. Their attempt was ill-advised, for the raging Hasan-bei killed one of them on the spot and seriously wounded the other. At this point, the bold Midhat Pasha returned with two of his adjutants. Hasan-bei shot them both dead, but once again he left Midhat Pasha himself untouched. The killer was eventually captured and bound, but only after he had killed one police officer and wounded seven soldiers. And all this time our friend Anwar was praying devoutly in the mosque, a fact confirmed by numerous witnesses.

Hasan-bei spent the night under lock and key in the guardroom, singing loud arias from Lucia di Lammermoor, by which they say Anwar-effendi was absolutely entranced. Anwar even tried to obtain a pardon for the valiant criminal, but the enraged ministers were adamant and in the morning the killer was hanged from a tree. The ladies of the harem, who loved their Circassian so passionately, came to watch his execution, weeping bitter tears and blowing him kisses from afar.

Henceforth there was no one to hinder Midhat's plans, apart from fate, which dealt him a blow from an entirely unexpected quarter. The great politician was let down by his own puppet, the new sultan Murad.

As early as the morning of the 31st of May, immediately following the coup, Midhat Pasha had paid a visit to Prince Murad, the nephew of the deposed sultan, and thereby frightened Murad quite indescribably. Permit me at this point to digress somewhat, in order to explain the pitiful plight of the heir to the throne of the Ottoman Empire.

The problem is that although the prophet Mohammed had fifteen wives, he did not have a single son, and he left no instructions concerning the succession to the throne. Therefore, down through the centuries, every one of the multitudinous sultanas has dreamed of placing her own son on the throne and attempted to eliminate the sons of her rivals by every possible means. There is even a special cemetery at the palace for innocent princes who have been murdered, so we Russians, with our Boris and Gleb and Tsarevich Dmitry, appear quite laughable by Turkish standards.

In the Ottoman Empire the throne is not transmitted from father to son, but from older brother to younger. When one line of brothers is exhausted, the next generation inherits, and again the throne passes from older brother to younger. Every sultan is mortally afraid of his younger brother or oldest nephew, and the chances of an heir actually living to reign are extremely slight. The crown prince is kept in total isolation and nobody is allowed to visit him; the scoundrels even try to ensure that his concubines are not capable of bearing children. According to an ancient tradition, the future padishah is attended by servants whose tongues have been cut out and whose eardrums have been punctured. You can imagine what effect this kind of upbringing has on their highnesses' state of mind. For instance, Suleiman II spent thirty-nine years in confinement, writing out and coloring in copies of the Koran. And when he finally did become sultan, it was not long before he began asking to go back and abdicated the throne. How well I understand him. Coloring in pictures is so much more pleasant.

However, let us return to Murad. He was a handsome youth, by no means stupid, and actually extremely well-read, although he had a tendency to drink to excess and suffered from an entirely justified persecution mania. He was delighted to entrust the reins of government to the wise Midhat, and so everything seemed to be continuing according to plan for our crafty conspirators. But the sudden elevation and remarkable death of his uncle had such a powerful effect on poor Murad that he began raving and lapsing into violent fits. The European alienists who visited the padishah in secret came to the conclusion that he was incurable and his condition could only deteriorate as time went on.

Now, note Anwar-effendi's incredible farsightedness. On the first day of Murad's reign, when the sky ahead was still bright and cloudless, our mutual friend had suddenly asked to be made secretary to Prince Abdul-Hamid, the sultan's brother and now heir to the throne. When I learned this, it became clear to me that Midhat Pasha was not certain of Murad V. After making a thorough assessment of the crown prince, Anwar evidently considered him acceptable, and Midhat set Abdul-Hamid a single condition: Promise that you will introduce a constitution, and you will be padishah. The prince naturally agreed.

What came after that you already know. On 31 August Abdul-Hamid II ascended the throne, replacing the insane Murad V; Midhat became grand vizier, and Anwar remained as the new sultan's puppet-master behind the scenes and undeclared chief of the secret police—in other words, Lavrenty (ha-ha!), your colleague.

It is indicative that in Turkey hardly anybody at all has even heard of Anwar-effendi. He does not call attention to himself or appear in public. I, for instance, have only seen him once, when I was presented to the new padishah. Anwar was sitting off to one side of the throne, wearing an immense black beard (I believe it was false) and dark glasses, which in general is a quite unprecedented breach of court etiquette. During the audience Abdul-Hamid glanced at him several times, as if he were seeking support or advice.

This is the man with whom you will be dealing from now on. If my intuition does not mislead me, Midhat and Anwar will continue to manipulate the sultan as they see fit, and in another year or two . . .

"Well, the rest is of no great interest," said Mizinov, breaking off his long recitation and wiping the sweat from his brow with a handkerchief. "Especially since the brilliant Nikolai Pavlovich was indeed misled by his intuition after all. Midhat Pasha failed to retain his grip on power and was exiled."

Erast Petrovich, who had listened very attentively and not moved even once the whole time (unlike Varya, who had fidgeted herself half to death on her hard chair), asked tersely: "The opening is clear, and so is the midgame. But what about the endgame?"

The general nodded approvingly.

"That is the whole point. The endgame proved to be so intricate that even Gnatiev, with all his experience, was taken by surprise. On the seventh of February this year, Midhat Pasha was summoned to the sultan, placed under armed guard, and put on board a ship, which carried off the disgraced head of government on a tour around Europe. And our Anwar, having betrayed his benefactor, from being the prime minister's éminence grise began playing the same role for the sultan. He did everything possible to provoke a rupture in relations between the Sublime Porte and Russia. And not long ago, when Turkey's fate was already hanging by a hair, according to information received from our agents, Anwar set out for the theater of military operations in order to intervene in the course of events by means of certain secret operations, the nature of which we can only guess."

At this point Fandorin began speaking rather strangely.

"No formal d-duties. That is one. Complete freedom of action. That is t-two. Reporting only to you. That is three."

Varya did not understand what these words meant, but the chief of gendarmes was delighted and promptly replied: "Well, that's just splendid! Now I recognize the old Fandorin. Why, my dear fellow, you'd become quite chilly and indifferent. Now don't hold this against me, I'm not talking as your superior, just as someone who is older, like a father. . . . You mustn't go burying yourself alive. Leave the graveyard for the dead. At your age, why, it doesn't bear thinking about! As the aria puts it, you have **toute la vie devant soi.**"

"Lavrenty Arkadievich!" In an instant the volunteer's pale cheeks flushed deep crimson and his voice grated like iron. "I do not b-believe that I invited any effusion of p-personal sentiment."

Varya thought his remark quite unforgivably rude and shrank down on her chair: Mizinov would be mortally offended by such an insult to his finer feelings. How he would roar!

But the satrap merely sighed and said dryly: "Your terms are accepted. You can have your freedom of action. That was actually what I had in mind. Just keep your eyes and ears open and if you notice anything unusual—well, you don't need me to tell you what to do."

"Aa-choo!" Varya sneezed and then shrank back down into her chair again in fright.

The general was even more frightened than she was. He started, swung round, and stared dumbfounded at the involuntary witness of his confidential conversation.

"Madam, what are you doing here? Why did you not leave the room with the lieutenant colonel? How dare you?"

"You ought to have looked," Varya replied with dignity. "I'm not some mosquito or fly that you can just choose to ignore. I happen to be under arrest, and no one has given me leave to go yet."

She thought she saw Fandorin's lips twitch ever so slightly. But no, she had imagined it—this specimen didn't even know how to smile.

"Very well then, all right." Mizinov's tone of voice held a quiet threat. "You, my dear nonrelative, have learned things you absolutely ought not to know. In the interests of state security, I am placing you under temporary administrative arrest. You will be taken under escort to the Kishinev garrison quarantine station and detained there under guard until the end of the campaign. And you have only yourself to blame."

Varya turned pale.

"But I haven't even seen my fiancé . . ."

"You'll see each other after the war," snapped Malyuta Skuratov, turning toward the door to summon his thugs, but then Erast Fandorin intervened.

"Lavrenty Arkadievich, I think it would be quite sufficient to ask Miss Suvorova to give her word of honor."

"I give my word of honor!" Varya cried, encouraged by this unexpected intercession on her behalf.

"I'm sorry, dear chap, we can't take the risk," the general snapped, without even looking at her. Then there's this fiancé of hers. And how can we trust a girl? You know what they say— 'the longer the braid, the dafter the maid.' "

"I don't have any braid! And that is a base insult to my intelligence!" Varya's voice trembled, threatening to break. "What do I want with all your Anwars and Midhats, anyway?"

"On my responsibility, your excellency. I vouch for Varvara Andreevna."

Mizinov said nothing, frowning in annoyance, and Varya realized that even among secret police agents there were clearly some people who were not entirely beyond salvation. After all, he was a Serbian volunteer.

"It's stupid," growled the general. He turned toward Varya and asked gruffly, "Do you know how to do anything? Is your handwriting good?"

"I qualified as a stenographer! I worked as a telegraphist! And a midwife!" said Varya, stretching the truth just a little.

"A stenographer and a telegraphist?" said Mizinov, surprised. "All the better, then. Erast Petrovich, I will allow this woman to remain here on one single condition: She will fulfill the duties of your secretary. You will in any case require some kind of courier or messenger who will not arouse unnecessary suspicion. Only bear in mind that you have vouched for her."

"Oh, no!" Varya and Fandorin exclaimed in a single voice. Then they continued speaking together, but saying different things.

Erast Petrovich said: "I have no need of a secretary."

Varya said: "I will not work for the Okhranka."

"As you wish," said the general, rising to his feet with a shrug. "Novgorodtsev, the escort!"

"I agree!" shouted Varya.

Fandorin said nothing.

# CHAPTER FOUR

—ɯ—

## In which the enemy strikes the first blow

## THE DAILY POST (London) 15 (3) July 1877

...An advance detachment of the dashing General Gurko's forces has captured Trnovo, the ancient capital of the kingdom of Bulgaria, and is pressing on apace towards the Shipka Pass, the gateway to the defenceless plains that extend to the walls of Constantinople itself. The military vizier Abdul Kerim Pasha has been removed from all his posts and committed for trial. Only a miracle can save Turkey now.

THEY HALTED BY THE PORCH. Some kind of understanding had to be reached.

Fandorin coughed to clear his throat and began.

"Varvara Andreevna, I very much regret that things have turned out like this. Naturally, you are entirely at liberty and I shall not oblige you to work for me in any way."

"Thank you," she replied coldly. "That is very noble of you. I must confess that for a moment I thought you had arranged all this deliberately. You could see perfectly well that I was there, and you must have anticipated how everything would turn out. Well, do you really need a secretary so badly?"

Once again, Erast Fandorin's eyes glinted briefly in a way that she might have taken for a sign of merriment in any normal man.

"You are most perceptive. But unjust. I was indeed guided by an ulterior motive, but I was acting entirely in your own interests. Lavrenty Arkadievich would quite certainly have banished you as far away as possible from the active forces. And Mr. Kazanzaki would have set a gendarme to guard you. But now you have a p-perfectly legitimate reason for remaining here."

Varya could hardly raise any objection to that, but she did not wish to thank this despicable spy.

"I see you are a truly subtle practitioner of

your despised profession," she said acidly. "You even managed to outwit the head ogre."

"By 'ogre' you mean Lavrenty Arkadievich?" Fandorin asked in surprise. "He hardly fits the p-part, I think. And then, what is so d-despicable about defending the interests of the state?"

What point was there in talking to someone like that?

Varya demonstratively turned away and ran her eyes over the camp: little white-walled houses, neat rows of tents, brand-new telegraph posts. She saw a soldier running along the street, waving his long, awkward arms in a very familiar-looking fashion.

"Varya, Varenka!" the soldier called out from a distance, pulling his long-peaked cap off his head and waving it in the air. "So you really did come!"

"Petya!" she gasped and, instantly forgetting Fandorin, she dashed toward the man for whose sake she had made the long journey of one and a half thousand versts.

They embraced and kissed, entirely naturally, with no awkwardness, in a way they never had before. It was a joy to see Petya's dear, plain face so radiant with happiness. He had lost weight and acquired a tan and he stooped more than he used to. The black uniform jacket with the red shoulder straps hung on him like a loose sack, but his smile was the same as ever, wide and beaming in adoration.

"So you accept, then?" he asked.

"Yes," Varya replied simply, even though she had been planning not to accept his proposal immediately, but only after a long and serious discussion; only after she had laid down certain conditions of principle.

Petya gave a childish squeal of joy and tried to hug her again, but Varya had already come to her senses.

"But we still have to discuss everything in detail. In the first place—"

"Of course we'll discuss everything, of course we will. Only not now, this evening. Why don't we meet in the journalists' tent? They have a kind of club there. You've met the Frenchman, haven't you? I mean Paladin. A splendid fellow. He's the one who told me you had arrived. I'm terribly busy right now; I just dashed away for a moment. If they notice, I'll really be for it. Till this evening, this evening!"

He ran off back the way he came, kicking up the dust with his heavy boots and glancing back at every second.

HOWEVER, THEY WERE NOT ABLE to meet that evening. An orderly brought a note from the staff building: "On duty all night. Tomorrow. Love. P."

There was nothing to be done, he was in the army now, so Varya began settling in. The nurses had taken her in to live with them. They were wonderful, caring women, but they were quite elderly—all about thirty-five—and rather dull. They collected together everything necessary to replace the things in her baggage appropriated by the enterprising Mitko—clothes, shoes, a bottle of eau-de-cologne (instead of her wonderful Parisian perfume!), stockings, underwear, a comb, hairpins, scented soap, powder, salve to protect against the sun, cold cream, emollient lotion to counteract the effect of wind, essence of chamomile for washing her hair, and other essential items. Of course, the dresses were quite awful, with the possible exception of only one, which was light blue with a little white-lace collar. After Varya had removed the old-fashioned cuffs, it actually turned out rather nice.

But, first thing in the morning, she already found herself at loose ends. The nurses had gone to the field hospital to tend two wounded men brought in from near Lovcha. Varya drank her coffee alone, then went to send a telegram to her parents: first so that they wouldn't go insane with worry; second to ask them to send some money (purely as a loan—let them not start thinking she had voluntarily returned to her cage). She went for a stroll around the camp, on her way gazing in fascination at a bizarre train with no tracks—a military transport drawn by traction engines that had arrived from the opposite bank of the river. The iron locomobiles with the huge wheels puffed heavily and panted out steam as they tugged along the heavy field guns and wagons of ammunition. It was an impressive spectacle—a genuine triumph of progress.

After that, for want of anything better to do, she called in on Fandorin, who had been assigned his own tent in the staff sector. Erast Petrovich was also idling the time away, lying on his camp bed and copying out words from a book in Turkish.

"Protecting the interests of the state, Mr. Policeman?" Varya asked. She had decided that it would be most appropriate to address the secret agent in a casually sarcastic tone of voice.

Fandorin stood up and threw on a military tunic with no shoulder straps (he had obviously had himself kitted out somewhere, too). Varya caught a glimpse of a thin silver chain in the opening of his unbuttoned collar. A cross? No, it looked more like a medallion. It would be interesting to take a glance at what it was exactly.

Could our sleuth possibly be of a romantic disposition?

The titular counselor buttoned up his collar and replied seriously: "If you live in a state, you should either ch-cherish it or leave it—anything else is either parasitism or mere lackeys' gossip."

"There is a third possibility," Varya parried, stung by the phrase "lackeys' gossip." "An unjust state can be demolished and a new one built in its place."

"Unfortunately, Varvara Andreevna, a state is not a house, it is more like a tree. It is not built, it grows of its own accord, following the laws of nature, and it is a long business. It is not a stonemason who is required, but a gardener."

Completely forgetting about her appropriate tone of voice, Varya exclaimed passionately: "But the times we live in are so oppressive and hard! Honest people are oppressed—they are crushed under the burden of tyrannical arrogance and stupidity. But you reason like an old man, with your talk about gardeners!"

Erast Petrovich shrugged.

"My dear Varvara Andreevna, I am tired of listening to whining about 'these difficult times' of ours. In Tsar Nicholas's times, which were far more oppressive than these, your 'honest people' marched in tight order and constantly sang the praises of their happy life. If it is now possible to complain about arrogance and tyranny, it means that times have begun getting better, not worse."

"Why, you're nothing but . . . nothing but . . . a lackey of the throne!" Varya hissed out this worst of all possible insults through her teeth, and when Fandorin did not even flinch, she explained it in words that he could understand. "A servile, loyal subject with no mind or conscience of his own!"

As soon as she had blurted it out, she took fright at her own rudeness, but Erast Petrovich was not angry in the least. He merely sighed and said: "You are unsure of how to behave with me. That is one. You do not wish to feel grateful, and therefore you get angry. That is two. If you will simply forget about your damnable gratitude, we shall g-get along very well. That is three."

Such blatant condescension only made Varya even more furious, especially since the cold-blooded secret agent was absolutely right.

"I noticed yesterday that you talk like a dancing teacher: one-two-three, one-two-three. Where did you pick up such a stupid mannerism?"

"I had my teachers," Fandorin replied

vaguely, and impolitely stuck his nose back into his Turkish book.

THE MARQUEE WHERE THE JOUR-NALISTS accredited to central headquarters gathered was visible from a distance. The entrance was festooned with the flags of various countries hanging on a long string, the pennants of magazines and newspapers, and even a pair of red suspenders decorated with white stars.

"I expect they were celebrating the success at Lovcha yesterday," volunteered Petya. "Someone must have celebrated so hard that he lost his suspenders."

He pulled aside the canvas flap and Varya glanced inside.

The club was untidy but quite cozy in its own way: wooden tables, canvas chairs, a bar counter with rows of bottles. It smelled of tobacco smoke, candle wax, and men's eau-de-cologne. There were heaps of Russian and foreign newspapers lying on a long table at one side. The newspapers looked rather unusual, because they were glued together out of telegraph tapes. On taking a closer look at the London **Daily Post,** Varya was surprised to see that it was that morning's issue. Evidently the newspaper offices forwarded them everything by telegraph. How wonderful!

Varya was particularly gratified to note that there were only two women present, both wearing pince-nez and no longer in the first flush of youth. But there were lots and lots of men, and she spied her acquaintances among them.

First of all there was Fandorin, still with his book. That was rather silly—he could have read it in his tent.

In the opposite corner a session of simultaneous chess was in progress. McLaughlin was striding up and down on one side of the table, smoking his cigar with a condescendingly good-natured expression, while seated along the other side, all concentrating intensely, were Sobolev, Paladin, and two other men.

"Bah, it's our little Bulgarian!" exclaimed General Michel, getting up from the chessboard with relief. "Why, how you have changed! All right, Seamus, we'll call it a draw."

Paladin smiled affably at the new arrivals and his gazed lingered on Varya (which was very pleasant), but then he continued with his game. However, a dark-complexioned officer in a positively dazzling uniform came dashing up to Sobolev, set a finger to one point of his over-exuberant waxed mustache, and exclaimed in French: "General, I implore you, introduce me

to your enchanting acquaintance! Extinguish
the candles, gentlemen! They are needed no
longer, for the sun has risen!"

Both the elderly ladies cast glances of extreme disapproval in Varya's direction, and in
fact even she was rather taken aback by such a
headlong assault.

"This is Colonel Lukan, the personal representative of our invaluable ally, His Highness
Prince Karl of Romania," said Sobolev with a
smile. "I must warn you, Varvara Andreevna,
that, when it comes to ladies' hearts, the colonel
is more deadly than any upas tree."

It was clear from his tone of voice that it
would be best not to lead the Romanian on, and
Varya replied coolly, leaning demonstratively on
Petya's arm: "Pleased to meet you. My fiancé,
volunteer Pyotr Yablokov."

Lukan took Varya's wrist gallantly between
his finger and thumb (a ring studded with a
very substantial diamond glittered on his hand),
but when he attempted to kiss her fingers, he
was instead duly rebuffed.

"In St. Petersburg, one does not kiss **modern**
women's hands."

But nonetheless, the company here was certainly intriguing, and Varya took a liking to the
correspondents' club. The only annoying thing
was that Paladin was still playing his infernal

game of chess. But the end was obviously close now: All of McLaughlin's other opponents had already capitulated, and the Frenchman's position was clearly hopeless. Even so, he did not seem downhearted, and he kept glancing in Varya's direction, smiling lightheartedly and whistling a fashionable little chansonette.

Sobolev stood beside him, looked at the board, and absentmindedly took up the refrain:

"Folichon-folichonet . . . give in, Paladin, this is your Waterloo."

"The Guards die before they surrender," said the Frenchman, tugging on his narrow, pointed beard, and finally decided on a move that made the Irishman frown and heave a sigh.

Varya went outside for moment to admire the sunset and enjoy the cool of the evening, and when she went back into the marquee, the chessboards had been cleared away and the conversation had moved on to the exalted topic of man's relations with God.

"Any kind of mutual respect is entirely out of the question," McLaughlin was saying passionately, evidently in response to some remark made by Paladin. "Man's relations with the Almighty are founded on the conscious acknowledgment of inequality. After all, children would never think of claiming equality with their parents! The child unconditionally accepts the supremacy of the parent and its dependence on him, it feels reverence for him and therefore obeys him—for its own good."

"Permit me, in replying, to employ your own metaphor," said the Frenchman, smiling as he drew on a Turkish **chibouk.** "All this is only correct with regard to little children. But when a child grows somewhat older, it inevitable begins to query the authority of its parent, even though the latter is still incomparably more wise and powerful. This is natural and healthy, for without it man would remain a little infant forever. This is the very stage to which mankind has progressed at the present time. Later, when mankind becomes even more mature, it will most certainly establish new and different relations with God, based on equality and mutual respect. And at some stage, the child will grow sufficiently mature not to have any further need of a parent at all."

"Bravo, Paladin, you speak as elegantly as you write!" Petya exclaimed. "But the whole point is surely that God does not exist, while matter and the elementary principles of decent behavior do. I advise you to use your concept for a feuilleton in the **Revue Parisienne;** it would make an excellent topic."

"One does not need a topic in order to write

a good feuilleton," the Frenchman declared. "One simply needs to know how to write well."

"Now that's going a bit too far," McLaughlin objected. "Without a topic, even a verbal acrobat such as yourself cannot produce anything worthwhile."

"Name any object you like, even the most trivial, and I will write you an article about it that my paper will be delighted to print," said Paladin, holding out his hand. "Shall we have a wager? My Spanish saddle for your Zeiss binoculars."

Everybody livened up remarkably at that.

"Two hundred rubles on Paladin," declared Sobolev.

"Any subject?" the Irishman said slowly. "Absolutely any subject at all?"

"Absolutely. Even that fly over there sitting on Colonel Lukan's mustache."

The Romanian hastily shook his moustache and said: "I bet three hundred on Monsieur McLaughlin. But what will the subject be?"

"Well, why not those old boots of yours," said McLaughlin, jabbing a finger in the direction of the Frenchman's ancient calf-leather footgear. "Try writing something about those that will send the reading public of Paris into raptures."

Sobolev threw his hands up in the air.

"Before they shake hands on it, I pass. Old boots are just too outlandish altogether."

In the end, a thousand rubles were bet on the Irishman, and the Frenchman was left without any backers. Varya felt sorry for poor Paladin, but neither she nor Petya had any money. She went across to Fandorin, who was still leafing through his pages of Turkish squiggles, and whispered angrily: "Why don't you do something? You must back him. I'm sure you can afford it. That satrap of yours must have given you a few pieces of silver. I'll pay you back later."

Erast Petrovich frowned and said in a bored voice: "A hundred rubles on M-monsieur Paladin." And then he went back to his fascinating reading matter.

"That makes the odds ten to one," Lukan summed up. "Not large winnings, gentlemen, but a sure thing."

At that moment, Varya's acquaintance Captain Perepyolkin came dashing into the marquee, changed beyond all recognition: a brand-new uniform, bright, shiny boots, an impressive black dressing over his eye (the bruising had clearly not healed yet), and a white bandage around his head.

"Your excellency, gentlemen, I come directly

from Baron Kriedener!" the captain announced impressively. "I have an important announcement for the press. You may make a note of my name—Captain of General Headquarters Perepyolkin, Operations Section. Pe-re-pyolkin. Nikopol has been stormed and taken! We have captured two pashas and six thousand soldiers! Our own losses are trifling. Victory, gentlemen!"

"Damnation! Again without me!" Sobolev groaned, and he dashed out without even saying good-bye.

The messenger watched the general leave with a rather bemused expression, but then he was besieged from all sides by journalists. Captain Perepyolkin began answering their questions with obvious enjoyment, flaunting his knowledge of French, English, and German.

Varya was amazed by Erast Petrovich's reaction.

He dropped his book on the table, forced his way resolutely through the gaggle of correspondents, and asked in a quiet voice: "P-pardon me, captain, but are you not mistaken? Kriedener was ordered to take P-Plevna. Nikopol is in entirely the opposite d-direction."

There was something in his voice that put the captain on his guard and made him forget about the journalists.

"Most certainly not, my dear sir. I personally received the telegram from the headquarters of the commander in chief. I was present while it was decoded and I delivered it to the baron myself. I remember the text perfectly: 'To the commander of the Western Division Lieutenant General Baron Kriedener. I order you to occupy Nikopol and secure your position there with a force of at least one division. Nikolai.'"

Fandorin turned pale.

"Nikopol?" he asked, even more quietly. "But what about Plevna?"

The captain shrugged.

"I have no idea."

There was a sudden stamping of feet and clanking of guns at the entrance. The flap was thrust open violently and Lieutenant Colonel Kazanzaki—the last person she wanted to see again!—looked into the marquee. The bayonets of an armed escort glinted behind the lieutenant colonel's back. The gendarme rested his gaze on Fandorin for a moment, looked straight through Varya, and smiled delightedly at Petya.

"Ah, there he is, the good fellow! Just as I thought. Volunteer Yablokov, you are under arrest. Take him," he ordered, turning to the men in the escort. Two gendarmes in blue uniforms promptly strode in and seized hold of Petya's elbows as he stood there, paralyzed with fright.

"You're out of your mind!" cried Varya. "Let him go this instant!"

Kazanzaki did not dignify her outburst with a reply. He snapped his fingers and the prisoner was quickly dragged outside while the lieutenant colonel remained behind, gazing around him with an equivocal smile.

"Erast Petrovich, what's happening?" Varya appealed to Fandorin, her voice trembling. "Say something to him!"

"Your grounds?" Fandorin asked darkly, staring at the gendarme's collar.

"In the message encoded by Yablokov, one word was changed. 'Plevna' was replaced by 'Nikopol,' nothing more. But only three hours ago, Osman Pasha's vanguard occupied the deserted town of Plevna and now threatens our flank. Those are my grounds, Mr. Observer."

"There you have it, McLaughlin, that miracle of yours that can save Turkey," Varya heard Paladin say in Russian that was quite correct, but with a charming Gallic roll to the r's.

"No miracle, **monsieur correspondent,** but perfectly straightforward treason," the lieutenant colonel said with a smile, looking at Fandorin as he spoke. "I simply cannot imagine, Mr. Volunteer, how you are going to explain yourself to his excellency."

"You t-talk too much, Lieutenant Colonel."

Erast Petrovich's glance slid even lower, to the top button of the gendarme's uniform jacket. "Personal ambition should not interfere with the p-performance of one's duty."

"What?" Kazanzaki's swarthy face began twitching. "You dare lecture me? Well, now! I've had time to make a few inquiries about you, Mr. Wunderkind. In the line of duty. And the character that emerges isn't exactly a highly moral one. Too sharp altogether, above and beyond the call of duty. Made a highly advantageous marriage, didn't you, eh? Doubly advantageous in fact—pocketed a nice fat dowry and still held on to your freedom. Very nice work indeed! My congrat—"

He never finished. Striking as deftly as a cat, Erast Petrovich swiped the palm of his hand across Kazanzaki's plump lips. Varya gasped, and several officers grabbed hold of Fandorin's arm, but immediately released it when he showed no signs of agitation.

"Pistols," Erast Petrovich pronounced in a humdrum tone of voice, looking the lieutenant colonel straight in the eye now. "Immediately. This very moment, before the command can interfere."

Kazanzaki had turned deep crimson. His eyes, as black as plums, flushed bright red with blood. After a moment's pause he swallowed and said: "By order of His Imperial Majesty, duels are absolutely forbidden for the duration of the war. As you, Fandorin, are perfectly well aware."

The lieutenant colonel went out and the canvas flap swung shut violently behind him. Varya asked: "Erast Petrovich, what are we going to do?"

# CHAPTER FIVE

—⟋ww⟍—

## In which the arrangement of a harem is described

## LA REVUE PARISIENNE (Paris) 18 (6) July 187
### Charles Paladin

## OLD BOOTS

### A FRONTLINE SKETCH

Their leather has cracked and turned softer than the skin on a horse's lips. In such boots one could not possibly appear in respectable company. And, of course, I don't—the boots are meant to serve a quite different purpose.

They were sewn for me ten years ago by an old Jew in Sofia. As he fleeced me of ten lire, he said: "Monsieur, long after the burdock is growing thick over my grave, you will still be wearing these boots and remembering old Isaac with a kindly word."

Less than a year passed before the heel of the left boot fell off in the excavation site of an Assyrian city in Mesopotamia. I was obliged to return to camp alone. As I hobbled across the burning sand, I cursed that old swindler from Sofia in the vilest possible terms and swore that I would burn those boots on the campfire.

The British archaeologists I was working with at the site never did get back to the camp. They were attacked by the horsemen of Rifat-bek, who regard all infidels as children of Satan, and every last one of them was butchered. I did not burn the boots; instead I replaced the heel and ordered silver heel plates.

In 1873, in the month of May, while I was on my way to Khiva, my guide, Asaf, decided to appropriate my watch, my rifle, and my black Akhaltekin stallion, Yataghan. At night, while I lay sleeping in my tent, Asaf dropped a carpet viper, whose bite is deadly, into my left boot. But the toe of the boot was gaping wide open, and the viper crawled away into the desert. In the morning Asaf himself told me what had happened, because he saw the hand of Allah in it.

Six months later the steamship **Adrianople** ran onto rocks in the Gulf of Therma. I drifted along the shoreline for two and a half leagues. The boots were pulling me down to the bottom, but I did not take them off, for I knew that act would be tantamount to capitulation, and then I would never reach land. Those boots gave me the strength not to give in. And I was the only one who made it ashore; everyone else was drowned.

Now I find myself in a place where men are being killed. The shadow of death hangs over us every day. But I am calm. I put on my boots, which in ten years have changed in color from black to red, and even under fire I feel as though I am gliding across a gleaming parquet floor in my dancing shoes.

And I never allow my horse to trample burdock—just in case it might be growing over old Isaac's grave.

VARYA HAD BEEN WORKING with Fandorin for two days now. She had to try to get Petya released, and, according to Erast Petrovich, there was only one way to do that: Find the true culprit in the case. So Varya herself had implored the titular counselor to take her as his assistant.

Things looked bad for Petya. They would not allow Varya to see him, but she knew from Fandorin that all the evidence was against the cryptographer. After receiving the commander in chief's order from Kazanzaki, Yablokov had set about encoding it immediately and then, following standing orders, he had personally delivered the message to the telegraph office. Varya suspected that the absentminded Petya could very well have confused the two towns, especially as everyone knew about the Nikopol fortress, but hardly anyone had ever heard of the little town of Plevna before. Kazanzaki, however, did not believe in absentmindedness, and Petya himself stubbornly insisted that he clearly remembered encoding the name "Plevna," because it sounded so funny. The worst thing of all was that, according to Erast Petrovich, who had attended one of the interrogation sessions, Yablokov was quite clearly hiding something, and doing it very clumsily indeed. Varya was well aware that Petya simply did not know how to lie. As things stood a court-martial seemed inevitable.

108 • *Boris Akunin*

Fandorin's way of seeking out the true culprit was rather strange. In the morning he arrayed himself in idiotic striped tights and performed a long sequence of English gymnastics. He lay for days at a time on his camp bed, occasionally visiting the headquarters operations section, and in the evenings he could always be found sitting in the journalists' club. He smoked cigars, read his book, drank wine without getting drunk, and only entered into conversation reluctantly. He didn't give her any instructions at all. Before he wished her good-night, all he said was: "I'll see you in the club tomorrow evening."

Varya was driven frantic by the realization of her own helplessness. During the afternoon she walked around the camp, keeping her eyes peeled for anything suspicious that might turn up. But nothing suspicious did turn up, and so, worn out, Varya would go to Erast Petrovich's tent to shake him up and spur him into action. The titular counselor's den was a truly appalling mess, a scattered confusion of books, three-verst maps, wickerwork-covered Bulgarian wine bottles, clothes, and cannonballs, which obviously served him as exercise weights. On one occasion Varya sat on a plate of cold pilaf, which for some reason was lying on a chair where she had failed to notice it. She flew into a terrible rage and afterward no matter how she tried she simply could not wash the greasy stain off her one and only decent dress.

On the evening of the seventh of July Colonel Lukan organized a party in the press club (as the journalists' marquee had come to be known, in the English fashion) in order to celebrate his birthday. To mark the occasion, three crates of champagne were delivered from Bucharest, for which the hero of the festivities claimed to have paid thirty francs a bottle. The money, however, was wasted, for the birthday boy was very soon forgotten—the true hero of the hour was Paladin.

In the morning, having armed himself with the Zeiss binoculars he had won from the humbled McLaughlin (note, by the way, that for his miserable hundred rubles Fandorin had won an entire thousand, and all thanks to Varya), the Frenchman had carried out an expedition of great daring: He had ridden unaccompanied to Plevna and, under the protection of his corre-spondent's armband, had penetrated to the en-emy's forward lines, even managing to interview the Turkish colonel.

"Monsieur Perepyolkin was kind enough to explain to me the best way of approaching the town without attracting a bullet," Paladin ex-plained to the rapt listeners surrounding him. "And it was really not difficult at all—the Turks had not even bothered to arrange proper patrols, and I only met my first **asker** on the outskirts of the town. 'What are you gawking at?' I yelled at him. 'Take me to your senior commander immediately.' In the East, gentlemen, the most important thing is to act like a padishah. If you shout and swear, then perhaps you may actually have a right to do it. They brought me to the colonel. His name is Ali-bei—a red fez, a big black beard, and a St. Cyr badge on his chest. Excellent, I thought, **la belle France** will come to my rescue. I put my situation to him. From the Parisian press. Abandoned by the malevolent fates in the Russian camp, where the boredom is absolutely intolerable and there are no exotic distractions at all, nothing but drunkenness. Would the honorable Ali-bei not agree to give an interview for the public of Paris? He would. So we sit there, drinking cold sherbet. My friend Ali-bei asks me: 'Is that wonderful café on the corner of the Boulevard Raspaille and the Rue de Sèvres still there?' To be quite honest, I don't have a clue whether it is or it isn't, it is such a long time since I was last in Paris, but I say: 'Why of course, and more prosperous than ever.' We speak about the boulevards, the can-can, the cocottes. The colonel becomes quite sentimental, his beard even becomes quite straggly—and it is a most distinguished beard, quite the Maréchal de Rey—and he sighs: 'Yes, the moment this cursed war is over, I shall go to Paris, to Paris.' 'Will it be over soon then, effendi?' 'Soon,' says Ali-bei, 'very soon. Once the Russians dislodge me and my wretched three **tabor**s from Plevna, you can write your conclusion. The road will be left open all the way to Sofia.' 'Aye-aye-aye,' I lament. 'You are a very brave man, Ali-bei, to face the entire Russian army with only three battalions! I shall certainly write to my newspaper about this. But where is the glorious Osman Nuri Pasha and his army corps?' The colonel took off his fez and waved one hand in the air: 'He promised to be here tomorrow, but he will not be in time—the roads are too bad. The evening of the next day, no sooner.' All in all, we had a splendid little chat. We talked about Constantinople and Alexandria. It cost me quite a struggle to get away—the colonel had already ordered a ram to be slaughtered. On Monsieur Perepyolkin's advice I have acquainted the grand duke's staff with the contents of my interview. They found my conversation with Ali-bei quite interesting," the correspondent concluded modestly. "I believe that tomorrow the Turkish colonel is due for a little surprise."

"Oh, Paladin, you old hothead you!" cried

Sobolev, advancing on the Frenchman to clutch him in a general's embrace. "A true Gaul! Let me kiss you!"

Paladin's face disappeared behind the general's immense beard and McLaughlin, who was playing chess with Perepyolkin (the captain had already removed his black bandage and was contemplating the board with both eyes screwed up in concentration), remarked dryly: "The captain ought not to have used you as a scout. I am not really certain, my dear Charles, that your escapade is entirely beyond reproach from the viewpoint of journalistic ethics. A correspondent from a neutral country has no right to take either side in a conflict, and especially to take on the role of a spy, insofar—"

But at this everyone, including Varya, fell upon the tiresome Celt in such a concerted attack that he was forced into silence.

"Oho, here's real revelry!" a confident, ringing voice declared.

Varya swung round to see a handsome officer of the hussars with black hair, a jaunty mustache, slightly slanting eyes with a devil-may-care glint to them, and a shiny new Order of St. George on his pelisse. This new arrival was not in the least embarrassed by the universal attention that he had attracted—on the contrary, he seemed to accept it as something entirely natural and undeserving of comment.

"Captain of the Grodno Hussars Regiment Count Zurov," the officer introduced himself with a salute to Sobolev. "Do you not remember me, your excellency? We marched on Kokand together and I served on Konstantin Petrovich's staff."

"Of course I remember you," said the general with a nod. "As I recall, you were tried for gambling while on the march and fighting a duel with some quartermaster."

"By God's mercy, nothing came of it," the hussar replied flippantly. "They told me my old friend Erasmus Fandorin is sometimes to be found in here. I hope they were not lying?"

Varya glanced quickly at Erast Petrovich, seated in the far corner. He stood up, gave an agonized sigh, and said in a faint voice: "Hippolyte? How do you c-come to be here?"

"There he is, damn me if he isn't!" The hussar dashed at Fandorin and began shaking him by the shoulders so enthusiastically that he set Erast Petrovich's head wobbling backward and forward.

"And they told me the Turks had set you on a stake in Serbia! Ah, but you've lost your looks, brother, I hardly knew you. Touch up the temples to make yourself a bit more impressive, is that it?"

My, but this titular counselor certainly did have a curious circle of acquaintances: the Vidin Pasha, the chief of gendarmes, and now this picture-postcard dandy with the swashbuckling manners. Varya crept a little closer, as if by chance, in order not to miss a single word.

"Life has certainly put us through the mill a bit, that it has." Zurov stopped shaking his old friend and began slapping him on the back instead. "But I'll tell you about my adventures some other time, tête-à-tête; they're not for a lady's ears." He gave Varya a mischievous sideways glance. "But anyway, they had the usual ending: I was left without a kopeck to my name, all on my lonely ownsome, with my heart shattered to tiny little pieces." (Another glance in Varya's direction.)

"Who c-could ever have imagined it?" commented Fandorin.

"Are you stammering? Concussion? Don't worry about it, it'll pass. Near Kokand a blast wave flung me against the corner of a mosque so hard my teeth were chattering for an entire month—would you believe, I couldn't even get a glass anywhere near my mouth. But after that I was all right; it passed."

"And where did you c-come from before here?"

"That, brother Erasmus, is a long story."

The hussar ran an eye over the club's habitués, who were observing him with undisguised curiosity, and said: "Don't be shy, gentlemen, come closer. I'm relating my Scheherazade to my friend Erasmus here."

"Odyssey," Erast Petrovich corrected him in a low voice, retreating behind the back of Colonel Lukan.

"An Odyssey is what happens in Greece, but what happened to me was a genuine Scheherazade." Zurov paused to whet his listeners' appetites and then launched into his narrative. "And so, gentlemen, as a result of certain circumstances known only to myself and Fandorin here, I found myself in Naples, totally washed up, high and dry. I borrowed five hundred rubles from the Russian consul—the old skinflint wouldn't give me any more—and set out for Odessa by sea. But along the way the devil prompted me to arrange a little game with the captain and the navigator. The scoundrels cleaned me out completely, right down to the very last kopeck. Naturally I protested vigorously and, having caused some minor damage to ship's property in the process, at Constantinople I was thrown off the ship. I mean to say, I was put ashore—without any money or any possessions, not even a hat. And it was winter then, gentlemen. A Turkish winter, but even so it was cold. There was nothing else to be done, so I set out for our embassy. Broke through all the barriers, went all the way up to the ambassador himself, Nikolai Pavlovich Gnatiev. A most understanding kind of fellow. I can't lend you any money, he says, on account of my being opposed in principle to lending of any kind, but if you like, count, I can take you on as my adjutant—I'm in need of a few valiant officers. In that case you will receive the usual start-up expenses and so on and so forth. And so I became an adjutant."

"To Gnatiev himself?" said Sobolev with a shake of his head. "The cunning old fox must clearly have seen something special in you."

Zurov shrugged modestly and continued.

"On my very first day in my new post I provoked an international conflict and an exchange of diplomatic notes. Nikolai Pavlovich sent me with a request to the well-known Russophobe and religious hypocrite Hassan Hairulla—he's the top Turkish priest, a bit like the pope in Rome."

**"Sheikh-ul-Islam,"** interjected McLaughlin,

scribbling in his notebook. "He's more like the chief procurator of your synod."

"That's it," Zurov agreed with a nod. "That's what I meant. This Hairulla and I took an immediate dislike to each other. I addressed him with appropriate respect, through the interpreter: 'Your Grace, an urgent letter from Adjutant General Gnatiev.' But the rotten dog blinks his eyes and answers me back in French—deliberately, so the dragoman can't moderate what he says: 'Now is the hour of prayer. Wait.' He squatted down with his face toward Mecca and started repeating over and over: 'Oh, great and all-powerful Allah, extend thy favor to thy faithful servant and let him live to see the vile infidels who are unfit to trample thy holy earth burning in hell.' Very nice indeed. Since when did they start praying to Allah in French? Very well, I think, in that case I can introduce something new into the Orthodox canon. Hairulla turns toward me, feeling very pleased with himself now that he's set the infidel in his place. 'Give me the letter from your general,' he says. **'Pardonnez-moi, éminence,'** I reply. 'This is the very time set for us Russians to say mass. Won't you pardon me for just a moment.' Down I go, bang, onto my knees and start praying in the language of Corneille and

Rocambole: 'Lord of all blessings, delight thy sinful servant the boyar, that is, the chevalier Hippolyte, and let him rejoice in the sight of Muslim dogs roasting in the frying pan.' In short, I caused complications in Russo-Turkish relations, which were already very far from straightforward. Hairulla refused to take the letter, began swearing loudly in his own language, and threw the dragoman and me out. Well, Nikolai Pavlovich gave me a dressing down for the sake of appearances, but I thought he seemed quite pleased. He obviously knew who to send to whom on what errand."

"Smartly done, Turkestan fashion," said Sobolev approvingly.

"But not very diplomatic," put in Captain Perepyolkin, gazing at the unduly familiar hussar disapprovingly.

"I didn't last too long as a diplomat," Zurov sighed, then added thoughtfully, "Obviously, that's not the way my path lies."

Erast Petrovich snorted rather loudly.

"There I am walking across the Galat Bridge one day, displaying the Russian uniform and taking a look at the pretty girls. They might wear veils, but the she-devils choose the most transparent fabric they can find, and that just makes the temptation even greater. Suddenly I see this divine creature riding toward me in a carriage, with huge velvet eyes sparkling over the top of her veil. And sitting beside her is this Abyssinian eunuch, a great huge brute, and behind them another carriage with the servant women. I stopped and bowed—in a dignified manner befitting a diplomat—and then she removed her glove and blew me a kiss" (Zurov pursed up his lips ) "with her little white hand."

"She removed her glove?" Paladin inquired in his French accent with the air of an expert. "That is no jest, gentlemen. The Prophet regarded fine, delicate hands as the most seductive part of the female body and categorically forbade noble Muslim women to go without gloves in order not to subject men's hearts to temptation. And so removing a glove—**c'est une grande signe,** like a European woman removing . . . But then, I had better refrain from drawing parallels." He stopped short, casting a sideways glance at Varya.

"There now, you see," put in the hussar. "After that, how could I possibly offend the lady by ignoring her? I take the shaft horse by the bridle and stop it, because I want to introduce myself. Then that eunuch, the boot-blacked oaf, lashes me smartly across the cheek with his whip. What would you have me do? I pulled out my sword, ran the lout through, wiped my blade on his silk caftan, and went home feeling sad at heart. No time for the pretty lady now. I had a feeling things would end badly. And it was prophetic—they turned out very nastily indeed."

"But why was that?" Lukan asked curiously. "Was she a pasha's wife?"

"Worse," sighed Zurov. "The wife of His Infidel Highness Abdul-Hamid II himself. And of course the eunuch was the sultan's, too. Nikolai Pavlovich did the best he could for me. He told the padishah in person: 'If my adjutant had accepted a blow with a whip from a slave, I myself would have torn off his shoulder straps for disgracing the name of a Russian officer.' But what do they know about the meaning of an officer's uniform? They threw me out within twenty-four hours. Off to Odessa on a packet boat. It was a good thing the war started soon anyway. When he said good-bye to me, Nikolai Pavlovich told me: 'You should thank God, Zurov, that it wasn't the senior wife, but only a "little lady," **kuchum kadineh.**' "

"Not **k-kuchum** but **kuchuk**," Fandorin corrected him, and suddenly blushed, which Varya thought strange.

Zurov whistled: "Oho! And how do you happen to know that?"

Erast Petrovich did not answer, but he looked highly disgruntled.

"Mr. Fandorin spent some time as the guest of a Turkish pasha," Varya declared provocatively.

"And the entire harem took care of you?" the count asked with keen interest. "Well, tell us about it, don't be such a swine."

"Not the entire harem, only a **kuchuk-hanum**," the titular counselor mumbled, clearly reluctant to go into the details. "A really splendid, good-hearted g-girl. And entirely modern. She knows French and English and is fond of Byron. She is interested in medicine."

This was a new and unexpected side to the secret agent, and one which for some reason was not at all to Varya's liking.

"A modern woman would never agree to live as the fifteenth wife in a harem," she snapped. "It's humiliating and altogether barbaric."

"I beg your pardon, mademoiselle, but that remark is not entirely fair," said Paladin, continuing to roll his Russian r's in the French manner. "You see, during my years of traveling in the East, I have made quite a serious study of the Muslim way of life."

"Yes, Charles, yes, do tell us about it," said McLaughlin. "I recall your series of essays on the life of the harem. It was quite excellent." The Irishman positively beamed at his own magnanimity.

"Any social institution, including polygamy, has to be viewed in historical context," Paladin began in a professorial tone, but Zurov pulled such a long face that the Frenchman thought better of it and began speaking like a normal human being. "Actually, in the conditions of the Orient, the harem is the only means capable of offering a woman a chance of survival. Judge for yourself—from the very beginning, Muslims have been a nation of warriors and prophets. Since the men spent their lives waging war, they died, and a huge number of women were widowed or were unable to find themselves a husband in the first place. Who was going to feed them and their children? Mohammed had fifteen wives, but not at all because of his excessively voluptuous inclinations. He accepted the responsibility of caring for the widows of his fallen comrades in arms, so these women could not even be called his wives in the Western sense. What, after all, is a harem, gentlemen? You imagine the soft murmuring of a fountain, seminaked odalisques indolently consuming Turkish delight, the tinkling of coin necklaces, the heady aroma of perfume, and the whole scene veiled in a dense haze of debauchery."

"And in the middle of it all, the lord and master of this henhouse, wrapped in his robe, with a hookah and a blissful smile on his bright red lips," Zurov mused dreamily.

"I am afraid I must disappoint you, captain. In addition to the wives, a harem is also poor female relatives, a throng of children, including other people's, countless female servants, old female slaves living out their final days, and God knows what else. And this entire horde has to be fed and supported by the breadwinner, the man. The richer and more powerful he is, the more dependents he has and the heavier the burden of responsibility he bears. The system of the harem is not only humane, it is the only possible system in the conditions of the East— without it many women would quite simply starve to death."

"What you describe is some kind of phalanstery, and you make the Turkish husband sound like Charles Fourier," Varya protested impatiently. "Would it not be better to give women the chance to support themselves, rather than keeping them in the position of slaves?"

"The society of the East is sluggish and little disposed to change, **Mademoiselle Barbara,**" the Frenchman replied deferentially, pronouncing her name so sweetly in French that it was quite impossible to be angry with him. "It has very few jobs, every one of which has to be fought for, and women would not survive in competition with the men. And in any case, a wife is by no means a slave. If a husband is not to her liking, she can always reclaim her freedom. All she need do is to make her husband's life so unbearable that he cries out angrily in the presence of witnesses: 'You are no longer my wife!' You must agree that it is not very difficult to reduce a husband to such a state. After that, she can collect her things and go. Divorce in the East is not what it is in the West; it is simple. And at the same time, the man is solitary, while the women form a collective. Is it any wonder, therefore, that the real power lies with the harem and not with its master? The most important figures in the Ottoman Empire are not the sultan and the grand vizier, but the padishah's mother and his favorite wife. And also, of course, the **kizlyar-agazi**—the head eunuch of the harem."

"And just how many wives is the sultan allowed to have?" Perepyolkin asked, with a guilty glance at Sobolev. "I'm only asking as a matter of information, of course."

"Four, like any true believer. But in addition to fully fledged wives, the padishah also has **ikbal**—something like his favorites—and very

young **gedikla**s, or 'maidens pleasing to the
eye,' who are aspirants to the role of the **ikbal.**"

"Now that's a bit more like it," said Lukan
with a satisfied nod. Spotting Varya's scornful
glance, he gave one side of his mustache a smart
twirl.

Sobolev (another fine goose) asked in a
voluptuous voice: "But surely in addition to
wives and concubines there are the slave girls?"

"All the sultan's women are slaves, but only
until a child is born. Then the mother immediately acquires the title of princess and all the
privileges that go with it. For instance, the all-
powerful Sultana Besma, mother of the late
Abdul-Aziz, was once a simple bathhouse atten-
dant, but she lathered Mehmed the Second so
successfully that first he took her as a concubine
and then he made her his favorite wife. The
career opportunities for women in Turkey are
truly unlimited."

"But, all the same, it must be devilishly tir-
ing, having a crowd like that hanging round
your neck," one of the journalists mused. "I'd
say it's a bit too much."

"Several sultans have also come to the same
conclusion," said Paladin with a smile. "Ibrahim
the First, for instance, grew terribly weary of all
his wives. It was easier for Ivan the Terrible or

Henry the Eighth to deal with such a situation—send the old wife to the block or to a convent, and then you can take a new one. But what can you do if you have an entire harem?"

"Yes, what can you do?" inquired one of the listeners.

"The Turks, gentlemen, do not surrender in the face of adversity. The padishah ordered all the women to be stuffed into sacks and drowned in the Bosphorus. When morning came his majesty was a bachelor again and he could acquire a new harem."

The men chortled, but Varya exclaimed: "You ought to be ashamed of yourselves, gentlemen. This is really quite appalling."

"But almost a hundred years ago, Mademoiselle Varya, manners at the sultan's court were moderated substantially," Paladin reassured her. "And all thanks to one exceptional woman who just happens to be a compatriot of mine."

"Then tell us about it," said Varya.

"The story is as follows. One of the passengers on board a French ship sailing the Mediterranean was an exceptionally beautiful seventeen-year-old girl whose name was Aimée Dubucque de Riverie. She was born on the magical island of Martinique, which has given the world many legendary beauties, including Madame de Maintenon and Josephine

Beauharnais. In fact our young Aimée knew the latter (at the time still plain Josephine de Taschery) very well; they were even friends. History has nothing to say on the subject of why this delightful Creole girl decided to set out on a voyage through seas teeming with pirates. All we do know is that off the coast of Sardinia the ship was seized by corsairs and Aimée found herself in the slave market of Algiers, where she was bought by the dey of Algiers himself—the very one who, according to Monsieur Popritschine, had a lump under his nose. The dey was old and no longer susceptible to female beauty, but he was very interested in good relations with the Sublime Porte, so poor Aimée made the journey to Istanbul as a living gift to Sultan Abdul-Hamid the First, the great-grandfather of the present-day Abdul-Hamid the Second. The padishah treated his captive gently, like a priceless treasure. He imposed no constraints on her and did not even oblige her to convert to Mohammedism. And for the patience shown by the wise ruler, Aimée rewarded him with her love. In Turkey she is known by the name of Nashedil-sultan. She gave birth to Prince Mehmed, who later ascended the throne and is known to history as a great reformer. His mother taught him French and gave him a taste for French literature and French freethinking.

Ever since then Turkey has looked toward the West."

"You're a great spinner of tales, Paladin," McLaughlin commented cantankerously. "No doubt you stretched the truth and embroidered it a little, as always."

The Frenchman smiled mischievously without saying a word, and Zurov, who for some time had been showing clear signs of impatience, exclaimed in sudden inspiration: "Yes, indeed, gentlemen, why don't we arrange a little game? All this talk, talk, talk. Really and truly, it's just not natural, somehow."

Varya heard Fandorin give a dull groan.

"Erasmus, you're not invited," the count added hastily. "The devil himself deals your hands."

"Your excellency," Perepyolkin protested. "I hope you will not permit gambling in your presence?"

Sobolev brushed his objections aside like an annoying fly.

"Stop that, Captain. Don't be such a pain in the neck. It's all very well for you, in your operations section. You at least have some kind of work to do, but I'm rusting away from sheer idleness. I don't play myself, Count—I'm far too impetuous—but I will certainly watch."

Varya saw Perepyolkin staring at the handsome general with the eyes of a beaten dog.

"Perhaps just for small stakes, then?" Lukan drawled uncertainly. "To reinforce the ties of soldierly comradeship."

"To reinforce the ties, of course, and just for small stakes," Zurov said with a nod, tipping several unopened decks of cards onto the table out of his sabretache. "A hundred in the pot. Who else—gentlemen?"

The bank was made up in a moment, and soon the marquee echoed with the magic phrases:

"There goes the old whore."

"We'll beat her with our little sultan here, gentlemen!"

**"L'as de carreau."**

"Ha ha, that's beaten it!"

Varya moved closer to Erast Petrovich and asked: "Why does he call you Erasmus?"

"It's just something that happened," said the secretive Fandorin, avoiding the question.

"Alas," Sobolev sighed loudly. "Kriedener's probably already advancing on Plevna, and I'm stuck in here like a low card in the discard pile."

Perepyolkin stuck close to his idol, pretending he was also interested in the game.

The angry McLaughlin, standing all alone with a chessboard under his arm, muttered something in English and then translated it into Russian himself.

"It used to be a press club; now it's a low gambling den."

"Hey, my man, do you have any Shustov cognac? Bring it over!" cried the hussar, turning to the bartender. "We might as well have some real fun while we're at it."

The evening was promising to turn out very cheerfully.


THE NEXT DAY, HOWEVER, the press club had changed beyond all recognition, with the Russians sitting there looking gloomy and depressed, while the correspondents were talking excitedly in low voices, and every now and then, when one of them learned some new details, he would go running to the telegraph office—what had happened was a sensation of the first order.

Already at lunchtime the dark rumors had begun to spread round the camp, and as Varya and Fandorin were walking back from the shooting range after five (the titular counselor was teaching his assistant to use a Colt revolver), they had been met by a sullenly agitated Sobolev.

"A fine business," he said, rubbing his hands together nervously. "Have you heard?"

"Plevna?" Fandorin asked forlornly.

"A total rout. General Schilder-Schuldner went at it all out—he wanted to catch Osman Pasha. We had seven thousand men, but the Turks had far more. Our columns attacked full on and were caught in a crossfire. Rosenbaum, the commander of the Arkhangelsk Regiment, was killed, Kleinhaus, the commander of the Kostroma Regiment, was fatally wounded, and Major General Knorring was brought back on a stretcher. A third of our men were killed. Absolute carnage. So much for those three battalions. And the Turks were different, too, not like before. They fought like devils."

"What about Paladin?" Erast Petrovich asked rapidly.

"He's all right. He turned bright green and kept babbling excuses; Kazanzaki's taken him away for interrogation. Well, now the real thing will start. Perhaps now they'll give me a posting. Perepyolkin hinted that there might be a chance." And the general set off toward the staff building with a spring in his step.

Varya had spent the time until evening in the hospital, helping sterilize surgical instruments. So many wounded had been brought in that they had been obliged to set up another two temporary tents. The nurses were dog-tired. The air was filled with the smell of blood and suffering and the screams and prayers of the wounded.

It was almost night before she was able to escape to the correspondents' marquee where, as has already been mentioned, the atmosphere was strikingly different from the day before.

The only place where life continued in full swing was at the card table, where the game was now in its second uninterrupted day. Pale-faced Zurov puffed on a cigar as he rapidly dealt out the cards. He had not eaten a thing, but he had been drinking incessantly without getting even slightly drunk. A tall heap of banknotes, gold coins, and promissory notes had sprung up beside his elbow. Sitting opposite him, tousling his hair in insane frenzy, was Colonel Lukan. Some officer or other was sleeping beside him with his light-brown head of hair slumped onto his folded arms. The bartender fluttered around them like a fat moth, plucking the lucky hussar's least wish out of the air on the wing.

Fandorin was not at the club, and neither was Paladin. McLaughlin was playing chess, while Sobolev, surrounded by officers, was poring over a three-verst map and hadn't even glanced at Varya.

Already regretting that she had come, she said: "Count, are you not ashamed? So many people have been killed."

"But we are still alive, mademoiselle," Zurov replied absentmindedly, tapping on a deck of cards with his finger. "What's the point of dying before your time has come? Oh, you're bluffing, Luke. I raise you two."

Lukan tugged the diamond ring off his finger.

"I'll see you." He reached out a trembling hand toward Zurov's cards, which were lying casually facedown on the table.

At that instant Varya saw Lieutenant Colonel Kazanzaki glide soundlessly into the tent, looking hideously like a black raven that has caught the sweet smell of a putrid corpse. Remembering what the gendarme's previous appearance had led to, she shuddered.

"Mr. Kazanzaki," said McLaughlin, turning toward the new arrival, "where is Paladin?"

The lieutenant colonel paused portentously, waiting for the club to become quiet. He answered curtly: "I have him. He is writing an explanation." He cleared his throat and added ominously, "And then we'll make up our minds."

The awkward silence that ensued was broken by Zurov's nonchalant light bass: "So this is the famous gendarme Kozinikinaki? Greetings to you, Mister Split-Lip." He waited, his eyes gleaming insolently as he stared expectantly at the lieutenant colonel's flushed features.

"And I have heard about you, Mister Brawler," Kazanzaki replied unhurriedly, also staring hard at the hussar. "A notorious character. Pray be so good as to hold your tongue, or I shall call the sentry and have you taken to the guardhouse for gambling in camp. And I shall arrest the bank."

"There's no mistaking a serious man," chuckled the count. "Understood, I'll be as silent as the grave."

Lukan finally turned over Zurov's cards, gave a protracted groan, and clutched his head in his hands. The count inspected the ring he had won with a skeptical eye.

"No, Major, no, there's no damned treason here!" Varya heard Sobolev say irritably. "Perepyolkin's right—he's the brains on the staff. Osman simply covered the ground at a forced march, and our blustering sabre-rattlers didn't expect that kind of energy from the Turks. We have a formidable enemy to fight now, and this war is going to be fought in earnest."

# CHAPTER SIX

—m—

## In which Plevna and Varya
## each withstand a siege

## DIE WIENER ZEITUNG (Vienna)
## 30 (18) July 1877

Our correspondent reports from Shumen, where the headquarters of the Turkish Army of the Balkans is located.

The fiasco at Plevna has left the Russians in an extremely foolish position. Their columns extend for tens and even hundreds of kilometers from the south to the north, their lines of communication are defenseless, their rear lines exposed. Osman Pasha's brilliant flanking maneuver has won the Turks time to regroup, and a little Bulgarian town has become a serious thorn in the shaggy side of the Russian bear. The atmosphere in circles close to the court in Constantinople is one of cautious optimism.

ON THE ONE HAND, things were going very badly; you might even say they could not possibly be any worse. Poor Petya was still languishing under lock and key—after the Plevna bloodbath the noxious Kazanzaki had lost interest in the cryptographer, but the threat of a court-martial remained as real as ever. And the fortunes of war had proved fickle—the golden fish that granted wishes had turned into a prickly scorpion fish and disappeared into the abyss, leaving their hands scratched and bleeding.

But on the other hand (this was something Varya was ashamed to admit even to herself) her life had never been so . . . interesting. That was the word: interesting. That was it exactly.

And the reason, in all honesty, was obscenely simple: It was the first time in Varya's life that she had been courted at the same time by so many admirers—and such admirers, too. Her recent traveling companions on the railway or the scrofulous students of St. Petersburg could not possibly compare. No matter how hard she tried to suppress them, these banal womanish feelings still sprang up like weeds in her vain, foolish heart. It was really awful.

For instance, on the morning of the eighteenth of June (a most important and memorable day, concerning which more below), Varya woke with a smile on her face. Before she was even fully awake and had barely even sensed the sunlight through her tightly shut eyelids, even as she was still stretching sweetly, she was already in a cheerful, happy, festive mood. It was only afterward, when her mind had woken up as well as her body, that she remembered about Petya and the war. With an effort of will, Varya forced herself to frown and think about sad realities, but something quite different kept creeping into her stubborn, drowsy head, in the manner of Agafya Tikhonovna: if she could add to Petya's devotion Sobolev's fame, and Zurov's daredevil panache, and Paladin's talent, and Fandorin's piercing glance . . . but no. Erast Petrovich did not suit the case, for not by any stretch of the imagination could she number **him** among her admirers.

Nothing really seemed clear as far as the titular counselor was concerned. Varya's position as his assistant remained, as ever, purely nominal. Fandorin did not initiate her into his secrets, although he was apparently dealing with serious business of some kind, not mere trivialities. He either disappeared for long periods or, on the contrary, simply sat in his tent receiving visits from Bulgarian peasants wearing smelly sheepskin hats. Varya guessed that they must be from Plevna, but her pride would not allow her to ask any questions. What was so remarkable about that, anyway? It wasn't as if people from Plevna were rare visitors to the Russian camp. Even McLaughlin had his own informant, who provided him with exclusive intelligence about life in the Turkish garrison. Of course, the Irishman did not share this knowledge with the Russian command, stubbornly citing his "journalistic ethics," but the readers of the **Daily News** knew all about Osman Pasha's order of the day and the massive redoubts that were springing up around the besieged town, growing more powerful by the hour.

This time, however, the Western Division of the Russian army was making thorough preparations for battle. The storming of Plevna was set for today, and everybody was saying that the "misunderstanding over Plevna" was certain to be cleared up. Yesterday Erast Petrovich had traced out a diagram of all the Turkish fortifications for Varya on the ground with a stick and explained that, according to absolutely reliable information in his possession, Osman Pasha had twenty-thousand **askers** and 58 artillery pieces, while Lieutenant General Kriedener had moved up thirty-two thousand soldiers and 176 field guns into the town, and the Romanians were due to arrive at any time. A cunning and strictly secret disposition of forces had been devised, involving a concealed outflanking maneuver and a diversionary attack. Fandorin had explained it all so well that Varya had immediately believed in the imminent victory of Russian arms and stopped paying much attention—she was more interested in watching the titular counselor and trying to guess what his relation was with the blond girl in his locket. Kazanzaki had said something odd about a marriage. Could she really be his wife? But she was too young; she was no more than a little girl.

Varya knew about her because three days earlier, when she looked into Erast Petrovich's tent after breakfast, she had seen him lying sound asleep on his bed, fully dressed, even wearing his dirty boots. He had been missing for the whole previous day, which meant he had probably only returned shortly before dawn. Just as she was about to creep quietly away, she had suddenly noticed the silver locket dangling out of the sleeping man's collar onto his chest. The temptation had been too great. Varya had tiptoed across to the bed, keeping her eyes fixed on Fandorin's face. Lying there, breathing regularly with his mouth slightly open, the titular counselor looked like a mischievous little boy who has smeared powder on his temples as a joke.

Varya had gingerly picked up the locket between her finger and thumb, clicked open the lid, and seen the tiny portrait. A pretty little china doll, a real Mädchen Gretchen: golden curls, little eyes and little mouth, tiny cheeks. Really nothing special. Casting a glance of disapproval at the sleeper, Varya had suddenly blushed bright red—the clear blue eyes with the pitch-black pupils were peering gravely at her from under their long lashes.

Trying to explain would have been stupid. Varya had simply fled, which wasn't so very clever either, but at least an unpleasant scene had been avoided. Strangely enough, afterward Fandorin had behaved as though the episode had never happened.

He was a cold, disagreeable man, he rarely joined in other people's conversations, and when he did he was bound to say something that made Varya's hackles rise. Take, for instance, that argument about parliament and the sovereignty of the people that had blown up during the picnic (a large party of them had gone off into the hills and dragged Fandorin along with them, although he had been dying to go back and skulk in his lair).

Paladin had started telling them about the constitution that had been introduced in Turkey the year before by the former grand vizier, Midhat Pasha. It was very interesting. Would you believe it—an uncivilized Asiatic country like that, but unlike Russia it actually had a parliament.

Then they had started arguing about which parliamentary system was the best. McLaughlin was for the British system and Paladin, even though he was a Frenchman, was for the American, while Sobolev campaigned for some indigenous Russian system involving the nobility and the peasantry.

When Varya had demanded suffrage for women, they had all made fun of her and that crude soldier Sobolev had started scoffing: "Oh, Varvara Andreevna, once you women are given the vote, you'll elect a parliament full of nothing but your own handsome little darlings and sweethearts. If you women had to choose between Fyodor Mikhailovich Dostoevsky and our Captain Zurov, who would you cast your vote for? You see?"

"Gentlemen, can people be elected to parliament compulsorily?" the hussar had asked in alarm, and the general mood had become even merrier.

Varya had struggled in vain to explain about

equal rights, citing the American territory of Wyoming, where women had been allowed to vote, and nothing terrible had happened to Wyoming as a result. No one had taken anything she said seriously.

"Why don't you say anything?" Varya had appealed to Fandorin, who had promptly distinguished himself by saying something that would have been better left unsaid altogether.

"Varvara Andreevna, I am opposed to democracy in general." (He had blushed even as he said it.) "One man is unequal to another from the very beginning, and there is nothing you can do about it. The democratic principle infringes the rights of those who are more intelligent, more talented, and harder working; it places them in a position of dependence on the foolish will of the stupid, talentless, and lazy, because society always contains more of the latter. Let our compatriots first learn to rid themselves of their swinish ways and earn the right to bear the title of citizen, and then we can start thinking about a parliament."

This absolutely outlandish declaration had left Varya completely flummoxed, but Paladin had come to the rescue.

"Nonetheless, if a country has already introduced voting rights," he had said gently (the conversation, of course, was conducted in

French), "it is surely unjust to disenfranchise half of mankind, and the better half at that."

Remembering those remarkable words, Varya smiled, turned on her side, and began thinking about Paladin.

Thank God Kazanzaki had finally left the man in peace. It had been General Kriedener's decision to base his strategy on the contents of some interview—poor Paladin had been eating his heart out and pestering absolutely everyone he met with his explanations and excuses. Varya liked him even more when he was feeling guilty and miserable like that. Previously she had thought him a tad too conceited, too accustomed to general admiration, and she had deliberately kept her distance, but now the need for that had fallen away and Varya had begun to behave quite naturally and affectionately with the Frenchman. He was cheerful and easy to be with, not like Erast Petrovich, and he knew such a terrible lot—about Turkey and the ancient history of the East, and French history. All those places he had seen, driven by his thirst for adventure! And how charmingly he narrated his little **récits drôles**!—so witty, so lively, without any posturing at all. How Varya adored it when Paladin responded to one of her questions with a significant pause and an intriguing smile and then said: **"O, c'est toute une histoire, made-**

**moiselle.**" And then, unlike the tight-lipped Fandorin, he would immediately tell her the story.

Most of the time the stories were funny, but sometimes they were frightening.

Varya remembered one of them particularly well.

"**Mademoiselle Barbara,** you berate Orientals for their lack of respect for human life, and you are quite right to do so." (They had been discussing the atrocities committed by the Bashi-Bazouks.) "But, after all, these are savages, barbarians, who have not yet developed much beyond the level of tigers or crocodiles. Let me describe to you a scene that I observed in that most civilized of countries, England. **O, c'est toute une histoire . . .** The British place such a high value on human life that they regard suicide as the most heinous of sins—and the penalty they apply for an attempt to do away with oneself is capital punishment. They have not yet gone that far in the East. Several years ago, when I was in London, a prisoner in the jail was due to be hanged. He had committed a terrible crime—somehow he had obtained a razor and attempted to cut his own throat. He had even been partly successful, but he was saved by the timely intervention of the prison doctor. Since I found the judge's logic in this case quite astounding, I decided I must watch the execution with my own eyes. And after using my connections to obtain a pass for the execution, I was not disappointed.

"The condemned man had damaged his vocal cords and could do no more than wheeze, so they dispensed with his final word. Quite a long time was spent on squabbling with the doctor, who claimed that the man could not be hanged—the cut would reopen and the hanged man would be able to breathe directly through his trachea. The prosecuting counsel and the governor of the prison consulted together and ordered the executioner to proceed. But the doctor was proved right: The pressure of the noose immediately reopened the wound and the man dangling at the end of the rope began sucking in air with an appalling whistling sound. He hung there for five, ten, fifteen minutes and still did not die, although his face turned blue.

"They decided to summon the judge who had passed sentence on him. But since the execution took place at dawn, a considerable time was required to wake the judge. He arrived an hour later and issued a verdict worthy of Solomon: Take the condemned man down from the gallows and hang him again, but this time tie the noose below the cut, not above it. They did as he said and the second attempt was successful. There you have the fruits of civilization."

Afterward, in the night, Varya had dreamed of a hanged man with a laughing throat. "There is no death," the throat said in Paladin's voice and began oozing blood. "You can only go back to the start line."

But those words about going back to the start line belonged to Sobolev.

"Ah, Varvara Andreevna, my entire life is an obstacle race," the young general had complained to her, shaking his close-cropped head bitterly. "But the umpire keeps disqualifying me and sending me back to the start line. Why, judge for yourself. I began in the Horse Guards and served with distinction against the Poles, but got involved in a stupid affair with a Polish girl, so it was back to the start line. I graduated from the General Headquarters Academy and was given a posting to Turkestan, and then there was a stupid duel with a fatal outcome, so it was back to the start line again, if you please. I married a prince's daughter and thought I would be happy—I was anything but. So there I was on my own again, right back where I started, my dreams shattered. I managed to have myself sent off to the desert again and I was as hard on myself as I was on everyone else. I only survived by a miracle, but I'm still empty-handed. Here I sit, vegetating like some useless hanger-on, and waiting for a new start. But will it ever come?"

Varya felt sorry for Paladin, but not for Sobolev. In the first place, Michel's complaints about being sent back to the start line were too melodramatic—at the age of thirty-two he was, after all, a general of the imperial retinue, with two Orders of St. George and a gold sword. And in the second place he was far too obviously playing for sympathy. When he was still a cadet his senior comrades had no doubt explained to him that victory in love could be won in two ways: either by a cavalry charge or by painstaking excavation of the approaches to the over-compassionate female heart.

Sobolev excavated his approaches rather ineptly, but Varya was flattered by his attentions—after all, he was a genuine hero, even if he did have that idiotic bush on his face. When it was tactfully suggested that the form of his beard might be modified, the general had taken to haggling: He would be willing to make such a sacrifice, but only in exchange for certain guarantees. However, the offering of guarantees did not enter into Varya's plans.

Five days earlier Sobolev had come to her in a happy mood—at long last he had been given his own detachment, of two Cossack regiments—and he was to take part in the storming of Plevna, covering the southern flank of the main corps. Varya had wished him a successful new start. Michel had told her he had taken Perepyolkin as his chief of staff and described the tedious captain as follows.

"He followed me around, whining and gazing into my eyes, so I took him. And what do you think, Varvara Andreevna? Eremei Ionovich Perepyolkin may be tedious, but he certainly is sound—he's on the general staff, after all. They know him in the operations section and they provide him with useful information. And then I can see that he is personally devoted to me— he hasn't forgotten who saved him from the Bashi-Bazouks. And, sinner that I am, I prize devotion above all else in my subordinates."

Sobolev had more than enough on his hands now, but only two days ago his orderly, Seryozha Bereshchagin, had delivered a sumptuous bouquet of scarlet roses from his excellency. The roses were still standing as firm as the heroes of the Battle of Borodino, showing no signs of drooping, and the entire tent was permeated with their dense, sensual scent.

The breach created by the general's withdrawal had been promptly filled by Zurov, a firm believer in the cavalry charge. Varya burst out laughing as she recalled how jauntily the

captain had carried out his initial reconnaissance.

"A veritable bellevue, mademoiselle. Nature!"
was what he had said that time when he followed Varya as she went out of the press club to
admire the sunset. Then, without wasting any
time, he had changed the subject. "Erasmus is a
wonderful chap, don't you think? A heart as
pure and white as a bedsheet. And a splendid
comrade, even if he is a bit sulky."

The hussar had paused and glanced expectantly at Varya with those insolently handsome eyes. Varya had waited to see what would
come next.

"A good-looking dark-haired man, too. Put
him in a hussar's uniform and he'd cut a fine figure altogether," said Zurov, doggedly pursuing
his theme. "He may go around looking like a
drowned chicken now, but you should have
seen the old Erasmus! An Arabian tornado!"

Varya had gazed at the tale-teller mistrust-
fully: She found it absolutely impossible to
imagine the titular counselor in the role of an
"Arabian tornado."

"What could possibly have brought about
such a change?" she had asked, hoping to
learn something about Erast Petrovich's mysterious past.

But Zurov had merely shrugged.

"The devil only knows. It's been a year since we last saw each other. It must be a fatal case of love. You think we men are all heartless, insensitive idiots, but in our souls we are ardent and easily wounded." He lowered his eyes sorrowfully. "A broken heart can make an old man of you even at twenty."

Varya had snorted: "At twenty, indeed! Trying to hide your age does not become you."

"Why, not me, I meant Fandorin," the hussar explained. "He's only twenty-one."

"Who, Erast Petrovich?" Varya had gasped. "Oh, come now, even I'm twenty-two."

"That's exactly what I mean," Zurov had said, brightening up. "What you need is someone a bit more mature, closer to thirty."

But she had stopped listening, astounded by what he had told her. Fandorin was only twenty-one? Twenty-one! Incredible! So that was why Kazanzaki had called him a wunderkind. Of course, the titular counselor had a boyish face, but the way he carried himself, that glance, those graying temples! What chill wind could have frosted your temples so early, Erast Petrovich?

Interpreting her bewilderment in his own way, the hussar had assumed a dignified air and declared: "What I'm leading up to is this. If that

rascal Erasmus has beaten me to it, then I withdraw immediately. Whatever his detractors may
claim, mademoiselle, Zurov is a man with principles. He will never try to poach anything that
belongs to his friend."

"Are you speaking of me?" Varya had asked
in sudden realization. "If I'm 'something that
belongs' to Fandorin, you won't try to poach
me, but if I'm not 'something that belongs' to
him, you will. Have I understood you cor-
rectly?"

Zurov raised his eyebrows diplomatically, but
without betraying the slightest sign of embarrassment.

"I belong and always will belong to nobody
but myself, but I do have a fiancé," Varya had
reprimanded the insolent lout.

"So I have heard. But I don't count monsieur
the detainee among my friends," the captain
had replied in a more cheerful voice, and the reconnaissance was complete.

The full-frontal assault had followed immediately.

"Would you care to wager with me, mademoiselle? If I can guess who will be first to come
out of the marquee, you will favor me with a
kiss. If I guess wrong, then I shall shave my head,
like a Bashi-Bazouk. Make up your mind! Of

course, the risk you would be taking is perfectly minimal—there are at least twenty people in the tent."

Varya had felt her lips curl into a smile despite herself.

"So who will be first?"

Zurov had pretended to be thinking hard and shook his head despairingly.

"Aah, farewell to my curly locks. . . . Colonel Sablin. No! McLaughlin. No—the bartender Semyon, that's who!"

He had cleared his throat loudly and a second later the bartender had come strolling out of the club, wiping his hands on the hem of his long-waisted silk coat. He had looked up briskly at the sky, muttered, "Oh, I hope it's not going to rain," and gone back inside without even glancing at Zurov.

"It's a miracle, a sign from above!" the count had exclaimed, stroking his mustache as he leaned toward the giggling Varya.

She had expected him to kiss her on the cheek, the way Petya always did, but Zurov had aimed for her lips and the kiss had proved to be long, quite extraordinary, and positively vertiginous.

Eventually, when she already felt that she was about to choke, Varya had pushed the impetuous cavalry officer away and clutched at her heart.

"Oh, I'll slap your face so hard," she had threatened in a feeble voice. "I was warned by decent people that you don't play fair."

"For a slap to the face I shall challenge you to a duel. And naturally I shall be vanquished," the count had purred, still ogling her.

It had been quite impossible to be angry with him.

A round face now appeared in the door of the tent. It was Lushka, the excitable and muddle-headed girl who performed the duties of maid and cook for the nurses, as well as lending a hand in the hospital when there was a large influx of wounded.

"There's a soldier waiting for you, miss," Lushka blurted out. "Dark-haired he is, with a mustache and a bunch of flowers. What shall I tell him?"

Speak of the devil, thought Varya, and smiled to herself again. She found Zurov's siege technology highly amusing.

"Let him wait. I'll be out soon," she said, throwing off her blanket.

But it was not the hussar strolling up and down beside the hospital tents, where all was in readiness to receive new wounded, it was the fragrantly scented Colonel Lukan, yet another ardent aspirant.

Varya heaved a heavy sigh, but it was too late to withdraw.

**"Ravissante comme l'aurore!"** the colonel exclaimed, first dashing to take her hand, then recoiling as he recalled the manners of modern women.

Varya shook her head in rejection of the bouquet, glanced at the gleaming gold braid of the Romanian ally's uniform, and asked coolly: "What are you doing all decked out like that first thing in the morning?"

"I am leaving for Bucharest, for a meeting of His Highness's military council," the colonel announced grandly. "I called around to say good-bye, and at the same time invite you to breakfast."

He clapped his hands and a foppish barouche wheeled into view from around the corner. The orderly sitting on the coach box was dressed in a faded uniform, but he was wearing white gloves.

"After you," Lukan said with a bow and Varya, intrigued despite herself, sat down on the springy seat.

"Where are we going?" she asked. "To the officers' canteen?"

The Romanian merely smiled mysteriously in reply, as though he were planning to whisk his companion away to the other side of the world.

The colonel had been behaving in a rather mysterious manner recently. He was still spending night after night without a break at the card table, but whereas during the initial days of his ill-starred acquaintance with Zurov there had been a hounded and downcast air about him, he seemed entirely recovered now, and although he was still throwing away substantial sums of money, he did not seem dispirited in the least.

"How did yesterday's game go?" asked Varya, looking closely at the dark circles under Lukan's eyes.

"Fortune has finally smiled on me," he replied, beaming. "Your Zurov's luck has run out. Have you ever heard of the law of large numbers? If you carry on betting large sums day after day, then sooner or later you are bound to win everything back."

As far as Varya could recall, Petya's exposition of this theory had been rather different, but it was hardly worth arguing about.

"The count has blind luck on his side, but I have mathematical reckoning and a huge fortune on mine. There, look." He held up his little finger. "I have won back my family ring. An Indian diamond, eleven carats. Brought back from the Crusades by one of my ancestors."

"What, did the Romanians actually take part in the Crusades?" Varya exclaimed rather too hastily and had to endure an entire lecture on the colonel's family tree, which proved to go all the way back to the Roman legate Lucian Mauritius Tulla.

Meanwhile, the barouche had driven out of the camp and halted in a shady grove. Standing there under an old oak tree was a table covered with a starched white cloth on which such an abundance of tasty things was laid out that Varya immediately began to feel hungry. There were French cheeses, and various fruits, and smoked salmon and pink ham, and crimson crayfish, and reclining elegantly in a little silver bucket was a bottle of Lafite.

It had to be admitted that even Lukan possessed certain positive qualities.

Just as they had raised their first glass, there was a deep rumbling far away in the distance, and Varya's heart skipped a beat. How could she have allowed herself to become so distracted? The storming of Plevna had begun! Over there the dead were falling, the wounded were groaning, while she . . .

Guiltily pushing away a bowl of emerald

green early grapes, Varya said: "My God, for their sake I hope everything goes according to plan."

The colonel drained his glass in a single swallow and immediately filled it again. Still chewing on something, he observed: "The plan is, of course, a good one. As His Highness's personal representative I am acquainted with it, and was even involved to some extent in drawing it up. The outflanking maneuver under cover of a range of hills is particularly original. Shakhovsky's and Veliaminov's columns advance on Plevna from the east. Sobolev's small detachment distracts Osman Pasha's attention in the south. On paper it all looks quite beautiful." Lukan drained his glass. "But war, Mademoiselle Varvara, is not fought on paper. And your compatriots will achieve absolutely nothing."

"But why?" Varya gasped.

The colonel chuckled and tapped the side of his head with one finger.

"I am a strategist, mademoiselle; I see further ahead than your general staff officers." He nodded toward his map case. "Over there I have a copy of the report I forwarded yesterday to Prince Karl. I predict a total fiasco for the Russians and I am certain that His Highness will be adequately appreciative of my perspicacity. Your commanders are too arrogant and self-assured; they overestimate their own soldiers and underestimate the Turks. And also their Romanian allies. But never mind—after today's lesson the tsar himself will ask for our help, you shall see."

The colonel broke off a handsome chunk of Roquefort and Varya's mood was finally ruined.

LUKAN'S GLOOMY PREDICTIONS proved correct.

In the evening Varya and Fandorin stood at the edge of the Plevna road as the wagons bearing the wounded drove past them in a never-ending line. The tally of casualties was not yet complete, but they had told her at the hospital that the ranks had been reduced by at least seven thousand men. They had also told her that Sobolev had distinguished himself by drawing the thrust of the Turkish counterattack—if not for his Cossacks, the rout would have been a hundred times more devastating. They were also amazed at the satanic precision demonstrated by the Turkish gunners, who had shelled columns while they were still making their approach, before the battalions had even been deployed for the attack.

Varya told all this to Erast Petrovich, but he

didn't say a word. Either he knew it all already or he was in a state of shock, she couldn't tell.

The column ground to a halt—one of the wagons had lost a wheel. Varya had been trying to look at the maimed and injured as little as possible, but now she glanced more closely at the lopsided wagon and gasped—she thought she recognized one wounded officer's face, a patch of dull white in the radiant dusk of summer. She moved closer and discovered she was right, it was Colonel Sablin, one of the regular visitors to the club. He was lying there unconscious, covered with a blood-soaked greatcoat. His body seemed strangely short.

"Someone you know?" asked the medical assistant accompanying the colonel. "A shell took both his legs off all the way up. Really bad luck."

Varya staggered back toward Fandorin and began sobbing convulsively.

She cried for a long time, until her tears had dried up and the air had turned cool, and still they kept on bringing back the wounded.

"In the club they take Lukan for a fool, but he turned out to be cleverer than Kriedener," said Varya, because she simply had to say something.

Fandorin looked at her inquiringly and she explained: "He told me this morning that the

attack would be a failure. He said the dispositions were good, but the commanders were
poor. And he said the soldiers weren't very—"

"He said that?" Erast Petrovich queried. "Ah,
so that's how things are. That changes—"

He broke off and knitted his brows.

"Changes what?"

No reply.

"Changes what? What?"

Varya was beginning to feel angry. "That's a
very stupid habit you have, saying 'A' without
going on to say 'B'! Tell me what's going on,
will you?"

She really felt like grabbing the titular counselor by the shoulders and giving him a good
shake. The pompous, ignorant little brat.
Trying to act as if he were the Indian chief
Chingachgook.

"It is treason, Varvara Andreevna," Erast
Petrovich declared, suddenly forthcoming.

"Treason? What do you mean, treason?"

"That is precisely what you and I are going
to find out." Fandorin rubbed his forehead.
"Colonel Lukan, by no means a towering intellect, is the only one to predict defeat for the
Russian army. That is one. He was acquainted
with the troop dispositions and as Prince Karl's
representative he even received a copy. That is
two. The success of the operation depended on

a secret maneuver carried out under the cover of a range of hills. That is three. The Turkish artillery shelled our columns by map coordinates, square after square, when they were out of their direct line of sight. That is four. The conclusion?"

"The Turks knew beforehand where to aim and when to fire," whispered Varya.

"And Lukan knew beforehand that the assault would be a failure. Oh, and by the way—five. In recent days this man has suddenly come into a lot of money."

"He is rich. Some kind of family fortune, estates. He told me about them, but I wasn't really listening."

"Varvara Andreevna, not very long ago the colonel tried to borrow three hundred rubles from me, and then in a matter of days, at least according to Zurov, he lost perhaps as much as fifteen thousand. Of course, Hippolyte could have been exaggerating . . ."

"He certainly could," Varya agreed. "But Lukan really did lose an awful lot. He told me so himself today, just before he left for Bucharest."

"He has gone away?"

Erast Petrovich turned away from her and began thinking, from time to time shaking his head. Varya tried approaching him from the side in order to see his face, but when she did she didn't notice anything particularly remarkable. Fandorin was standing with his eyes half-closed, staring up at the bright light of Mars.

"I tell you what, my d-dear Varvara Andreevna," he said, speaking slowly, and Varya felt a warm glow in her heart—first because he had said "my dear," and second because he had begun to stammer again. "It appears I shall have to ask for your assistance after all, although I promised—"

"Why, I'll do anything at all!" she exclaimed rashly, then added quickly, "in order to save Petya."

"Well, that's splendid." Fandorin looked into her eyes searchingly. "But it is a very difficult task, and not a very pleasant one. I want you to go to Bucharest as well, to look for Lukan and try to investigate him. Shall we say, try to find out if he really is so rich. Exploit his vanity, boastfulness, and foolishness. After all, he has told you more than he should once already. He is sure to spread his tail feathers for you to admire." Erast Petrovich hesitated. "After all, you are a young and at-t-tractive individual . . ."

At this point he coughed and broke off, because Varya had whistled in amazement. She had finally won a compliment from the commendatore's statue after all. Of course, it was a feeble sort of compliment—"a young and attractive individual"—but even so, even so . . .

Then Fandorin immediately had to go and spoil everything.

"Naturally, you cannot travel on your own, and it would l-look strange. I know that Paladin is planning to go to Bucharest. He will certainly not refuse to take you with him."

No, he is definitely not a human being, he is a block of ice, thought Varvara. Imagine trying to thaw out someone like that! Could he really not see that the Frenchman was already circling around her? Of course he could, he saw everything, it was simply, as foolish Lushka would put it, that he couldn't give a tinker's damn.

Erast Petrovich apparently interpreted her dissatisfied expression in his own way.

"Don't worry about money. There is a salary due to you, with traveling expenses and so forth. I shall issue it to you. You can buy something while you are there, amuse yourself a little."

"Oh, I shall have no reason to be bored in Charles's company," Varya said vengefully.

# CHAPTER SEVEN

—⁓—

## In which Varya
## forfeits the name
## of a respectable woman

## THE MOSCOW PROVINCIAL
## GAZETTE
### 22 JULY (3 AUGUST) 1877

### SUNDAY FEUILLETON

When your humble servant discovered that this city, which has become home-from-home to our rear-line community in recent months, was founded in times of old by Prince Vlad, dubbed the Impaler, and otherwise known by the name of Dracula, many things suddenly became clear. It is now clear to him, for instance, why in Bucharest you are fortunate if you can get three francs for your ruble, why an appalling lunch at an inn costs the same

as a banquet at Moscow's Slavyansky
Bazaar, and why you pay as much for a
hotel room as it would cost to rent the
whole of Buckingham Palace. The accursed vampires lick their lips with great
relish as they suck voraciously on savory
Russian blood, only pausing every now
and then to spit. And most unpleasant
of all is the fact that since electing a tin-
pot German prince as its ruler, this
Danubian province, which owes its autonomy entirely to Russia, has developed a distinct odor of wurst and brawn.
The gaze of the noble hospodars is fixed
admiringly on Herr Bismarck, and for
the good citizens of Bucharest a Russian
is no better than a contemptible goat;
they turn their noses up as they tug on
its udder. As though sacred Russian
blood were not even now being spilled
on the fields of Plevna for the cause of
Romanian freedom. . . .

ALAS, VARYA WAS MISTAKEN, seriously
mistaken. The journey to Bucharest proved to
be boring in the extreme.

In addition to Paladin, several other correspondents had decided to seek diversion in the
Romanian capital. It was clear to everyone that

166 • *Boris Akunin*

during the days, and even weeks, that lay immediately ahead, nothing of any real interest would
take place in the theater of military operations,
and once the journalistic fraternity realized that
the Russians would need some time to recover
from the bloodbath at Plevna, it made tracks for
the fleshpots of the rear lines.

They had taken a long time over their preparations, only starting out two days later. As a
lady, Varya was seated in the britzka beside
McLaughlin, while everyone else set off on
horseback, and she could only gaze from a distance at the Frenchman on his noble mount,
Yataghan (who found the slow pace irksome),
and make conversation with the Irishman. He
discussed every possible aspect of the climatic
conditions of the Balkans, London, and Central
Asia, told her all about the arrangement of the
springs on his carriage, and analyzed several extremely complicated chess problems in close detail. All this put Varya in a very bad mood, and
during their halts she regarded the boisterous
travelers, including even Paladin, with his
cheeks flushed from the moderate exertion,
with a jaundiced eye.

On the second day of the journey—they had
already passed Alexandria—she began to feel a
little better, because the cavalcade was overtaken
by Zurov. He had distinguished himself in ac-

tion and for his bravery been made Sobolev's adjutant. The general had apparently even wanted to recommend him for the Order of St. Anne, but the hussar had managed to wangle himself a week's leave in lieu—a chance to stretch his legs properly, as he put it.

At first the captain amused Varya with his fancy trick riding—plucking bluebells at full gallop, juggling gold imperials, and standing erect in the saddle. Then he made an attempt to swap places with McLaughlin, and when he was phlegmatically but unambiguously rebuffed, he moved the meek coachman onto his own chestnut mare and seated himself on the coach box, twisting his head round all the time to regale Varya with amusing stories of his own heroism and the dark machinations of the jealous "Jerome" Perepyolkin, with whom the newly appointed adjutant was at daggers drawn. And in this manner the journey was completed.

As Erast Petrovich had predicted, Lukan did not prove hard to find. Following her instructions, Varya took a room in the most expensive hotel, the Royale, and when she inquired after the colonel at the reception desk, it transpired that **"son excellence"** was well known there—he had been carousing in the restaurant the previous day and the day before that, and he was certain to be there today as well.

Since there was still a long time left until the evening, Varya set out for a stroll along the fashionable Calea Mogoshoaiei, which after life under canvas seemed to her like Nevsky Prospect: smart carriages, striped awnings above the shop windows, dazzling southern beauties, picturesque dark-haired men in light blue, white, and even pink frock coats, and uniforms, uniforms, uniforms everywhere. The sound of Romanian speech was swamped by Russian and French. Varya drank two cups of hot chocolate in a genuine café, ate four little cakes, and was on the point of dissolving in utterly blissful contentment when she happened to glance into a mirror on a pillar beside a hat shop and gasped in horror. No wonder all the men were looking straight through her as if she were not even there!

The bedraggled creature in the faded blue dress and battered straw hat was an insult to the name of Russian womanhood. And the pavements were full of sultry Messalinas sauntering along in very latest Paris fashions!

VARYA WAS TERRIBLY LATE arriving at the restaurant. She had agreed with McLaughlin to meet at seven, and it was already nine when she appeared. As a perfect gentleman, the **Daily**

**Post** correspondent had agreed to the rendezvous without a murmur (she could hardly go to the restaurant alone—she would have been taken for a demimondaine), nor did he utter a single word of reproach for her lateness, although he did look absolutely miserable. But never mind—after tormenting her all the way here with his meteorological expertise he owed her a favor, and now he could make himself useful.

Lukan wasn't in the room yet, and out of natural human consideration Varya asked McLaughlin to explain to her once again how the Old Persian Defence went. The Irishman, completely failing to notice Varya's dramatic transformation (on which she had spent six whole hours and almost all her traveling allowance—six hundred eighty-five francs), coolly remarked that he was not aware of the existence of any such defence. She was therefore obliged to inquire as to whether it was always this hot in late July in this part of the world. It turned that it was, but it was absolutely nothing in comparison with the humid heat of Bangalore.

When the gilt-wood doors finally swung open at half-past ten and the Roman legate's descendant entered the hall in a somewhat tipsy condition, Varya felt as delighted as if he were her closest friend. She leapt to her feet and waved to him with genuine warmth.

There was, however, an unforeseen complication in the form of a plump brown-haired woman hanging on the colonel's arm. The complication glanced at Varya with undisguised venom, and Varya felt embarrassed—it had somehow never entered her head that Lukan might be married.

The colonel settled this minor difficulty with true martial resolve—he gave his companion a gentle slap just below her ample bustle, and after hissing something vitriolic, the complication made an indignant exit. Apparently she was not his wife. Varya felt even more embarrassed.

"Our wildflower has unfurled its petals to become a delightful rose!" Lukan wailed as he dashed toward Varya across the entire width of the room. "What a dress! And that hat! My God, can I really be on the Champs-Elysées?

He was a coarse, vulgar showoff, of course, but it was pleasant to hear nonetheless. For the good of the cause Varya even compromised her principles and allowed him to press his lips to her hand. The colonel nodded to the Irishman with casual benevolence (he was not a rival) and sat down at the table without waiting to be invited. Varya thought that McLaughlin also seemed glad to see the Romanian. Could he really be weary of discussing meteorological matters? No, surely not.

The waiters were already bearing away the coffee and cake ordered by the thrifty correspondent and bringing wines, sweets, fruit, cheeses.

"You will not forget Bucharest!" Lukan promised. "In this town everything belongs to me!"

"In what sense?" the Irishman asked. "Do you happen to own extensive property in the city?"

The Romanian did not even dignify the question with an answer.

"Congratulate me, mademoiselle! My report has been appreciated at its true worth, and in the very near future I may expect an advancement."

"What report is that?" McLaughlin inquired again. "What kind of advancement?"

"All of Romania is expecting an advancement," the colonel declared with a solemn expression. "It is now absolutely clear that the emperor of Russia has overestimated the strength of his army. I have learned from absolutely reliable sources," he said, dropping his voice dramatically and leaning over so that the curl of his mustache tickled Varya's cheek, "that General Kriedener will be relieved of the command of the Western Division, and the forces besieging Plevna will be placed under the leadership of our own Prince Karl."

McLaughlin took a pad out of his pocket and began taking notes.

"Mademoiselle Varvara, can I perhaps interest you in a nocturnal excursion through the streets of Bucharest?" Lukan whispered in her ear, taking astute advantage of the opportune pause. "I can show you things you have never seen in that boring northern capital of yours. I swear it will be a night to remember."

"Is that the decision of the Russian emperor or simply the wish of Prince Karl?" the inquisitive journalist asked.

"The wish of His Highness is more than enough," snapped the colonel. "Without Romania and her army of fifty thousand valiant warriors, the Russians are helpless. Let me tell you, Mister Correspondent, that my country has a great future ahead of it. Soon, very soon, Prince Karl will become king. And your humble servant," he added, turning toward Varya, "will become an extremely important person. Possibly even a senator. The perspicacity I have demonstrated has been adequately appreciated. Now, what do you say to that romantic drive? I positively insist."

"I'll think about it," she promised evasively,

desperately trying to think of a way to channel the conversation in the required direction.

At that moment Zurov and Paladin entered the restaurant—most inopportunely, from the point of view of the cause, but Varya was glad to see them anyway: In their company Lukan would be a bit less brazen.

Following the direction of her glance, the colonel muttered gloomily.

"They're letting absolutely anyone into the Royale nowadays. We should have taken a private room."

"Good evening, gentlemen," Varya greeted her acquaintances cheerfully. "What a small town Bucharest is, to be sure! The colonel was just boasting to me of his perspicacity. He forecast in advance that the storming of Plevna would end in defeat."

"Did he, indeed?" asked Paladin, looking closely at Lukan.

"You look absolutely magnificent, Varvara Andreevna," said Zurov. "What's that you have there—Martell? Waiter, some glasses over here!"

The Romanian took a drink of cognac and contemplated the two other men glumly.

"When did you make this prediction? Who did you tell?" asked McLaughlin, peering through half-closed eyes.

"It was in a report addressed to his sovereign," Varya explained. "And now the colonel's perspicacity has been adequately appreciated."

"Eat and drink to your heart's content, gentlemen," said Lukan, inviting them with a broad sweep of his arm as he rose abruptly to his feet. "It will all go on my bill. Miss Suvorova and I are going for a drive. She has promised me."

Paladin raised his eyebrows in astonishment and Zurov exclaimed suspiciously.

"What's this I hear, Varvara Andreevna? You, going for a drive with Luke?"

Varya was close to panic. If she left with Lukan, her reputation would be ruined forever, and there was no telling where it might lead. But if she refused, her mission would end in failure.

"I shall be back in a moment, gentlemen," she said dejectedly and walked across to the exit as quickly as she could. She needed to gather her thoughts.

In the foyer she halted beside the tall mirror with the bronze scrolls and flourishes and pressed a hand to her blazing brow. How should she proceed? Go up to her room, lock herself in, and refuse to answer the door! I'm sorry Petya; please don't be angry with me, Mister Titular Counselor, Varya Suvorova is simply not cut out to be a spy.

The door creaked ominously and the colonel's red, angry face appeared in the mirror immediately behind her.

"I'm sorry, mademoiselle, but nobody treats Mikhai Lukan like that. First you make advances to me after your own fashion, and then you take it into your head to disgrace me in public? You've picked the wrong man this time! You're not in your scurvy press club now—this is my home ground!"

Not a trace was left of the future senator's former gallantry. His yellowish-brown eyes rained bolts of lightning down on her.

"Let's go, mademoiselle, the carriage is waiting." A swarthy, hirsute hand descended onto Varya's shoulder, clutching it with surprisingly powerful fingers that seemed to be forged of iron.

"You have lost your mind, Colonel! I am no courtesan!" Varya shrieked, glancing around.

There were quite a lot of people in the foyer, mostly gentlemen in light summer jackets and Romanian officers. They were observing the titillating scene with interest, but apparently had no intention of intervening on behalf of the lady (if, indeed, she was a lady).

Lukan said something in Romanian and the onlookers laughed knowingly.

"Had a bit too much to drink, Marusya?"

one of them asked in Russian, and they all laughed even louder.

The colonel grabbed Varya masterfully round the waist and led her off toward the exit, performing the maneuver so adroitly that it was quite impossible to resist.

"You insolent lout!" Varya exclaimed and tried to hit Lukan on the cheek, but he grabbed hold of her wrist. His face was close now, smelling of a mixture of stale alcohol and eau de cologne. I'm going to be sick, Varya thought in fright.

But a moment later the colonel's hands released their grip of their own accord. First there was a loud slap, then a resounding crunch, and Varya's assailant went flying back against the wall. One of his cheeks was bright red from the slap and the other was stark white from a heavy punch. She saw Paladin and Zurov standing shoulder to shoulder two paces away. The correspondent was shaking the fingers of his right hand; the hussar was massaging his right fist.

"The allies have just had a falling out," Hippolyte declared. "And that's only the beginning. You won't get away with just a black eye, Luke. People who treat ladies like that end up with holes in their hide."

Paladin did not say a word. He simply

pulled off one white glove and threw it in the colonel's face.

Lukan shook his head, straightened up, and rubbed his temple. He looked from one of them to the other. What astounded Varya most of all was that all three of them seemed to have completely forgotten that she even existed.

"Am I being challenged to a duel?" The Romanian forced the French words out hoarsely, as though with a great effort. "Both of you at once? Or one at a time?"

"Choose whichever you like the look of," Paladin replied coolly. "And if you're lucky with the first, you'll have the second to deal with."

"O-oh no," the count objected. "That won't do. I was the first to bring up the subject of his hide, and I'm the one he'll go shooting with."

"Shooting?" Lukan exclaimed with an unpleasant laugh. "Oh no, Mister Cardsharp, the choice of weapons is mine. I know perfectly well that you and Monsieur Scribbler here are crack shots. But this is Romania, and we'll fight our way, the Wallachian way."

He turned toward the watching crowd and shouted something, at which several Romanian officers promptly drew their sabers from their scabbards and held them out hilt-first.

"I choose Monsieur Journalist," said the

colonel, cracking his knuckles and laying a hand on the handle of his saber. He was growing more sober and more elated even as they watched. "Choose any of these swords you like and be so kind as to follow me out into the yard. First I'll skewer you, and then I'll slice off this brawler's ears."

There was a murmur of approval in the crowd and someone even shouted, "Bravo!"

Paladin shrugged and took hold of the nearest saber.

McLaughlin pushed his way through the idle onlookers.

"Stop this! Charles, you must be insane! This is barbarous! He'll kill you! Fighting with sabers is the Balkan national sport—you don't have the skill."

"I was taught to fence with a spadroon, and that's almost the same thing," the Frenchman replied imperturbably, weighing the blade in his hand.

"Gentlemen, don't!" said Varya, at last recovering her voice. "This is all because of me. The colonel had taken a little drink, but he did not mean to offend me, I am sure. Stop this immediately, it's absolutely absurd! Think of the position you are putting me in!" Her voice trembled piteously, but her entreaty fell on deaf ears.

Without even glancing at the lady whose

honor was the reason for all the commotion, the knot of men trooped off down the corridor, talking excitedly, in the direction of the small inner courtyard. Varya was left alone with McLaughlin.

"This is stupid," he said angrily. "Spadroons, he says! I've seen the way the Romanians handle a saber. They don't assume the third position and say 'en garde.' They slice you up like blood sausage. Oh, what a writer will be lost—because of that idiotic French conceit. And it won't do that turkey-cock Lukan's prospects any good, either. They'll stick him in jail and there he'll stay until the victory's won and an amnesty's signed. Back in Britain—"

"My God, my God, what can I do," Varya muttered in dismay, not listening to him. "I'm the one to blame for everything."

"Flirting, madam, is certainly a great sin," the Irishman unexpectedly agreed. "Ever since the Trojan war—"

She heard a throng of male voices howl in the courtyard.

"What's happening? Surely it can't be over already?" Varya cried, clutching at her heart. "So quickly! Go and take a look, Seamus. I beg you!"

The correspondent said nothing. He was listening, his genial features set in a mask of alarm.

McLaughlin clearly did not wish to go out into the yard.

"What are you waiting for?" said Varya, trying to stir him into action. "Maybe he needs medical assistance. Oh, you're useless!"

She darted into the corridor and saw Zurov coming toward her, his spurs jangling.

"Oh, what a terrible shame, Varvara Andreevna," he shouted out to her from a distance. "What an irreparable loss!"

She slumped against the wall in black despair and her chin began to tremble.

"How on earth could we Russians have allowed ourselves to abandon the tradition of dueling with sabers," Hippolyte continued with his lament. "Such brilliance and pageantry, such elegance! Not just a bang and a puff of smoke and that's the end of it. Why it's a ballet, a poem, the Fountain of Bakhchisarai!"

"Stop babbling, Zurov!" Varya sobbed. "Tell us what's happened!"

"Oh, you should have seen it!" said the captain, gazing excitedly at Varya and McLaughlin. "It was all over in ten seconds. Just imagine the scene. A dark, gloomy courtyard. The broad flagstones lit by lanterns. We spectators are up on the gallery with only Paladin and Luke down below. The Romanian vaults to and fro, brandishing his saber and tracing out a figure eight in the air, tosses up an oak leaf and slices it in half. The audience applauds in delight. The Frenchman simply stands there, waiting for our peacock to stop his strutting. Then Luke bounded forward, embellishing the atmosphere with a treble clef, but without even moving from the spot Paladin leaned backward to dodge the blow and then, with such lightning speed that I couldn't even see how he did it, he flicked the cutting edge of his sword right across the Romanian's throat. Luke gurgled a little, fell flat on his face, jerked his legs a couple of times, and that was it. Retired without a pension. End of the duel."

"Did they check? Is he dead?" the Irishman asked quickly.

"Dead as dead can be," the hussar assured him. "The blood would have filled Lake Ladoga. Why, Varvara Andreevna, you're upset! You look as pale as a ghost! Here, come lean against me." And he promptly slipped his arm round Varya's waist, which in the circumstances was entirely appropriate.

"What about Paladin?" she murmured.

Zurov edged his hand a little higher, as though inadvertently, and said with a casual air: "What about him? He's gone to the commandant's office to hand himself in. That's the way it goes, you know; nobody's going to give him a pat on the back for this. That was no junior cadet he killed, it was a colonel. They'll pack him off back to France at the very least. Why don't I unfasten one of your buttons so you can breathe more easily?"

Varya couldn't see or hear a thing. I'm disgraced, she thought. She had forfeited the name of a respectable woman forever. She had bungled her spying, played with fire, and now look where it had got her. She was far too frivolous— and men were all beasts. Someone had been killed because of her. And she would never see Paladin again. But the worst thing of all was that the thread leading into the enemy's web had been snapped.

What would Erast Petrovich say?

# CHAPTER EIGHT

—⁓—

## In which Varya
## sees the angel of death

## THE GOVERNMENT HERALD
### (ST. PETERSBURG)
### 30 JULY (11 AUGUST) 1877

Defying excruciating bouts of epidemic gastritis and bloody diarrhea, our Sovereign has spent the last few days visiting hospitals that are filled to overflowing with typhus victims and the wounded. His Imperial Majesty's heartfelt sympathy for their suffering is so sincere that these scenes bring an involuntary glow to the heart. The soldiers throw themselves on their gifts with all the naive joy of little children, and the author of these lines has on several occasions witnessed the Emperor's wonderful blue eyes moistened with a tear. It is impossible to observe such occasions without experiencing a peculiarly tender reverence.

WHAT ERAST PETROVICH SAID WAS THIS:

"You took quite a long time getting back, Varvara Andreevna, and you have missed some very interesting developments. The moment I received your telegram, I gave orders for a thorough search to be made of the dead man's tent and personal belongings, but nothing of any particular interest was found. The day before yesterday, however, the papers found on Lukan were delivered from Bucharest. And what d-do you think?"

Varya apprehensively raised her eyes to look the titular counselor in the face for the first time. But she detected no pity or—which would have been even worse—scorn in Fandorin's expression, only concentration and something very like excitement. Her initial relief was immediately succeeded by a sense of shame: She had taken her time because she dreaded coming back to the camp. She had sniveled and moped about her precious reputation and not given a single thought to the cause. What an appalling egotist!

"Tell me, then!" she urged Fandorin, who

was observing with interest the tear slowly sliding down Varya's cheek.

"I beg your gracious forgiveness for involving you in such an unpleasant business," Erast Petrovich said contritely. "I expected almost anything, b-but not—"

"What have you discovered in Lukan's papers?" Varya interrupted him angrily, feeling that if the conversation didn't change direction immediately she was certain to burst into tears.

Fandorin either guessed what might happen or simply decided that the subject was closed, but in any case he made no attempt to delve any further into the Bucharest episode.

"Some extremely interesting entries in his notebook. Here, take a look."

He took a fancy little book bound in brocade out of his pocket and opened it at a page with a bookmark. Varya ran her eyes down the column of numbers and letters:

$$19 - Z - 1500$$
$$20 - Z - 3400 - i$$
$$21 - J + 5000\ Z - 800$$
$$22 - Z - 2900$$
$$23 - J + 5000\ Z - 700$$
$$24 - Z - 1100$$
$$25 - J + 5000\ Z - 1000$$

$$26 - Z - 300$$
$$27 - J + 5000 \; Z - 2200$$
$$28 - Z - 1900$$
$$29 - J + 15000 \; Z + i$$

She read it through again more slowly, and then again. She wanted desperately to demonstrate her keen acumen.

"Is it a cipher? No, the numbers run consecutively . . . A list? The numbers of regiments? Numbers of troops? Perhaps casualties and reinforcements?" Varya chattered, wrinkling her forehead. "So Lukan was a spy after all? But what do the letters mean—Z, J, i? Or perhaps they are formulas or equations?"

"You flatter the departed, Varvara Andreevna. It is all much simpler than that. If these are equations, then they are extremely simple. But with one unknown."

"Only one?" Varya asked, astonished.

"Take a closer look. The first c-column, of course, consists of dates. Lukan follows them with a long dash. From the nineteenth to the twenty-ninth of July in the Western style. How was the colonel occupied on those days?"

"How should I know? I didn't follow him around." Varya thought for a moment. "Well, he was probably in the staff building, and perhaps he visited the forward positions."

"I never once saw Lukan visit the forward positions. In fact, I really only ever came across him in one place."

"In the club?"

"Precisely. And what did he do there?"

"Nothing—he played cards."

"B-bravo, Varvara Andreevna."

She glanced at the page again.

"So he kept notes of his gambling accounts! Z is always followed by a minus sign, and J always by a plus sign. So he marked his losses with the letter Z and his winnings with the letter J? Is that all?" Varya shrugged in disillusionment. "What has that got to do with espionage?"

"There was no espionage. Espionage is a high art, but here we are dealing with elementary bribery and treason. The swashbuckling Zurov appeared in the club on the nineteenth of July, the day before the first assault on Plevna, and Lukan was drawn into the game."

"That means Z is Zurov!" Varya exclaimed. "Wait a moment . . ." She began whispering to herself, gazing at the figures. "Forty-nine . . . carry seven . . . A hundred and four . . ." She summed up: "In all, he lost 15,800 rubles to Zurov. That seems about right—Hippolyte also said something about fifteen thousand. But then what is the 'i'?"

"I p-presume that is the infamous diamond ring—**'inel'** in Romanian. Lukan lost it on the twentieth of July and on the twenty-ninth he won it back again."

"But then who is 'J'?" Varya asked, rubbing her forehead. "I don't think there was any J among the card players. And Lukan won . . . mmm . . . Oho!—thirty-five thousand rubles from this man. I don't recall the colonel ever having such large winnings. He would have been certain to brag about it."

"This was nothing to brag about. Those are not his winnings, they are his fee for treason. The first time the m-mysterious J paid the colonel was on the twenty-first of July, when Zurov completely cleaned Lukan out. After that the deceased received sums of f-five thousand from his unknown patron on the twenty-third, twenty-fifth, and twenty-seventh, that is, every second day. That was how he was able to carry on playing with Hippolyte. On the twenty-ninth of July Lukan received fifteen thousand all at once. The question is, why so much, and why precisely on the twenty-ninth?"

"He sold the plan of battle for the second assault on Plevna!" Varya gasped. "The disastrous assault took place the next day, on the thirtieth."

"Bravo yet again. And there you have the secret of Lukan's much-vaunted perspicacity, and the incredible accuracy of the Turkish gunners, who shelled our columns by map coordinates while they were still making their approach."

"But who is J? You must have some suspect in mind, surely?"

"Well, of course," Fandorin muttered indistinctly. "I er . . . have my suspicions. But the pieces don't all fit together yet."

"But it means that all we have to do is find this J and then they'll let Petya go, take Plevna, and the war will be over?"

Erast Petrovich thought for a moment, wrinkling his smooth forehead, and said quite seriously: "The sequence of your logic is not entirely beyond reproach, but in principle it is quite correct."

VARYA DID NOT DARE show up at the press club that evening. She was sure everyone there must blame her for Lukan's death (after all, they didn't know about his treason) and the banishment of the universal favorite, Paladin, who had not returned from Bucharest. According to Erast Petrovich, the duelist had been arrested and ordered to leave the territory of the principality of Romania within twenty-four hours.

Hoping to run into Zurov or at least McLaughlin and find out from them just how censoriously public opinion was inclined to regard her criminal self, poor Varya strolled in circles around the marquee with its brightly colored pennants, maintaining a distance of a hundred paces from it. She had absolutely nowhere else to go, and she certainly didn't want to go back to her own tent. Those wonderful but limited creatures, the sisters of mercy, would start up their interminable discussions about which of the doctors was a sweetheart and which was an ogre, and whether the one-armed Lieutenant Strumpf from Ward Sixteen was serious when he proposed to Nastya Pryanishnikova.

The flap of the marquee fluttered and Varya glimpsed a stocky figure in a blue gendarme's uniform. She hastily turned away, pretending to admire the quite wretched view of the village of Bogot, home to the commander in chief's headquarters. Where, she wondered, was the justice in it all? That base schemer and thug Kazanzaki could visit the club without the slightest fuss, while she—essentially an innocent victim of circumstances—was left loitering outside in the dust like some kind of homeless dog! Varya shook her head in violent indignation and had just made her mind up to drop the whole business and go home when she heard the odious Greek's ingratiating voice call out behind her: "Miss Suvorova! What a pleasant surprise."

Varya swung around and assumed a sour look, certain the lieutenant colonel's unusual politeness was merely the prelude to the venomous strike of a serpent.

Kazanzaki looked at her, stretching his thick lips into a smiling expression that was almost ingratiating.

"All the talk in the club is of nothing but you. Everyone is impatient to see you. After all, it's not every day that swords are crossed over a beautiful lady, and with a fatal outcome, too."

Varya frowned suspiciously, anticipating some trick, but the gendarme only smiled all the more sweetly.

"Only yesterday Count Zurov gave us a quite brilliantly colorful account of the entire escapade, and now this article today—"

"What article?" Varya asked, seriously alarmed.

"Haven't you heard? Our disgraced Paladin has excelled himself, filling an entire page in the **Revue Parisienne** with a description of the duel. Very romantic it is, too. You are referred to exclusively as '**la belle mademoiselle S.**'"

"Do you mean to say," Varya asked in a voice that trembled slightly, "that no one blames me?"

Kazanzaki raised his immensely thick eyebrows.

"No, apart, perhaps, from McLaughlin and Eremei Perepyolkin. But everybody knows McLaughlin is an old grouch, and Perepyolkin rarely comes unless he's with Sobolev. By the way, Perepyolkin was awarded the medal of St. George for the last action. Now, what on earth did he do to deserve that? It just goes to show how important it is to be in the right place at the right time."

The lieutenant colonel smacked his lips enviously and cautiously broached the subject that interested him most: "Everybody's wondering where the heroine of the episode could have disappeared to, but it appears that our heroine is occupied with important state business. Well, now, what does the subtle Mr. Fandorin have in mind? What hypotheses does he entertain concerning Lukan's mysterious notes? Don't be surprised, Varvara Andreevna. After all, I **am** the head of the special section."

So that's it, Varya thought to herself, looking at the lieutenant colonel sullenly. I told you so. He likes to have his work done for him.

"Erast Petrovich tried to explain something to me, but I didn't really understand it," she told him with a naive flutter of her eyelashes. "Something to do with a 'Z' and a 'J.' You really ought to ask the titular counselor yourself. In any case, Pyotr Afanasievich is not guilty of anything, at least that much is now clear."

"He may not be guilty of treason, but he is most certainly guilty of criminal negligence." The gendarme's voice had assumed its familiar steely ring. "It's best that your fiancé stays in jail for the time being—no harm will come to him there." But then Kazanzaki immediately changed his tone, evidently recalling that today he was playing a very different role. "Everything will be all right, Varvara Andreevna. I'm not proud and I'm always willing to admit my mistakes. Take, for instance, the peerless Monsieur Paladin. I admit I interrogated him and I suspected him—there were good grounds for it. Because of his famous interview with the Turkish colonel, our command made a mistake and people died. My hypothesis was that Colonel Ali-bei was a mythical character invented by the Frenchman, out of either journalistic vanity or other, less innocent, considerations. Now I see that I was unfair to him." He lowered his voice confidentially. "We have received information from agents in Plevna. Osman Pasha really does have a certain Ali-bei as either his deputy or his adviser. He almost never appears in public. Our man only saw him from a distance; all he could make out was a bushy black beard and dark glasses. Paladin mentioned the beard, too, by the way."

"A beard and dark glasses?" Varya echoed, also lowering her voice. "Could it possibly be that—what is his name now—Anwar-effendi?"

"Shsh-sh," said Kazanzaki, glancing around nervously and lowering his voice even further. "I'm certain it's him. A very shrewd gentleman. Pulled the wool over our correspondent's eyes very smartly indeed. Only three **tabor**s, he says, and the main forces will not get here soon. A simple enough ploy, but very elegant. And, like dummies, we took the bait."

"But then, if Paladin is not to blame for the failure of the first assault and Lukan is the traitor, surely it means they were wrong to banish Paladin for killing him?" Varya asked.

"Yes, it does. It's very tough luck on the poor fellow," the lieutenant colonel said casually, edging a bit closer. "See how frank I am with you, Varvara Andreevna. And note that I've even shared some secret information. Perhaps you might be willing to let me have just a little something in return? I copied out that page from the notebook and I've been struggling with it for two days now, and all to no avail. First I thought it was a cipher, but it doesn't look like one. A list of army units or their movements? Casualties and reinforcements? Tell me, now, what ideas has Fandorin come up with?"

"I'll tell you only one thing. It is all much simpler than that," Varya quipped condescendingly, then she adjusted her hat and set off with a sprightly stride toward the press club.

THE PREPARATIONS FOR the third and final assault on the fortress of Plevna continued throughout a sultry August. Although these preparations were shrouded in the strictest secrecy, everybody in the camp was saying that the battle would definitely take place on the thirtieth day of the month, the date of His Majesty the Emperor's name day. From dawn until dusk the infantry and cavalry practised joint maneuvers in the surrounding valleys and hills; by day and night, field guns and siege guns were moved up. The exhausted soldiers were a pitiful sight in their sweaty tunics and kepis gray with dust, but the general mood was one of vengeful glee: We've put up with enough of this—we Russians may be slow off the mark, but once we get moving we'll squash that pesky fly of Plevna with a single tap of our mighty bear's paw.

In the club and the officers' canteen, where

Varya took her meals, everyone was suddenly transformed into military strategists—they drew diagrams, dropped the names of Turkish pashas in every sentence, and tried to guess from which side the main blow would be struck. Sobolev visited the camp several times, but he maintained an enigmatic distance. He didn't play chess anymore, only glanced occasionally at Varya in a dignified manner, and no longer complained about his cruel fate. A staff officer whom Varya knew whispered to her that the major general would be assigned, if not the key role in the forthcoming assault, than at least a highly important one, and he was now in command of two whole brigades and a regiment. Mikhail Dmitrievich had at last earned the recognition that he deserved.

The entire camp was in a state of high animation, and Varya tried her very best to feel inspired by the universally optimistic mood, but somehow she couldn't. If the truth were told, she was bored to death by all this talk of reserves, troop positions, and lines of communication. She was still not allowed to see Petya, Fandorin was walking around with a face as dark as thunder and answering questions in an incomprehensible mumble, and Zurov only appeared in the company of his patron, Sobolev. He cast sideways glances at Varya like a caged wolf and made pitiful faces at the bartender Semyon, but he didn't play cards or order any wine—Sobolev's detachment ran under iron discipline. The hussar complained in a whisper that "Jerome" Perepyolkin had taken over "the entire works" and wouldn't allow anyone space to draw breath. And his protector Sobolev wouldn't allow anyone to thrash some sense into him. The sooner the assault came, the better.

The only uplifting event of recent days had been the return of Paladin, who had apparently sat out the storm in Kishinev and then hurried back to the theater of military operations as soon as he heard he had been totally rehabilitated. Varya had been genuinely delighted to see the Frenchman, but even he seemed changed. He no longer entertained her with amusing little stories, avoided talking about the incident in Bucharest, and spent all his time racing about the camp, catching up on what he had missed during his month's absence and dashing off articles for his **Revue.** All in all, Varya felt much the same as she had in the restaurant of the Hotel Royale when the men had caught the scent of blood and gone wild, entirely forgetting that she even existed. Yet another proof that by his very nature man was closer to the animal world than woman, that the feral principle was more pronounced in man, and therefore the true variety of **Homo sapiens** was indeed woman—the more advanced, subtle, and complex being. It was such a shame that she had no one with whom she could share her thoughts. Words like that only made the nurses giggle into their hands, and Fandorin merely nodded absentmindedly.

In short, nothing was happening and she was bored witless.

AT DAWN ON THE THIRTIETH OF August Varya was woken by an appalling rumbling. The first cannonade had begun. The previous eve-ning Erast Petrovich had explained to her that, in addition to the usual artillery preparation, the Turks would be subjected to psychological pressure—that was the very latest word in the art of war. At the first ray of sunlight, when the Muslim faithful were supposed to perform their **nimaz,** three hundred Russian and Romanian guns would start raining a hail of fire on the Turkish fortifications; at precisely nine hundred hours, the cannonade would cease. In anticipation of an attack, Osman Pasha would dispatch fresh troops to his forward positions, but nothing would happen. The allies would stay put and silence would reign over the open expanses of Plevna. At precisely eleven hundred hours, the bewildered Turks would be deluged by a second hail of fire that would continue until one in the afternoon. That would be followed by another lull. The enemy would be carrying away his wounded and dead, hastily patching up the damage, bringing up new guns to replace those that had been destroyed, but still the assault would not come. The Turks, who were not notable for their strong nerves and, as everybody knew, were capable of a brief impulsive effort but balked at the prospect of any prolonged exertion, would naturally be thrown into confusion, perhaps even panic. The entire Mohammedan command would probably ride down to the front line and gaze through their binoculars, wondering what was happening. And then, at fourteen hundred thirty hours, the enemy would be hit with a third hail of fire, and half an hour later the assault columns would rush at the Turks, whose nerves by this time would be frayed to tatters.

Varya had squirmed, imagining herself in the place of the poor defenders of Plevna. It would be really terrible, waiting for the decisive events for an hour, two hours, three hours, and all in vain. She certainly wouldn't have been able to stand it. It was a cunningly conceived plan—you had to give the genuises at HQ their due.

"Ba-boom! Ba-boom!" rumbled the heavy

siege guns. "Boom! Boom!" the field guns echoed more thinly. This will go on for a long time, Varya thought; I ought to have some breakfast.

Not having been informed beforehand of the artful plan of artillery preparation, the journalists had left to take up their position before it was light. The location of the correspondents' observation point had to be agreed in advance with the command, and following long discussions it had been decided by a majority of votes to request a small hill located between Grivitsa, which was at the center of the forward positions, and the Lovcha highway, beyond which lay the left flank. At first most of the journalists had wished to be sited closer to the right flank, since the main blow was obviously going to be struck from that side, but McLaughlin and Paladin had succeeded in changing their colleagues' minds, their main argument being that the left flank might well be of secondary importance, but Sobolev was there, which meant that there was bound to be a sensation of some kind in that direction.

After taking breakfast with the pale-faced nurses, who shuddered at every explosion, Varya set out to look for Erast Petrovich. She did not find the titular counselor in the staff building or in the special section. On the off chance he might be at home, Varya glanced into Fandorin's tent and saw him calmly seated in a folding chair, holding a book in his hand and dangling a moroccan-leather slipper with a curled-up toe from his foot as he drank his coffee.

"When are you going to the observation point?" Varya asked, seating herself on the camp bed because there was nowhere else to sit.

Erast Petrovich shrugged. His fresh, rosy cheeks were positively glowing. The ex-volunteer was obviously thriving on camp life.

"Surely you're not going to sit here all day? Paladin told me that today's battle will be the largest assault on a fortified position in all of history. Even more stupendous than the capture of Malakhov."

"Your Paladin likes to exaggerate," replied the titular counselor. "Waterloo and Borodino were on a larger scale, not to mention the Leipzig Battle of the Nations."

"You're an absolute monster! The fate of Russia hangs in the balance, thousands of people are dying, and he just sits there reading his book! It's positively immoral!"

"And is it moral to sit and watch from a safe distance while people k-kill one another?"

It was a miracle. There was actually a trace of human feeling—irritation—in Erast Petrovich's voice. "Thank you very k-kindly, I have already observed this spectacle and even p-participated in it. I did not like it. I prefer the company of T-Tacitus." And he demonstratively stuck his nose back in his book.

Varya leapt up, stamped her foot, and strode toward the door, but just as she was on the point of leaving Fandorin said: "Take care out there, will you? Don't wander from the correspondents' viewing point. You never know."

She halted and glanced back at Erast Petrovich in amazement.

"Are you showing concern?"

"B-but honestly, Varvara Andreevna, what business do you have up there? First they'll shoot their cannon for a long time, then they'll run forward and there'll be clouds of smoke so that you won't be able to see anything, you'll just hear some of them shouting 'Hurrah!' and others screaming in agony. Very interesting, I'm sure. Our work is not up there, but here, in the rear."

"A rear-line rat." Varya uttered the phrase that suited the occasion and left the miserable misanthrope alone with his Tacitus.

The small hill occupied by the correspondents and military observers from neutral countries proved easy to find—Varya spotted the large white flag in the distance while she was

still on the road that was choked solid with ammunition wagons. It was flapping feebly in the
wind, and below it she could make out the dark
mass of a fair-sized crowd, perhaps a hundred
people, maybe more. The controller of traffic, a
captain wearing a red armband on his sleeve
who was hoarse from shouting as he directed
the shells to their initial destinations, smiled
briefly at the pretty young lady in the lace hat
and waved his hand.

"That way, that way, mademoiselle. But be
sure not to turn off the track. The enemy artillery won't fire at a white flag, but a shell or two
could land anywhere else once in a while. Just
where do you think you're going, you stupid oaf?
I told you, six-pound shells go to the sixth bat-
tery."

Varya shook the reins of the meek little light-
chestnut horse she had borrowed from the infirmary stables and set off toward the flag, gazing
around her curiously.

The entire valley on this side of the range of
low hills, beyond which lay the approaches to
Plevna, was dotted with strange-looking islets.
It was the infantry lying on the grass by companies, waiting for the order to attack. The soldiers were talking among themselves in low
voices and every now and then she heard unnat-
urally loud laughter from one side or another.

The officers were gathered together in small groups of several men, smoking **papyrosa**s. They looked at Varya, riding past sidesaddle, with surprise and mistrust, as if she were a creature from some other, unreal world. The sight of this stirring, droning valley made Varya feel a bit sick and she clearly glimpsed the angel of death circling above the dusty grass, gazing into the men's faces and marking them with its invisible sign.

She struck the little horse with her heel in order to get through this ghastly waiting room as quickly as possible.

But then, at the observation point, everybody was excited and full of gleeful anticipation. There was a picnic atmosphere, some people had even made themselves comfortable beside white tablecloths spread out on the ground and were already tucking in. "I didn't think you were coming," said Paladin, greeting the new arrival. He was as agitated as all the others, and Varya noted that he was wearing his famous old rust-colored boots.

"We've been hanging around here like idiots since the crack of dawn, and the Russian officers only began moving up at midday. Mr. Kazanzaki paid us a visit a quarter of an hour ago and we learned from him that the assault will only begin at three o'clock," the journalist prattled on cheerfully. "I see you were also aware in advance of the plan of battle. It's too bad of you, **Mademoiselle Barbara**—you could have given us a friendly warning. I rose at four o'clock, and for me that is worse than death."

The Frenchman helped the young lady dismount, seated her on a folding chair, and began to explain: "Over there, on the hills opposite us, are the Turkish fortified positions. You see, where the shell bursts fly up in the air like fountains? That is the very center of their position. The Russo-Romanian army extends in a parallel line about fifteen kilometers long, but from here we can only survey a part of that immense space. Note that round hill—no, not that one, the other one, with the white tent. That is the command post, the temporary headquarters. The commander of the Western Division, Prince Karl of Romania, is there, and so are the commander in chief, Grand Duke Nicholas, and the emperor Alexander himself. Oh, the rockets, there go the rockets! A most picturesque spectacle, is it not?"

Lines of smoke were traced out in the air above the empty stretch of land that separated the opposing sides, as if someone had cut the vault of heaven into slices like a watermelon or a round loaf of bread. Lifting her head, Varya saw three colored balls high above her—one close, the next a little further away, above the imperial headquarters, and the third right on the very horizon.

"Those, Varvara Andreevna, are balloons," said Kazanzaki, who had appeared beside her. "They correct the artillery fire from them using signaling flags."

The gendarme looked even more repulsive than ever, cracking his knuckles in his excitement and flaring his nostrils nervously. He had caught the scent of human blood, the vampire. Varya demonstratively moved her chair farther away, but he appeared not to notice the maneuver. He came up to her again and pointed off to one side beyond the low hills, where the rumbling sounded particularly loud.

"As always, our mutual friend Sobolev has sprung a surprise of his own. According to the plan of action, his role is to appear to threaten the Krishin redoubt, while the main forces strike their blow in the center. But our ambitious little general couldn't wait, and this morning he launched a frontal attack. Not only has he broken away from the main forces and got himself cut off by the Turkish cavalry, he has put the entire operation in jeopardy! Well, now, he'll hear about that, all right!"

Kazanzaki took a gold watch out of his

pocket, tugged agitatedly on the peak of his kepi, and crossed himself.

"Three o'clock! They'll go in now!"

Varya looked around and saw that the entire valley had begun to move: The islets of white tunics began heaving and fluttering, moving up quickly to the front line. Pale-faced men were running past the low hill, following an elderly officer with a long drooping mustache who was limping along nimbly at the front.

"Keep up, get those bayonets higher!" he shouted in a shrill, piercing voice, glancing around behind him. "Sementsov, keep formation or I'll rip your head off!"

And now there were other company-sized columns running past, but Varya carried on gazing after that first one, with the elderly officer and the unknown Sementsov.

The company spread out into a line and set off at a slow run toward the distant redoubt, where the fountains of earth began spurting up even more furiously.

"Right—now he'll give it to them," someone said beside her.

In the distance the shells were already bursting fast and furiously and Varya could not see much through the smoke spreading across the ground, but her company was still running in neat formation and nobody seemed to be shelling it.

"Come on, Sementsov, come on," Varya whispered, clenching her fist tight.

Soon "her" men were completely hidden from sight by the backs of other columns that had spread out into lines to advance. When the open space in front of the redoubt was full to the halfway mark with white tunics, shell bursts began springing up like neatly trimmed bushes in among the mass of men: a first, a second, a third, a fourth. And then again, a little bit closer: a first, a second, a third, a fourth. And again. And again.

"He's combing them fine," Varya heard someone say. "So much for the artillery preparation. They shouldn't have wasted time showing off with their damned idiotic psychology. They should have just kept pounding them."

"They've run! They're running!" Kazanzaki grabbed Varya's shoulder and squeezed it tightly.

She glanced up at him indignantly, but realized the man was completely carried away. Somehow she managed to free herself and looked in the direction of the field.

It was hidden under a veil of smoke through which she caught brief glimpses of something white, and black lumps of earth were flying through the air.

All talk on the hill stopped. A crowd of silent men came running out of the blue-gray mist, skirting the observation point on both sides. Varya saw red blotches on the white tunics and cringed.

The smoke thinned a little and the valley was exposed, covered with the black rings of shell craters and white dots of soldiers' tunics. Varya noticed that the white dots were moving and she heard a dull howling sound that seemed to come from out of the earth itself—the cannon had just that moment stopped firing.

"The first trial of strength is over," said a major she knew who had been attached to the journalists from central headquarters staff. "Osman is well dug in; it'll take some effort to budge him. First more artillery preparation, and then 'hurrah-hurrah' again."

Varya felt sick.

# CHAPTER NINE

—m—

## In which Fandorin
## receives a reprimand
## from his chief

## THE RUSSIAN GAZETTE
### (ST. PETERSBURG)
### 31 AUGUST (12 SEPTEMBER) 1877

Recalling the paternal parting words of his ardently adored commander, the intrepid youth exclaimed: "I will get the message through, Mikhail Dmitrich, if it costs me my life!" The nineteen-year-old hero leapt up onto his Cossack steed and galloped off across the valley swept by winds of lead, to where the main forces of the army lay, beyond the Bashi-Bazouks lurking in ambush. Bullets whistled over the rider's head, but he only spurred on his fiery steed, whispering: "Faster! Faster! The outcome of the battle depends on me!"

But alas, malign fate is more powerful than courage. Shots rang out from the ambush, sending the valiant orderly crashing to the ground. Drenched in blood, he leapt to his feet and dashed at the Mohammedan infidels, sword in hand, but like black kites the cruel enemy flung themselves on him and slew him, then hacked at his lifeless body with their swords.

Such was the death of Sergei Bereshchagin, the brother of the illustrious artist.

Thus there perished in the bud a most promising talent, fated never to blossom.

So fell the third of the riders dispatched by Sobolev to the emperor . . .

SOMETIME AFTER SEVEN in the evening she found herself back at the familiar fork in the road, but instead of the hoarse-voiced captain she found an equally hoarse lieutenant, giving instructions. He was having an even harder time than his predecessor, because now he had to direct two opposed streams of traffic: the line of ammunition wagons still moving up to the front line and the wounded being evacuated from the battlefield.

After the first attack Varya had lost her nerve

and she realized that another terrible spectacle like that would be too much for her. She had set out for the rear, even crying a little along the way—fortunately there was nobody she knew anywhere nearby. But she hadn't gone all the way back to the camp, because she felt ashamed.

Shrinking violet, prim young lady, weaker sex, she rebuked herself. You knew you were going to a war, not a garden party at Pavlovsk Park. And on top of everything, she desperately did not want to give the titular counselor the satisfaction of knowing that he had been proved right yet again.

And so she turned back.

She rode her horse at a walk, her heart sinking lower and lower as the sounds of battle drew nearer. In the center the rifle fire had almost died away and there was only the rumbling of cannon, but from the Lovcha highway, where Sobolev's isolated detachment was fighting, there came constant volleys of shots and the incessant roar of a multitude of voices, only faintly audible at such a distance. General Michel was apparently not having an easy time.

Suddenly Varya was startled by the sight of McLaughlin emerging from the bushes on his horse, spattered with mud. His hat had slipped over to one side of his head, his face was red, and sweat was streaming down his forehead.

"What's happening? How's the battle going?" Varya asked, catching the Irishman's horse by the bridle.

"Well, I think," he replied, wiping his cheeks with a handkerchief. "Oof—I got stuck in some kind of undergrowth and just barely managed to get out again."

"Well, you say? Have the redoubts been taken?"

"No, the Turks stood firm in the center, but twenty minutes ago Count Zurov galloped past our observation point in a great hurry to get to headquarters. All he shouted was: 'Victory! We are in Plevna! No time now, gentlemen, an urgent dispatch!' Monsieur Kazanzaki set off after him. No doubt that highly ambitious gentleman wishes to be there beside the bearer of good news in case some of the glory rubs off on him." McLaughlin shook his head disapprovingly. "And then the gentlemen of the press went dashing off helter-skelter—every one of them has his own man among the telegraphists. Take my word for it, telegrams reporting the capture of Plevna are winging their way to their newspapers at this very moment."

"Then what are you doing here?"

The correspondent replied with dignity: "I never rush things, Mademoiselle Suvorova. You have to check all the details thoroughly first.

Instead of a bald statement of fact, I shall send an entire article, and it will be in time for the same morning edition as their skimpy telegrams."

"So we can go back to the camp?" Varya asked in relief.

"Yes, I believe so. We'll find out more at the staff building than out here in this savannah. And it will be dark soon, too."

HOWEVER, AT THE STAFF BUILDING no one really knew anything, because no dispatches about the capture of Plevna had been received from field headquarters—quite the contrary, in fact. All the major thrusts of the offensive had apparently been repulsed and the losses were absolutely astronomical, at least twenty thousand men. They said the emperor had completely lost heart and responded to questions about Sobolev's success with a shrug: How could Sobolev take Plevna with his two brigades if sixty battalions in the center and on the right flank had not even been able to take the first line of redoubts?

It didn't make any sense at all. McLaughlin was triumphant, delighted at his own circumspection, but Varya was furious with Zurov:

That braggart and liar had only confused everybody with his arrant nonsense.

Night fell and the dispirited generals returned to staff headquarters. Varya saw Grand Duke Nikolai Nikolaevich enter the little operations-section building, surrounded by his adjutants. His equine face was twitching spasmodically between the thick sideburns.

Everyone was talking in whispers about the huge losses—the news was that a quarter of the army had been killed. But out loud they spoke about the heroism displayed by the officers and men. A great deal of heroism had been displayed, especially by the officers.

Shortly after twelve, Varya was sought out by Fandorin. He looked dejected.

"Come with me, Varvara Andreevna. The chief wants to see us."

"Us?" she asked, surprised.

"Yes, the entire staff of the special section. And that includes both of us."

They walked quickly to the mud-walled hut where Lieutenant Colonel Kazanzaki's department was located.

The officers and staff of the Special Section of the Western Division were all gathered in the familiar room, but their commanding officer was not among them.

However, Lavrenty Arkadievich Mizinov was there, scowling menacingly behind the desk.

"Ah-hah, the titular counselor and his lady secretary have decided to join us," he said acidly. "Wonderful—now we only have to wait for His Worship the lieutenant colonel to arrive and we can begin. Where's Kazanzaki?" barked the general.

"Nobody has seen Ivan Kharitonovich this evening," the most senior officer present replied timidly.

"Magnificent. Fine protectors of secrets you all are."

Mizinov jumped up and began walking around the room, stamping his feet loudly.

"This isn't an army, it's a circus, a cabaret show with escape artists! Whenever you want to see someone, they tell you he isn't here. He's disappeared! Without trace!"

"Your excellency, you are sp-speaking in riddles? What is the m-matter?" Fandorin asked in a low voice.

"I don't know, Erast Petrovich, I don't know!" exclaimed Mizinov. "I was hoping that you and Mr. Kazanzaki would tell me that." He stopped for a moment to get a grip on himself and then continued more calmly: "Very well. We're not waiting for anyone else. I've just come from the emperor, where I witnessed a most interesting scene: Major General of His Imperial Majesty's retinue Sobolev the Second shouting at His Imperial Majesty and His Imperial Highness, and the tsar and the commander in chief apologizing to him."

"Impossible!" one of the gendarmes gasped.

"Silence!" shrieked the general. "Be quiet and listen! Apparently, sometime after three o'clock this afternoon, Sobolev's detachment, having taken the Krishin redoubt by a frontal attack, broke through into the southern outskirts of Plevna at the rear of the main force of the Turkish army, but was forced to a halt by a lack of infantry and artillery support. Sobolev dispatched several riders with a request to send reinforcements immediately, but they were intercepted by the Bashi-Bazouks. Finally, at six o'clock, Adjutant Zurov, accompanied by fifty Cossacks, managed to break through to the central army group positions. The Cossacks went back to Sobolev because he needed every man he could get, and Zurov galloped on to headquarters alone. In Plevna they were expecting reinforcements to arrive at any minute, but they never came. And that is not surprising, because Zurov never reached headquarters and we never learned about the breakthrough on the left flank. In the evening the Turks redeployed their forces to bring their full might to bear on

Sobolev; shortly before midnight, having lost most of his men, he withdrew to his initial position. But we had Plevna in the bag! A question for all of you here: What could have happened to Adjutant Zurov, in broad daylight, in the very center of our positions? Who can answer me that?"

"Evidently Lieutenant Colonel Kazanzaki can," said Varya, and everyone turned to look at her.

She related excitedly what she had heard from McLaughlin.

After a prolonged pause, the chief of gendarmes turned to Fandorin:

"Your conclusions, Erast Petrovich?"

"The battle has been lost, there is no p-point in wailing and beating our chests—emotions merely hinder the effort of investigation," the titular counselor replied coolly. "What we need to do is this. Divide up the t-territory between the correspondents' observation point and the field headquarters into squares. That's the first thing. At the first light of d-dawn, search every last centimeter of each square. That's the second thing. If the b-bodies of Zurov or Kazanzaki are found, nothing must be touched and the ground around them must not be trampled— that's the third thing. And, just to be certain, search for both of them among the seriously wounded in the infirmaries—that's the fourth thing. For the moment, Lavrenty Arkadievich, there is n-nothing more to be done."

"What do you suggest I should report to His Majesty? Treason?"

Erast Petrovich sighed.

"More likely s-sabotage. But in any case we shall find out in the morning."

THEY DID NOT SLEEP that night. There was a lot of work to be done; the members of the special section divided the area up into half-verst squares on a map and allocated people to the search teams, while Varya rode around to all six hospitals and infirmaries and checked the officers who had been brought back unconscious. The sights she saw were so horrible that by dawn she had slipped into a peculiar numb stupor, but she had not found either Zurov or Kazanzaki, although she had seen quite a number of her acquaintances among the wounded, including Perepyolkin. The captain had also attempted to break out and bring help, but for his pains he had received a blow from a crooked saber across the collarbone—he had no luck where the Bashi-Bazouks were concerned. The poor man was lying on his bed, pale-faced and miserable, and the expression in his sunken brown eyes was almost as mournful as on that unforgettable day when they first met. Varya dashed across to him, but he turned away and said nothing. What had she done to make him dislike her?

The first rays of the sun found Varya on a bench beside the special-section building. Fandorin had virtually forced her down onto it and ordered her to rest, and Varya had slumped, weary and numb, against the wall and sunk into a restless half-sleep. Her entire body ached and she felt a little sick—after all the nervous strain and a sleepless night, that was hardly surprising.

The search teams had set out for their squares before first light. At a quarter past seven a messenger from Section Fourteen arrived at a gallop and ran into the hut; Fandorin came dashing out, buttoning up his tunic on the run.

"Let's go, Varvara Andreevna, they've found Zurov," he said tersely.

"Is he dead?" she sobbed.

Erast Petrovich did not answer.

The hussar was lying on his stomach with his head twisted to one side. Even from a distance Varya spotted the silver handle of the Caucasian dagger thrust deep into his left shoulder. When she dismounted, she saw his face in profile: the beautiful glint of the glassy eye staring in surprise, the dark powder burn ringing the gaping bullet wound in the temple.

Varya sobbed again without crying and turned away from the terrible sight.

"We haven't touched anything, Mr. Fandorin, just as you ordered," the gendarme in charge of the team reported. "He had only one verst left to ride to the command post. This area's in a hollow; that's why no one saw anything. And as for the shot, there was so much shooting going on. . . . The picture's quite clear: He was stabbed in the back with the dagger unexpectedly, taken by surprise. Then they finished him off with a bullet in the left temple at point-blank range."

"Mm-hmm," Erast Petrovich replied vaguely, leaning down over the body.

The officer lowered his voice: "It's Lieutenant Colonel Kazanzaki's dagger; I recognized it immediately. He showed it to us, said it was a present from a Georgian prince."

To that Erast Petrovich replied: "Splendid."

Varya felt sicker than ever now, and she squeezed her eyes shut to fight off the nausea.

"Are there any hoofprints?" asked Fandorin, squatting down on his haunches.

"Unfortunately not. As you can see, the bank of the stream here is nothing but gravel, and further up the whole area is trampled—the cavalry squadrons must have come this way yesterday."

The titular counselor straightened up and stood by the sprawling corpse for about a minute. His face was fixed and expressionless, the same gray color as his temples. And he's hardly more than twenty, thought Varya with a shudder.

"Very well, Lieutenant. Transfer the body to the camp. Let's go, Varvara Andreevna."

On the way she asked him: "Surely Kazanzaki isn't a Turkish agent? It's unbelievable! He is repulsive, of course, but even so . . ."

"Not to that extent?" asked Fandorin with a humorless chuckle.

Just before noon the lieutenant colonel was also found—after Erast Petrovich had given orders for the small grove of trees and the bushes near the spot where poor Hipppolyte had died to be searched again, this time more thoroughly.

From what Varya was told (she didn't go to see for herself), Kazanzaki was half-sitting, half-lying with his back slumped against a boulder. He had a revolver in his right hand and a hole in his forehead.

The meeting to discuss the results of the search was led by Mizinov himself.

"First of all, I must say that I am extremely

dissatisfied with the results of Titular Counselor Fandorin's work," the general began in a voice that boded no good. "Erast Petrovich, a dangerous and sophisticated enemy has been operating right under your very nose, inflicting severe damage on our cause and putting the success of the entire campaign in jeopardy, and you have still not identified him. Certainly this was no easy task, but then you are by no means what I would call a beginner. I can't expect any more from the rank-and-file members of the special section. They were recruited from various provincial offices, where for the most part they were previously involved in standard investigations. But for you, with your exceptional abilities, this is quite inexcusable."

Varya pressed a hand to her throbbing temple and cast a sideways glance at Fandorin. He appeared entirely unperturbed, but his cheekbones had turned ever-so-slightly pink (probably nobody but Varya would have noticed that)—his chief's words had obviously cut him to the quick.

"And so, gentlemen, what do we have? We have a fiasco entirely without precedent in world history. The head of the secret Special Section of the Western Division, the most important formation in the entire Army of the Danube, was a traitor."

224 • *Boris Akunin*

"Can we regard that as established fact, your excellency?" the most senior gendarme officer present asked timidly.

"Judge for yourself, major. Of course, the fact that Kazanzaki was Greek by origin and that there are many Turkish agents among the Greeks is not in itself proof. But remember the mysterious letter 'J' that figured in Lukan's notes. Now we can see what that J meant—'gendarme.' "

"But the word 'gendarme' is written with a 'G'," the major with the gray mustache persisted.

"It is written that way in French, but in Romanian it is written with a J—'jandarm,' " his chief explained condescendingly. "Kazanzaki was the puppet-master who pulled the Romanian colonel's strings. And in addition: Who was it that went dashing after Zurov when he was on his way to deliver the message on which the outcome of the battle, perhaps even the whole war, depended? Kazanzaki. And in addition. Whose dagger was used to kill Zurov? Your superior's. And in addition—what else in addition? When he was unable to extract the knife from his victim's shoulder blade, the killer realized there was no way he could avoid suspicion and he shot himself. By the way, there are two bullets missing from the chamber of his revolver."

"But an enemy spy would not have killed himself. He would have tried to hide," the major objected timidly.

"Where, by your leave? He could not get across the front line, and in our rear lines as of today he would have been a wanted man. He could not hide with the Bulgarians and he could not reach the Turks. Better a bullet than the gallows—he was certainly right about that. Apart from which, Kazanzaki was not a spy, but a traitor. Novgorodtsev," said the general, turning to his adjutant, "where's the letter?"

Novgorodtsev extracted a snow-white sheet of paper folded in quarters from his file.

"Discovered in the pocket of the suicide," explained Mizinov. "Read it out, Novgorodtsev."

The adjutant peered dubiously at Varya.

"Read it, read it," the general urged him. "This isn't a college for daughters of the nobility, and Miss Suvorova is a member of the investigative group."

Novgorodtsev cleared his throat and blushed bright red as he began to read: " 'My deer hart Vanchik-Kharitonchik—' Gentlemen," the adjutant commented, "the spelling is quite appalling, but I shall do my best to read it as it is written. Such terrible scrawl. Hmm . . . 'My deer hart. Life withowt yoo will be enuff to mayk me lay hands on miself, rather than carrie on living like this. You kissed me and keressed me and I did you, but that scowndrel fayt was watching us envyously and hideing his nife behind his back. Withowt you I am meer dust, the dirt on the grownd. I beg yoo come back soon. But if yoo fynd sumone else in that lowsy Kishinev, I will come and I sware on my muther I will rip your guts out. Yors for a thowsand yeers, Shalunishka.' "

"A strange letter from a mistress," commented the major.

"It's not from a woman, it's from a man," said Mizinov with a crooked smile. "That's the whole point. Before he went to the Kishinev office of gendarmes, Kazanzaki served in Tiflis. We sent an inquiry immediately and already have a reply. Read out the telegram, Novgorodtsev."

Novgorodtsev clearly read the new document with greater pleasure than the love letter.

" 'To His Excellency Adjutant General L. A. Mizinov in reply to an enquiry of the 31st of August, received at 52 minutes past one o'clock in the afternoon. Extremely urgent. Top secret.

" 'I beg to report that during his term of duty in the Tiflis office of the gendarmes from

January 1872 to September 1876, inclusive, Ivan Kazanzaki proved himself to be a capable and energetic worker and no sanctions or penalties were ever applied to him. On the contrary, for his services he was awarded the Order of St. Stanislav, third class, and received two official expressions of thanks from His Imperial Highness the vice-regent of the Caucasus. However, according to information provided in summer 1876 by agents in the field, he had perverted leanings and was supposedly even involved in an unnatural relationship with the well-known Tiflis pederast Prince Vissarion Shalikov, alias Shalun Beso. I would not normally have given any credence to such rumors, unsupported as they were by any proof; however, bearing in mind that despite his mature age Lieutenant Colonel Kazanzaki was unmarried and had never been observed to be involved with women, I decided to conduct a secret internal investigation. It was established that Lieutenant Colonel Kazanzaki was indeed acquainted with Shalun, although the existence of an intimate relationship was not confirmed. Nonetheless, I decided the best thing would be to request Lieutenant Colonel Kazanzaki's transfer to another office without any adverse consequences for his service record.

" 'Commander of the Tiflis Office of Gendarmes Colonel Panchulidzev.' "

"SO THERE YOU HAVE IT," Mizinov summed up bitterly. "He fobbed off a dubious member of his department on someone else and concealed the reason from his superiors. And now the entire army is suffering the consequences. Because of Kazanzaki's treason, we've been stuck at blasted Plevna for two months now and there's no telling how much more time we'll have to waste here. The emperor's name-day celebrations have been ruined. Today His Majesty was even speaking of retreat—can you imagine that?" He swallowed convulsively. "Three failed assaults, gentlemen! Three! Do you recall, Erast Petrovich, that it was Kazanzaki who delivered the first order to take Plevna to the coding room? I don't know how he managed to substitute 'Nikopol' for 'Plevna,' but that Judas clearly had a hand in it somehow!"

Varya thought with a start that now there seemed to be a new glimmer of hope for Petya. But the general chewed on his lips and continued: "I shall of course have Colonel Panchulidzev committed for trial as a lesson to anyone else who covers things up, and will insist on his being reduced to the ranks. But his telegram does, at least, allow us to reconstruct the chain of events. It is all quite simple. The Turkish agents who infest the Caucasus so thickly must have discovered Kazanzaki's secret vice and recruited the lieutenant colonel by blackmailing him. It's a story as old as the world. 'Vanchik-Kharitonchik'! God, what disgusting filth! Better if it had been done for money!"

Varya was just about to open her mouth to intercede for the devotees of single-sex love, who were, after all, not to blame that nature had made them different from everyone else, when Fandorin rose to his feet.

"May I take a look at the letter?" he said, then took the sheet of paper, turned it over in his hands, ran a finger along the crease, and asked: "And where is the envelope?"

"Erast Petrovich, you amaze me," the general said, flinging up his arms. "How could there be an envelope? Such missives are not sent by the post."

"So it was simply lying in his inside pocket? Well, well." And Fandorin sat back down.

Lavrenty Arkadievich shrugged.

"I'll tell you what you had better do, Erast Petrovich. I think it possible that, apart from Colonel Lukan, the traitor may also have recruited someone else. Your job is to discover whether there are any more dragon's teeth lying in or around headquarters. Major," he said, addressing the senior officer present, who jumped to his feet and stood to attention, "I appoint you acting head of the special section. Your job is the same. Provide the titular counselor every possible assistance."

"Yes, sir!"

There was a knock at the door.

"With your permission, your excellency?" The door opened a little and a face wearing blue spectacles appeared in the gap.

Varya knew he was Mizinov's secretary—a quiet little functionary with a name that was hard to remember whom everybody disliked and feared.

"What is it?" the chief of gendarmes asked guardedly.

"An emergency at the guardhouse. The commandant has come to report it. He says one of his prisoners has hanged himself."

"Are you out of your mind, Przebiševski? I have an important meeting and you interrupt me with drivel like this?"

Varya clutched at her heart in fright, and the secretary immediately spoke the very words she was afraid to hear: "But it is the cryptographer Yablokov who has hanged himself, the very same . . . He left a note which has a direct bearing . . . That was why I took it on myself . . . But if this is a bad moment, please forgive me, I will leave." The functionary gave an offended sniff and made as if to retreat behind the door.

"Give me the letter!" the general roared. "And send the commandant in!"

Everything went hazy in front of Varya's eyes. She struggled to get to her feet, but she could not; she was numbed by some bizarre paralysis. She saw Fandorin leaning over her and tried to say something to him, but she could only move her lips weakly without making a sound.

"Now it's quite clear that Kazanzaki altered the order!" Mizinov exclaimed after he had run his eyes over the note. "Listen: 'Again, thousands of dead killed and all because of my blunder. Yes, my guilt is appalling and I will no longer deny it. I committed a fatal error—I left the encoded order to take Plevna on my desk while I absented myself on personal business. While I was gone someone altered one word in the message and I delivered the message without even checking it! Ha-ha, I, Pyotr Yablokov, am the genuine savior of Turkey, not Osman Pasha. Do not bother to examine my case, judges, I have pronounced judgment on myself!' Ah, how very elementary it all is. The boy went off on his own business and Kazanzaki promptly altered the message. It would only take a moment!"

The general crushed the note and tossed it on the floor at the feet of the commandant of the guardhouse, who was standing rigidly to attention.

"Er . . . Erast Pet . . . rovich, what has—happened?" Varya mumbled, scarcely able to force out the words. "Petya!"

"Captain, how is Yablokov? Is he dead?" Fandorin asked, addressing the commandant.

"How could he be dead when he can't even tie a noose properly?" the commandant barked. "They've taken Yablokov down and they're reviving him now!"

Varya pushed Fandorin away and dashed to the door. She collided with the doorpost, ran out onto the porch, and was blinded by the bright sunlight. She had to stop. Fandorin appeared beside her again.

"Varvara Andreevna, calm down; everything is all right. We will go there together now, but first you must catch your breath. You look terrible."

He took her gently by the elbow, but for some reason the entirely gentlemanlike touch of his hand provoked an overwhelming attack of nausea. She doubled over and vomited copiously all over Erast Petrovich's boots. Then she sat on the step, trying to understand why no-body was sliding down off the ground when it was sloping at such an angle.

Varya felt something pleasant and ice-cold touch her forehead, and gave a low moan of pleasure.

"A fine business," she heard Fandorin's hollow voice say. "This is typhus."

— ෴ —

# CHAPTER TEN

**In which the emperor
is presented with a golden sword**

THE DAILY POST (LONDON)
9 DECEMBER (27 NOVEMBER) 1877

For the last two months the siege of Plevna has effectively been commanded by the old, experienced General Totleben, well-remembered by the British from the Sebastopol campaign. Being rather more of an engineer than a military leader, Totleben has abandoned the tactic of frontal attacks and subjected the army of Osman Pasha to a strict blockade. The Russians have lost a great deal of precious time, for which Totleben has been subjected to severe criticism, but now it must be acknowledged that the cautious engineer is right. Since the Turks were finally cut off from Sofia one month ago, Plevna has begun to suffer from hunger and a shortage of ammunition. Totleben is referred to ever more often as the second Kutuzov (the Russian field marshal who exhausted Napoleon's forces by retreating incessantly in 1812—Editor's note). Osman and his army of fifty thousand are expected to surrender any day now.

IT WAS AN ABOMINABLY COLD and unpleasant day (gray sky, icy sleet, and squelching mud) when Varya made her way back to the army positions in a specially hired cab. She had spent an entire month on a hospital bed in the Trnovo Epidemiological Hospital, where she could quite easily have died, because many people did die of typhus, but she had been lucky. Then she had spent another two months dying of boredom while she waited for her hair to grow, because she certainly couldn't go back with her head shaved like a Tatar's. Her accursed hair had grown back far too slowly, and even now it stood up on her head like a crew cut or the bristles of a brush. In fact, she looked perfectly absurd, but her patience had run out—one more week of idleness and Varya would have been driven absolutely insane by the sight of the crooked little streets of that horrid little town.

Petya had managed to get away to visit her once. He was still officially under investigation, but he had been let out of the guardhouse now and gone back to work—the army had expanded rapidly and there was a shortage of cryptographers. Petya was greatly changed: He had let his beard grow, but it was sparse and straggly and really didn't suit him at all, and he had wasted half away, and he mentioned either God or service to the people with every second breath. What had shocked Varya most of all was that when they met her fiancé had kissed her on the forehead. Did he really have to treat her like a corpse in a coffin? Had her looks really suffered that much?

The Trnovo highway was choked with strings of army wagons and her carriage was barely crawling along, so, since she was familiar with the area, Varya ordered the coachman to turn off on to a track that led south around the camp. It was longer that way, but they would get there sooner.

On the empty road the horse broke into a lively jog and the rain almost stopped. In another hour or two she would be home. Varya snorted. A fine home—a damp tent open to all the winds under heaven!

After they passed Lovcha they began meeting individual riders, for the most part foragers and brisk, bustling orderlies, and soon Varya saw the first person she knew.

There was no mistaking that lanky figure in the bowler hat and the redingote, perched awkwardly on the dejected chestnut mare—McLaughlin! Varya had a sudden sense of déjà vu. During the third assault on Plevna, when she was returning to the army positions just as she was today, she had encountered the Irishman in precisely the same way. Only then it had been hot, and now it was cold, and she had probably looked better then.

But it really was very fortunate that McLaughlin would be the first to see her. He was unaffected and forthright; his reaction would tell her straightaway whether she could show herself in society with her hair like this, or whether she ought to turn back. And she could find out all about the latest news . . .

Varya courageously grabbed the cap off her head, exposing her shameful brush—she might as well do things properly.

"Mr. McLaughlin!" she shouted out, half-rising from her seat as her carriage overtook the correspondent. "It's me! Which way are you headed?"

The Irishman looked around and raised his bowler hat.

"Oh, Mademoiselle Varya, I'm very glad to

see you in good health. Did they crop your hair like that for reasons of hygiene? I can hardly recognize you."

Varya felt a cold shiver inside.

"Why, is it so terrible?" she asked dejectedly.

"Not at all," McLaughlin hastened to reassure her. "But you look much more like a boy now than you did when we first met."

"Are we going the same way?" she asked. "Get in with me and we can talk. Your horse doesn't look too good."

"A sad old nag. My Bessie managed to get herself in the family way by a dragoon's stallion and she blew up like a barrel. And the headquarters groom, Frolka, doesn't like me because I never give him bribes—what you might call tips—as a matter of principle, so he palms me off with these dreadful jades! I don't know where he gets them from! And right now I'm in a great hurry on extremely important secret business."

McLaughlin paused provocatively, and it was clear he was positively bursting to tell her just how important and secret his business was.

The contrast with the son of Albion's habitual stolid reserve was striking—the journalist really must have discovered something quite extraordinary.

"Get in for just a minute," Varya wheedled.

"Let the poor animal have a rest. I have some jam pies here, and a thermostatic flask full of coffee with rum."

McLaughlin took a watch on a silver chain out of his pocket.

"Haf pust seven—Anatha foty minits to get thea. Oll rait, then, haf an aua. Etl be haf pust eit . . ." he muttered to himself in that incomprehensible foreign tongue of his and sighed. "Oh, all right, but just for a minute. I'll ride with you as far as the fork in the road and then turn off for Petyrnitsy."

He hitched his reins to the carriage and took a seat beside Varya, swallowed one pie whole, bit off half of a second, and gulped down a mouthful of hot coffee from the lid of the flask with great relish.

"Why are you going to Petyrnitsy?" Varya asked casually. "Are you meeting your informant from Plevna again?"

McLaughlin gave her a searching glance and adjusted his steamed-up glasses.

"Give me your word you won't tell anyone—at least not until ten o'clock," he demanded.

"My word of honor," Varya said immediately. "But what's the big mystery?"

McLaughlin began huffing and puffing, taken aback by the casual way in which the promise had been given, but it was too late for him to back out now, and he was obviously longing to confide in someone.

"Today, the tenth of December, or in your style the twenty-eighth of November 1877, is a historic day," he began, and then lowered his voice to a whisper. "But as yet there's only one man in the entire Russian camp who knows it—your humble servant. Oh, McLaughlin doesn't give people tips just for performing their duty, but for good work McLaughlin pays very well, mark my words. No more, no more, not another single word about that!" He held up his hand to forestall the question that Varya was about to blurt out. "I won't tell you the name of my source. I will only say that he has been tested many times and has never once let me down."

Varya recalled one of the journalists saying enviously that the source of the **Daily Post** correspondent's information on life in Plevna was not some Bulgarian, but a Turkish officer or something of the kind. Not many people had really believed it, though. But what if it were true?

"Well, tell me then. Don't keep me in suspense."

"Remember, not a word to anyone until ten o'clock this evening. You gave me your word of honor."

Varya nodded impatiently—oh, these men and their stupid rituals. Of course she wouldn't tell anyone.

McLaughlin leaned right down to her ear.

"This evening, Osman Pasha will surrender."

"I don't believe it!" Varya squealed.

"Quiet! At precisely ten o'clock this evening, the commander of the corps of grenadiers, Lieutenant General Ganetsky, whose forces occupy a position on the left bank of the Vid, will be approached by the truce envoys. I shall be the only journalist to witness this great event. And I shall also forewarn the general—at half-past nine and no sooner—so that the patrols don't open fire on the envoys by mistake. Can you imagine what an article it will make?"

"Yes, I can," said Varya with a nod of delight. "And I can't tell absolutely anyone at all?"

"It would be the end of me!" McLaughlin exclaimed in panic. "You gave me your word!"

"Very well, very well," she reassured him. "Until ten o'clock my lips are sealed."

"Ah, here's the fork. Stop here!" said the correspondent, prodding the coachman in the back. "You're going to the right, Mademoiselle Varya, and I'm going to the left. I can just imagine the scene. There I am, sitting with the general, drinking tea and making idle conversation about this and that, and at half-past nine I take out my watch and casually remark: 'By the way, Ivan Stepanovich, in half an hour or so you will have visitors from Osman Pasha.' Not bad, eh?"

McLaughlin began laughing excitedly as he stuck his foot in the stirrup.

A few moments later, he was lost to view behind the gray curtain of the intensifying downpour.

IN THREE MONTHS the camp had changed beyond recognition. The tents were all gone and in their place stood neat files of wooden huts. Everywhere there were paved roads, telegraph poles, and neat signposts. It was a good thing for an army to be commanded by an engineer, thought Varya.

In the special section, which now occupied three whole buildings, she was told that Mr. Fandorin had been allocated a separate cottage (the duty officer pronounced this new foreign word with obvious relish) and shown how to get there.

Cottage Number 158 proved to be a one-room prefabricated hut on the very edge of the headquarters staff village. The master of the house was at home; he opened the door himself and looked at Varya in a way that gave her a warm feeling inside.

"Hello, Erast Petrovich, here I am, back again," she said, for some reason feeling terribly anxious.

"Glad to see you," Fandorin said briefly and moved aside to let her in. It was a very simple room, but it had a set of wall bars and an entire arsenal of gymnastic apparatus. There was a three-verst map on the wall.

Varya explained: "I left my things with the nurses. Petya is on duty, so I came straight to you."

"I can see you are well." Erast Petrovich looked her over from head to toe and nodded. "A new hairstyle. Is that the fashion now?"

"Yes. It's very practical. And what's been happening here?"

"Nothing much. We're still besieging the Turk." Varya thought the titular counselor's voice sounded bitter. "One month, t-two months, three months now. The officers are taking to drink out of boredom, the quartermasters are p-plundering the supplies, the public coffers are empty. In short, everything is perfectly normal. War the Russian way. Europe has already heaved a sigh of relief and is happily watching as Russia's l-lifeblood drains away. If Osman Pasha holds out for another t-two weeks, the war will be l-lost."

Erast Petrovich sounded so peevish that

Varya took pity on him and whispered: "He won't hold out."

Fandorin started and looked into her eyes inquisitively.

"Do you know something? What? Where from?"

And so she told him. She could tell Erast Petrovich, surely—he wouldn't run off to tell everybody about it.

"To Ganetsky? Why to G-Ganetsky?" the titular counselor said with a frown when he had heard her out.

He walked across to the map and muttered under his breath: "It's a long way to G-Ganetsky. Right out on the flank. Why not go to command headquarters? Wait! Wait!"

A resolute expression appeared on the titular counselor's face; he tore his greatcoat down from its hook and dashed toward the door.

"What? What is it?" Varya cried, running after him.

"A trap," Fandorin muttered curtly, without stopping. "Ganetsky's defences are thinner. And beyond them lies the Sofia highway. They are not surrendering—they are trying to break out. They have to dupe Ganetsky so that he won't fire."

"Oh!" she gasped. "And they won't really be

envoys at all. Where are you going? To the headquarters building?"

Erast Petrovich halted.

"It's twenty to nine. At headquarters, things
take a long time. From one chief to another. It
would take too long. We can't reach Ganetsky in
time. We'll go to Sobolev! Half an hour at a gallop. Sobolev won't waste time asking permission
from headquarters. He'll take the risk. Strike the
first blow. Engage the enemy. If he can't help
Ganetsky, at least he'll be able to strike at the
flank. Trifon, my horse!"

My goodness, he has an orderly now, thought
Varya, bewildered.


THE RUMBLING IN the distance went on all
night long, and at dawn news came that Osman
had been wounded in the battle and surrendered with his entire army: Ten pashas and
forty-two thousand fighting men had laid down
their arms.

It was the end; the siege of Plevna was over.

There were many killed: Ganetsky's corps,
caught off guard by the unexpected attack, had
been almost completely wiped out. But the
name on everyone's lips was the White General,
the invulnerable Russian Achilles, Sobolev the

Second, who at the decisive moment had taken the risk of striking through Plevna, already deserted by the Turks, straight into Osman's unprotected flank.

FIVE DAYS LATER, on the third of December, the emperor, who was leaving for the theater of military action, held a farewell parade for the guards in Paradim. Individuals close to the throne and heroes who had distinguished themselves in the final battle were invited. Lieutenant General Sobolev himself sent his carriage for Varya. His star may have soared directly to its zenith, but the resplendent Achilles had apparently not forgotten his old friend.

Never before had Varya found herself in such distinguished society. She was positively blinded by the glitter of all the epaulettes and medals. To be quite honest, she had never suspected there were so many generals in the Russian army. The senior military commanders stood in the front row, waiting for the members of the imperial family to appear, among them Michel, who looked quite offensively young standing there in his customary white uniform with no greatcoat, even though the day had turned out bright but frosty. All eyes were fixed on the savior of the Fatherland, who seemed to Varya to have become much taller and broader across the shoulders, with a much graver expression than he had before. The French were obviously right when they said that the finest yeast was fame.

Close by, two ruddy-cheeked aides-de-camp were conversing in low voices. Varya found it pleasant that one of them kept glancing across at her with his rakish black eyes.

". . . and the emperor said to him: 'As a mark of respect for your valor, **mushir,** I return to you your saber, which you may wear here in Russia, where I trust you will have no cause for any dissatisfaction.' Such a fine scene—what a pity you weren't there."

"Ah, but then I was on duty in the council on the twenty-ninth," his companion replied jealously. "And with my own ears I heard the emperor say to Miliutin: 'Dmitry Alexandrovich, I request your permission, as the senior cavalier of St. George here present, to adorn my saber with the sword-knot of St. George. I believe I have earned it.' 'I request your permission'! How do you like that?"

"Yes, that's bad, all right," the black-eyed one agreed. "They really ought to have thought of it themselves. He's more like some sergeant major than a minister. His Majesty has shown such great generosity! Totleben and Nepokoinitsky—Orders of St. George, second class. Ganetsky—St. George, third class. And this is a mere sword-knot."

"And what will Sobolev receive?" Varya asked keenly, although she was not acquainted with these gentlemen. Never mind, this was the army, and it was a special occasion.

"Our Ak Pasha is quite sure to receive something special," the black-eyed man readily replied, "if his chief of staff, Perepyolkin, has skipped a rank. That's quite understandable, of course—a mere captain can't hold an appointment like that. But the prospects opening up for Sobolev are positively breathtaking. He has luck on his side, there's no denying it. If only he weren't spoiled by a passion for such vulgar ostentation . . ."

"Hush!" his companion hissed. "They're coming!"

Four soldiers emerged onto the porch of the unprepossessing house that was grandly titled "the field palace": the emperor, the commander in chief, the tsarevich, and the prince of Romania. Tsar Alexander Nikolaevich was in his winter uniform coat and Varya caught a glimpse of a bright-orange patch on the hilt of his saber—the sword-knot.

The orchestra struck up the solemn "Preobrazhensky March."

A colonel of the guards strode out to the front, saluted, and rapped out in a ringing voice trembling with excitement:

"Your Im-perial Majesty! Permit the officers of your personal escort to present you with a gold sword with the inscription 'For bravery'! In commemoration of our service together! Purchased with the officers' own personal funds!"

One of the aides-de-camp whispered to Varya: "Now that's neatly done. Good for the escort!"

The emperor accepted the gift and wiped away a tear with his glove.

"Thank you, gentlemen, thank you. I am touched. I shall send you all a saber from myself. For six months, so to speak, through thick and—"

He broke off and gestured with his hand.

People around her began sniffing with emotion, someone even sobbed, and Varya suddenly spotted Fandorin, standing in the crowd of officials, right beside the porch. What was he doing here? A titular counselor was hardly a figure of any great significance. Then she suddenly noticed the chief of gendarmes beside Fandorin, and everything became clear. After all, the true hero of the capture of the Turkish army was Fandorin. If not for him, there wouldn't have been any parades here today. He would probably receive an award, too.

Erast Petrovich caught Varya's eye and pulled a long-suffering face. He clearly did not share the general jubilation.

After the parade, when she was cheerfully beating off the advances of the black-eyed aide-de-camp, who insisted on trying to identify their mutual acquaintances in St. Petersburg, Fandorin came up to her, bowed rapidly, and said: "I beg your pardon, Colonel. Varvara Andreevna, the emperor wishes to see both of us."

—⁓—

# CHAPTER ELEVEN

**In which Varya
infiltrates the supreme
sphere of politics**

## THE TIMES (London)
## 16 (4) December 1877

## DERBY AND CAERNARVON
## THREATEN TO RESIGN

At yesterday's meeting of the cabinet, Lord Beacons-field proposed a demand for six million pounds of emergency credits from parliament in order to equip an expeditionary force which could be sent to the Balkans in the near future in order to protect the interests of the empire against the inordinate pretensions of Tsar Alexander. The decision was taken despite the opposition of the foreign secretary, Lord Derby, and the colonial secretary, Lord Caernarvon, who opposed any direct confrontation with Russia. Upon finding themselves in the minority, both ministers tendered their resignations to Her Majesty. The queen's response is as yet unknown.

VARYA HAD PUT ON all her best finery for the parade in the presence of His Imperial Majesty, and so she would have no cause to blush for her costume in front of her sovereign—that was the first thought that came into her head. The pale lilac hat with the watered silk ribbon and veil, the violet dress with the embroidery on the bodice and the moderate train, the black boots with the mother-of-pearl buttons. Modest and unaffected, but decent enough—thanks to the shops of Bucharest.

"Are we going to be decorated?" she asked Erast Petrovich on the way.

He was also decked out in his finest: creased trousers, boots polished like mirrors, an order of some kind in the buttonhole of his neatly ironed frock coat. There was no denying that the titular counselor looked every inch the part, except that he was so extremely young.

"Hardly."

"Why not?" asked Varya in astonishment.

"We're not important enough," Fandorin

replied thoughtfully. "They still haven't decorated all the generals, and we come low down on the list."

"But after all, if it weren't for us . . . I mean, if it weren't for you, Osman Pasha would have been bound to break out. Just think what would have happened then!"

"I realize that. But after a victory people don't usually think of such things. No, trust me, my experience tells me that this smacks of politics."

There were only six rooms in the "field palace," and therefore the function of the waiting room was assumed by the porch, where a dozen or so generals and senior officers were already shuffling their feet as they waited for their invitation to present themselves to the royal gaze. They were all wearing rather silly, delighted expressions—there was a whiff of decorations and promotions in the air. The waiting men stared at Varya with understandable curiosity. She glanced haughtily over their heads at the low winter sun: Let them rack their brains trying to guess who this young woman in the veil was and why she had presented herself for an audience.

The wait stretched out, but it wasn't boring at all.

"Who has been in there for so long, General?" Varya asked grandly, addressing a tall old man with tangled masses of whiskers at the sides of his mouth.

"Sobolev," said the general, putting on a significant expression. "He went in half an hour ago." He drew himself erect and touched a hand to the brand-new decoration with the black-and-orange bow on his chest. "Pardon me, madam, I have not introduced myself. Ivan Stepanovich Ganetsky, commander of the grenadier corps." He paused expectantly.

"Varvara Andreevna Suvorova," said Varya with a nod. "Pleased to meet you."

At this point Fandorin demonstrated a brusqueness quite untypical of him in normal circumstances and pushed forward, preventing her from finishing what she was going to say.

"Tell me, General, just before the assault, was the **Daily Post** correspondent, McLaughlin, at your headquarters?

Ganetsky glanced in annoyance at this civilian whippersnapper, but then clearly decided that not just anybody would be invited to see His Majesty and replied politely: "Why yes, he was. He was the reason it all happened."

"What, exactly?" Erast Petrovich asked with a rather stupid expression.

"Why, surely you must have heard?" This was evidently not the first time the general had told the tale. "I know McLaughlin from St.

Petersburg. A serious man and a friend of Russia, even though he is a subject of Queen Victoria. When he told me that Osman was going to surrender to me at any moment, I sent off runners to the forward edge of our lines, so that no one, God forbid, would open fire. And, like an old fool, I went to put on my dress uniform." The general gave an embarrassed smile, and Varya decided that he was really terribly nice. "So the Turks took the patrols without a single shot being fired. It was a good job my grenadiers didn't let me down; fine lads—they held out until Mikhail Dmitrievich attacked Osman from the rear."

"What happened to McLaughlin?" the titular counselor asked, staring fixedly at Ganetsky with his cold blue eyes.

"I didn't see," said the general with a shrug. "I was busy. My God, but it was a fine mess. The Bashi-Bazouks reached our actual headquarters; I was lucky to get away with my life in my dress tunic."

The door opened and Sobolev emerged onto the porch, with a red face and a special, unusual gleam in his eyes.

"On what shall we congratulate you, Mikhail Dmitrievich?" asked a general of Caucasian appearance in a Circassian coat with a gilded cartridge belt.

Everybody held their breath, but Sobolev was in no hurry to answer. He paused for effect, glancing round at all of them and winking gaily at Varya.

But she did not discover exactly how the emperor had honored the hero of Plevna, because the dull, workaday features of Lavrenty Arkadievich Mizinov appeared behind the Olympian's shoulder. The chief gendarme of the empire beckoned with one finger to Fandorin and Varya. Her heart began to race.

As they were walking past Sobolev, he whispered quietly: "Varvara Andreevna, I will wait for you without fail."

From the entrance hall they stepped straight into the aide-de-camp's room, where the duty general and two officers were sitting at a table. The emperor's personal apartments were on the right, his study was on the left.

"Answer questions loudly, clearly, and fully," Mizinov instructed them as they walked along. "In detail, but without deviating from the subject."

There were two people in the simple study furnished with portable items of Karelian birch. One was sitting in an armchair, the other was standing with his back to the window. Varya naturally glanced first at the seated individual, but he was not Alexander; he was a wizened old man wearing gold-rimmed glasses, with an intelligent, thin-lipped face and eyes of impenetrable ice. State Chancellor Prince Korchakov in person, exactly the way he looked in his portraits, except perhaps rather more delicate—a legendary individual in his own way. Varya believed he had been minister of foreign affairs before she was even born. But most important of all, he had studied at the Lycée with the Poet. He was the one who was "the darling of fashion, friend of high society, observer of its dazzling ways." Although at the age of eighty the "darling of fashion" put her more in mind of a different poem that was included in every grammar-school textbook:

**Which one of you, as feeble age advances,**
**Is doomed to greet our Lycée Day alone?**
**Ill-fated friend! To those new generations**
**A tedious guest, unwelcome and despised,**
**Calling to mind our former congregations,**
**One trembling hand shading his**
**rheumy eyes . . .**

The chancellor's hand really was trembling. He took a cambric handkerchief out of his pocket and blew his nose, which not did hinder him from surveying first Varya and then Erast Petrovich in the most censorious manner—and, moreover, the legendary's person's gaze lingered for a long moment on Fandorin.

Spellbound by the sight of the alumnus of the Lycée at Tsarskoe Selo, Varya had entirely forgotten the most important individual present. Embarrassed, she turned toward the window, thought for a moment, and then curtseyed—as they used to do in grammar school when the headmistress entered the classroom.

Unlike Korchakov, His Majesty demonstrated distinctly more interest in her person than in Fandorin's. The famous Romanov eyes—piercing, mesmerizing, and distinctly slanted—gazed at her with fastidious severity. They see into your very soul, she thought, that's the expression, and then she immediately felt quite angry with herself for slipping into the slave mentality of ignorant prejudice. He was simply imitating the "basilisk stare" that his father—may he lie uneasy in his grave—had been so proud of. And she began demonstratively inspecting the man whose will governed the lives of eighty million subjects.

The first observation: Why, he was really old! Puffy eyelids, sideburns, a mustache with curly ends and a pronounced sprinkling of gray, knotty, gouty fingers. But then, of course, next year he would be sixty—almost as old as her grandmother.

The second observation: He didn't look as kind as the newspapers said he was. He seemed indifferent and weary. He'd seen everything in the world there was to see; nothing could surprise him, nothing could make him feel particularly happy.

The third observation, and the most interesting: Despite his age and his imperial lineage, he was not indifferent to the female sex. Otherwise, why, Your Majesty, would you be running your eyes over my breasts and my waist like that? It was obviously true what they said about him and Princess Dolgorukova, who was only half his age. Varya stopped being even slightly afraid of the tsar-liberator.

Their chief introduced them.

"Your Majesty, this is Titular Counselor Fandorin, the one you have heard about. With him is his assistant, Miss Suvorova."

The tsar did not say hello or even nod. He concluded his inspection of Varya's figure without hurrying, then turned his head toward Erast Petrovich and said in a low voice modulated like an actor's: "I remember—Azazel. And Sobolev was just telling me."

He sat down at the desk and nodded to Mizinov.

"You begin. Mikhail Alexandrovich and I will listen."

He might offer a lady a chair, even if he is an emperor, Varya thought disapprovingly, abandoning her final shred of belief in the monarchic principle.

"How much time do I have?" the general asked respectfully. "I am aware, Your Majesty, just how busy you are today. And the heroes of Plevna are waiting."

"As much time as is needed. This is not merely a strategic matter, but a diplomatic one, too," the emperor rumbled, then glanced at Korchakov with an affectionate smile. "Mikhail Alexandrovich here has come from Bucharest specially. Rattling his old bones in a carriage."

The prince stretched his mouth in a clearly habitual manner to form a smile devoid of the slightest sign of merriment, and Varya remembered that the previous year the chancellor had suffered some kind of personal tragedy. Someone close to him had died—either his son or his grandson.

"Pray do not take this amiss, Lavrenty Arkadievich," the chancellor said in a doleful voice, "but I am having doubts. It all sounds rather too shady, even for Mr. Disraeli. And the heroes can wait. Waiting for a decoration is quite the most pleasant of pastimes. So please let us hear what you have to say."

Mizinov straightened up his shoulders smartly and turned, not to Fandorin, but to Varya: "Miss Suvorova, please tell us in detail about both of your meetings with the correspondent of the **Daily Post,** Seamus McLaughlin—during the third assault on Plevna and on the eve of Osman Pasha's breakout."

And so Varya told them.

It turned out that the tsar and the chancellor were both good listeners. Korchakov only interrupted her twice. The first time he asked: "Which Count Zurov is that? Not Alexander Platonovich's son?"

The second time he asked: "McLaughlin knew Ganetsky well, then, if he referred to him by his first name and patronymic?"

But His Majesty slapped his palm on the table in irritation when Varya explained that many of the journalists had acquired their own informants in Plevna.

"You still haven't explained to me, Mizinov, how Osman managed to organize his entire army for a breakout and your scouts failed to inform you in time!"

The chief of gendarmes started and prepared to make his excuses, but Alexander gestured to stop him.

"Later. Continue, Suvorova."

"Continue"—how do you like that! Even in the first class at school they had been more polite to her. Varya paused demonstratively to make the point, then went on to finish her story nonetheless.

"I think the picture is clear," said the tsar, glancing at Korchakov. "Let Shuvalov draw up a note."

"But I am not convinced," the chancellor replied. "Let us hear what arguments our inestimable Lavrenty Arkadievich has to offer."

Varya struggled in vain to understand where exactly the point of disagreement between the emperor and his senior diplomatic adviser lay. Mizinov cleared up the matter for her.

He took several sheets of paper out of his cuff, cleared his throat, and began speaking in the manner of a student who is top of the class: "With your permission, I will move from the specific to the general. Very well. First of all, I must confess my own failings. All the time our army was besieging Plevna, a cunning and merciless enemy was operating against us and my department failed to expose him in time. It was the intriguing of this cunning and clandestine enemy that resulted in our losing so much time and so many men and almost letting the fruits of many months of effort slip through our fingers on the thirtieth of November."

At these words the emperor crossed himself.

"God has preserved Russia."

"After the third assault, we—or rather, I, for the conclusions drawn were mine—made a serious mistake in concluding that the main Turkish agent was Lieutenant Colonel of Gendarmes Kazanzaki, thereby granting the genuine culprit full freedom of action. It is now not open to doubt that from the very beginning we have been sabotaged by the British subject McLaughlin, who is quite certainly an absolutely top-class agent, and an exceptional actor who spent a long time training thoroughly for his mission."

"How did this person ever come to be with our army in the field?" His Majesty asked, displeased. "Were correspondents given visas entirely without verification?"

"Naturally, a check was carried out, and an extremely thorough one," the chief of gendarmes said with a shrug. "A list of publications was requested from the editorial offices of all the foreign journalists and cross-checked with our embassies. Every one of the journalists is a well-known professional of good repute who has no history of hostility to Russia. McLaughlin in

particular. As I said, a most thorough gentleman. He was able to establish friendly relations
with many Russian generals and officers during
the Central Asian campaign. And his article last
year about Turkish atrocities in Bulgaria earned
McLaughlin the reputation of a friend of the
Slavs and a genuine supporter of Russia.
Whereas in fact all this time he must have been
acting on secret instructions from his government, which is well known for its undisguised
hostility to our Eastern policy.

"Initially, McLaughlin restricted his activities
purely to spying. Of course, he was passing information about our army to Plevna, for which
purpose he made full use of the freedom that
was so precipitately afforded to foreign journalists. Yes, many of them did have contacts with
the besieged town that were not controlled by
us, and this did not arouse the suspicions of our
counterintelligence agents. We shall draw the
appropriate conclusions for the future. Again I
must accept the blame.

"For as long as he could, McLaughlin used
others to do his dirty work. Your Majesty will
of course recall the incident involving the
Romanian Colonel Lukan, whose notebook included references to a certain mysterious 'J.' I
precipitately decided that the person concerned
was the gendarme Kazanzaki. Unfortunately I

was mistaken. J stood for 'journalist'—in other words, our British friend.

"However, during the third assault the fate of Plevna and the entire war hung by a thread, and McLaughlin changed his tactics to outright sabotage. I am sure he did not simply act on his own discretion, but had instructions on what to do from his superiors. I regret that I did not put the British diplomatic agent Colonel Wellesley under secret observation from the very beginning. I have previously reported this gentlemen's anti-Russian maneuverings to Your Majesty. It is quite clear that Turkish interests are closer to his heart than are ours.

"Now let us reconstruct the events of the thirtieth of August. General Sobolev, acting on his own initiative, broke through the Turkish defences and reached the southern outskirts of Plevna. This is understandable, since Osman had been warned by his agent of our general plan of attack and drawn all his forces into the center. Sobolev's attack caught him by surprise. However, our command was not informed of this success in time, and Sobolev had insufficient strength to continue his advance. McLaughlin and the other journalists and foreign observers—who included, I note in passing, Colonel Wellesley—happened by chance to be at the crucial point on our front, between the center and the left flank. At six o'clock, Count Zurov, Sobolev's adjutant, broke through the Turkish covering forces. As he rode past the journalists, whom he knew well, he shouted out the news of Sobolev's success. What happened after that? All the correspondents dashed to the rear in order to telegraph home as soon as possible the news that the Russian army was winning. All of them—except for McLaughlin. Suvorova met him about half an hour later, alone, spattered with mud, and, strangely enough, riding out of the undergrowth. There is no doubt that the journalist had both the time and the opportunity to overtake the messenger and kill him, together with Lieutenant Colonel Kazanzaki, who to his own misfortune had set out in pursuit of Zurov. Both of them knew McLaughlin very well and could not possibly have anticipated any treachery from him. It was not difficult to stage the lieutenant colonel's suicide—he dragged the body into the bushes, fired twice into the air with the gendarme's revolver, and it was done. And that was the bait we swallowed."

Mizinov lowered his eyes contritely, but then continued without waiting for His Majesty to rebuke him: "As for the recent attempted breakout, in this case McLaughlin was acting by agreement with the Turkish command. He could well be described as Osman's trump card. Their calculations were simple and accurate. Ganetsky is a distinguished general but—I beg your pardon for my bluntness—no towering intellect. As we know, he accepted the information conveyed to him by the journalist at face value without doubting it for a second. We have the resolve of Lieutenant General Sobolev to thank—"

"It is Erast Petrovich whom you have to thank!" Varya exclaimed, unable to restrain the mortal outrage she felt for Fandorin's treatment. He just stood there and said nothing, not even standing up for himself. Why had he been brought here—as a piece of furniture? "It was Fandorin who galloped to Sobolev and persuaded him to attack!"

The emperor stared in amazement at her for this brazen violation of etiquette, and old Korchakov shook his head reproachfully. Even Fandorin looked embarrassed and shifted his weight from one foot to the other. It seemed that everyone was displeased with her.

"Continue, Mizinov," he emperor said with a nod.

"By your leave, Your Majesty," said the wrinkled chancellor, raising a finger. "If McLaughlin had undertaken such a substantial act of sabotage, why would he need to inform this young woman of his intentions?" The finger inclined in Varya's direction.

"Why, that's obvious," said Mizinov, wiping the sweat from his brow. "He calculated that Suvorova would spread this astounding news around the camp immediately and that it would quickly reach the headquarters staff. Wild jubilation and confusion. They would think the cannonade in the distance was a salute. Perhaps, even, in their joy they would not believe the first report of an attack from Ganetsky and would wait to confirm it. A small detail of improvisation by a cunning intriguer."

"Possibly," the prince conceded.

"But where has this McLaughlin got to?" asked the tsar. "That is who we need to interrogate. And arrange a face-to-face meeting with Wellesley. Oh, we wouldn't want the colonel to slip away!"

Korchakov sighed pensively: "Yes, a **compromization** like this, as they call it in the Zamoskvorechie district, would allow us to neutralize British diplomacy completely."

"Unfortunately McLaughlin has not been found, either among the prisoners or among the wounded," said Mizinov, sighing in a different key. "He managed to get away, I have no idea how. He's a cunning serpent. Nor is Osman Pasha's infamous adviser, Ali-bei, among the prisoners—the bearded gentleman who ruined our first assault for us, and whom we assume to be the alter ego of Anwar-effendi. I have already presented Your Majesty with a report concerning the latter."

The emperor nodded.

"What say you now, Mikhail Alexandrovich?"

The chancellor half-closed his eyes.

"That an interesting scheme could be made of this, Your Majesty. If it is all true, then this time the English have allowed themselves to get carried away and overstepped the line. With a bit of careful planning, we could still benefit from all this."

"Well then, well then, what exactly are you scheming?" Alexander asked curiously.

"Sire, with the capture of Plevna the war has entered its concluding phase. The final victory over the Turks is only a matter of weeks away. I emphasize: **over the Turks.** But we must avoid the same thing happening as in fifty-three, when we began with a war against the Turks and ended up fighting the whole of Europe. Our finances could not bear the strain of such a conflict. You are already aware of how much this campaign has cost us."

The tsar frowned as if he had a toothache and Mizinov shook his head sadly.

"I am greatly alarmed by the resoluteness and callousness with which this McLaughlin acts," Korchakov continued. "It indicates that in her desire to prevent us from reaching the straits, Britain is prepared to resort to any measures, even the most extreme. Let us not forget that the English have a naval squadron in the Bosphorus. And, at the same time, our dear friend Austria has its guns trained on our rear, having stabbed your father in the back once already. To be quite honest, while you have been fighting Osman Pasha, I have been thinking more and more about a different war, a diplomatic one. After all, we are spilling blood, expending enormous funds and resources, and we may well end up with nothing even so. That accursed Plevna has devoured precious time and besmirched the reputation of our army. Please forgive an old man, Your Majesty, for being such a prophet of doom on a day like today."

"Enough of that, Mikhail Alexandrovich," sighed the emperor, "we are not on parade. Do you think I don't see?"

"Until I heard the explanations offered by Lavrenty Arkadievich, I was inclined to be very skeptical. If someone had said to me an hour ago: 'Tell me, old fox, what can we count on after the victory?'—I would have replied honestly: 'Bulgarian autonomy and a little piece of the Caucasus, that is the maximum possible, a paltry return for tens of thousands killed and millions wasted.' "

"And now?" asked Alexander, leaning forward slightly.

The chancellor looked quizzically at Varya and Fandorin.

Mizinov caught the meaning of his glance and said: "Your Majesty, I understand what Mikhail Alexandrovich has in mind. I had come to the same conclusion, and I did not bring Titular Counselor Fandorin with me by chance. But I think we could perhaps allow Miss Suvorova to leave now."

Varya snorted indignantly. Apparently, she wasn't trusted here. How humiliating to be thrown out of the room—and just at the most interesting point!

"Please p-pardon my impertinence," said Fandorin, opening his mouth for the first time in the entire audience, "but that is not reasonable."

"What precisely is not?" asked the emperor, knitting his gingerish brows.

"One should not trust an employee halfway, Your M-Majesty. It creates unnecessary resentment and is harmful to the cause. Varvara Andreevna knows so much already that she will q-quite easily guess the rest."

"You are right," the tsar conceded. "Go on, Prince."

"We must exploit this business to shame Britain in front of the entire world. Sabotage, murder, a conspiracy with one of the combatants in contravention of declared neutrality—it is quite unprecedented. To be honest, I am astounded at Lord Beaconsfield's rashness. What if we had captured McLaughlin and he had testified? What a scandal! What a nightmare! I mean, for England, of course. She would have had to withdraw her navy squadron and justify her actions to the whole of Europe, and she would still have been licking her wounds for a long time after that. In any case, the British Cabinet would have been obliged to give up interfering in the Eastern conflict. And without London, the ardor of our Austro-Hungarian friends would have cooled immediately. Then we would have been able to exploit the fruits of victory to the full and—"

"Dreams," said Alexander, interrupting the old man rather sharply. "We do not have McLaughlin. The question is, what are we to do now?"

"Get him," Korchakov replied imperturbably.

"But how?"

"I don't know, Your Majesty, I am not the head of the Third Section." The chancellor fell silent, folding his hands complacently across his skinny stomach.

"We are certain of the Englishman's guilt and we have circumstantial evidence of it, but no solid proof," said Mizinov, picking up where the chancellor had left off. "That means we shall have to obtain it—or create it. Hmm . . ."

"Explain your meaning," the tsar pressed him, "and do not mumble, Mizinov. Speak straight out, we are not playing forfeits."

"Yes, Your Majesty. McLaughlin is now either in Constantinople or, most likely, making his way to England, since his mission has been accomplished. In Constantinople we have an entire network of secret agents, and kidnapping the scoundrel will not be too difficult. In England it is a harder proposition, but with sensible organization—"

"I do not wish to hear this!" Alexander exclaimed. "What sort of abominations are you talking?"

"Sire, you did order me not to mumble," said the general with a shrug.

"Bringing McLaughlin back in a sack wouldn't be such a bad thing," the chancellor mused, "but it's too bothersome and unreliable.

We could find ourselves caught up in a scandal. Yes, that kind of thing is fine in Constantinople, but I wouldn't recommend it in London."

"Very well," said Mizinov with a vehement shake of his head. "If McLaughlin is found in London, we shall not touch him. But we will stir up a scandal in the English press about the British correspondent's inappropriate behavior. The English public will not approve of McLaughlin's exploits, because they do not fit their much-vaunted idea of fair play."

Korchakov was pleased: "Now that's more to the point. In order to tie Beaconsfield's and Derby's hands, all we need is a good scandal in the newspapers."

While this conversation was going on, Varya had been imperceptibly edging closer to Erast Petrovich until now she finally found herself right beside the titular counselor.

"Who is this Derby?" she asked in a whisper.

"The foreign secretary," Fandorin hissed, scarcely even moving his lips.

Mizinov glanced round at the whisperers and knitted his brows in a threatening frown.

"This McLaughlin of yours is clearly an old hand with no particular prejudices or sentiments," said the chancellor, continuing with his deliberations. "If he is found in London, then, before there is any scandal, we could have a confidential chat with him. Present him with the evidence, threaten him with exposure . . . After all, if there is a scandal, he's finished. I know how the British are about such things—no one in society will ever offer him their hand again, even if he is covered with medals from head to foot. And then again, two murders is no laughing matter. There is the prospect of criminal proceedings. He is an intelligent man. If we also offer him a good sum of money and present him with an estate somewhere beyond the Volga, he might give us the information we need, and Shuvalov could use it to put pressure on Lord Derby. If he threatened to expose them, the British cabinet would suddenly turn as meek as lambs. What do you think, General, would a combination of threats and bribery work on McLaughlin?"

"They would be bound to," the general promised confidently. "I have also considered this option, which is why I brought Erast Fandorin with me. I did not dare appoint a man to such a delicate mission without Your Majesty's approval. There is far too much at stake. Fandorin is resourceful and determined, he has an original mind, and, most important of all, he has already worked on one highly com-

276 • *Boris Akunin*

plex secret mission in London and managed it
quite brilliantly. He knows the language. He
knows McLaughlin personally. If necessary, he
will kidnap him. If that is not possible, he will
come to terms with him. If he cannot come to
terms, then he will assist Shuvalov to arrange a
fine scandal. He can even testify against
McLaughlin as a direct eyewitness. He possesses
exceptional powers of persuasion."

"And who's Shuvalov?" Varya whispered.

"Our ambassador," the titular counselor
replied absentmindedly, thinking of something
else. He didn't really seem to be following what
the general was saying.

"Well, Fandorin, can you manage that?" the
emperor asked. "Will you go to London?"

"Yes, I will go, Your Majesty," said Erast
Petrovich. "Certainly I will go."

The autocrat eyed him keenly, having caught
the echo of something left unsaid, but Fandorin
did not add anything else.

"Well, then, Mizinov, act along both lines,"
said Alexander, summing up. "Look for him in
Constantinople and in London. Only do not
waste any time—we have very little left."


WHEN THEY CAME OUT into the aide-
de-camp's room, Varya asked the general:

"But what if McLaughlin can't be found at all?"

"You can rely on my instinct, my dear," the general sighed. "We will definitely be seeing that gentleman again."

# CHAPTER TWELVE

—✺—

## In which events take
## an unexpected turn

## THE ST. PETERSBURG GAZETTE
### 8 (20) January 1878

### TURKS SUE
### FOR PEACE!

After the capitulation of Vessel Pasha, the capture of Philippopol, and the surrender of ancient Adrianople, which yesterday flung open its gates to admit the Cossacks of the White General, the outcome of the war has finally been settled, and this morning a train carrying the Turkish truce envoys arrived at the positions of our valiant forces. The train was detained at Adrianople and the pashas were transferred from there to the headquarters of the Commander in Chief, currently quartered in the village of Germanly. When the head of the Turkish delegation, 76-year-old Namyk Pasha, learned the provisional terms of the peace settlement, he exclaimed in despair: **"Votre armée est victorieuse, votre ambition est satisfaite et la Turkie est détruite!"**

Well, now, say we, that is no more than Turkey deserves.

THEY HADN'T SAID GOOD-BYE PROPERLY. Sobolev had collected Varya from the porch of the "field palace," enveloped her in his magnetic aura of success and glory, and whisked her away to his headquarters to celebrate the victory. She had barely even had time to nod to Erast Petrovich, and in the morning he was no longer in the camp. His orderly Trifon said: "His honor has gone away. Call back in a month."

But a month had passed, and the titular counselor had still not returned. Evidently it was not proving so easy to find McLaughlin in England.

It wasn't that Varya actually missed him. On the contrary: Once they decamped from Plevna, life had become quite fascinating. Every day there were moves to new places, new cities, stu-

pendous mountain landscapes, and endless celebrations of almost daily military victories. The
commander in chief's headquarters first moved
to Kazanlyk, beyond the Balkan range, and then
still further south, to Germanly. Here there was
no winter at all. The trees were all green and the
only snow to be seen was on the summits of the
distant mountains.

Without Fandorin there was nothing that
Varya had to do. She was still, however, officially attached to the headquarters staff and
she received her salary punctually for December and January, plus traveling expenses, plus
a bonus for Christmas. She had accumulated
quite a tidy sum, but she had nothing to
spend it on. Once, in Sofia, she had wanted to
buy a charming copper lamp (it was exactly
like Aladdin's), but Paladin and Gridnev
hadn't allowed her. In fact, they had almost
come to blows over who would present Varya
with the trinket, and she had been obliged to
give way.

Concerning Gridnev. The eighteen-year-old
ensign had been attached to Varya by Sobolev.
The hero of Plevna and Sheinov was kept busy
day and night with army affairs, but he had not
forgotten about Varya. Whenever he could find
a free moment to visit headquarters, he always
called in to see her, sent her gigantic bouquets

of flowers, and invited her to celebrations (they saw in the New Year twice, once according to the Western calendar and once according to the Russian calendar). But this was still not enough for the tenacious Michel, so he had placed one of his orderlies at Varya's disposal—"for assistance on the road and for protection." At first the ensign had sulked and glared hostilely at his superior in a skirt, but quite soon he had grown tame, and even seemed to have developed certain romantic feelings for her. It was funny, of course, but flattering. Gridnev wasn't handsome. That strategist Sobolev would not have sent anyone handsome, but he was as lovable and eager to please as a puppy. In his company, twenty-two-year-old Varya felt like a very grown-up and worldly-wise woman.

She was in a rather strange position now. At headquarters they apparently assumed that she was Sobolev's mistress, but since everyone regarded the White General with indulgent adoration, no one condemned her for it. On the contrary, some small portion of Sobolev's halo seemed to extend to her as well. Many of the officers would probably have been quite indignant if they had discovered that she dared to refuse to enter into intimate relations with the glorious Russian Achilles and was remaining faithful to some lowly cryptographer.

But, to be honest, things were not going all that well with Petya. No, he didn't get jealous and he didn't make scenes, but since his failed suicide Varya found it hard to be with him. In the first place, she hardly ever saw him—Petya was atoning for his guilt with work, since it was impossible to atone for it with blood in the cryptography section. He worked two consecutive shifts each day, slept at his post on a folding bed, no longer visited the journalists in their club, and took no part in the general carousing. She had been obliged to celebrate Christmas and Epiphany without him. At the sight of Varya, his face lit up with a gentle, quiet joy. And he spoke to her as if she were an icon of the Virgin of Vladimir: She was the light of his life, and his only hope, and without her he would never have survived.

She felt terribly sorry for him. Only more and more often now she found herself pondering the troublesome question of whether it was possible to marry out of pity, and the answer was always that it wasn't. But it was even more unthinkable to say: "You know, Petya, I've changed my mind and decided not to be your wife." It would be just like putting down a wounded animal. She was caught on the horns of a dilemma.

A substantial gathering still convened as before in the press club as it migrated from place to place, but it was not as boisterous as in Zurov's unforgettable time. They gambled with restraint, for small stakes, and the chess sessions had ceased with McLaughlin's disappearance. The journalists did not mention the Irishman, at least in the company of Russians, but the two other British correspondents had been made the object of a demonstrative boycott and stopped coming to the club altogether.

Of course, there had been drinking sprees and scandals. Twice matters had almost reached the point of bloodshed, and both times, alas, because of Varya.

The first time, when they were still at Kazanlyk, a newly arrived adjutant, who had not fully grasped Varya's status, made an unfortunate attempt to joke by calling her "the duchess of Marlborough," with the obvious implication that Marlborough himself was Sobolev. Paladin demanded an apology from the insolent fellow, who proved stubborn in his drunken stupor, and they had stepped out to fight a duel with pistols. Varya was not in the marquee at the time, or else she would, of course, have put a stop to this idiotic conflict straightaway. Fortunately, no harm was done:

284 · *Boris Akunin*

The adjutant shot wide, and when Paladin fired in reply he shot the adjutant's forage cap neatly off his head, after which the offending party sobered up and admitted his error.

On the second occasion it was the Frenchman who was challenged, and once again for a joke, only this time it was quite a funny one, or at least Varya thought so. It happened after the youthful Gridnev had begun to accompany her everywhere. Paladin rashly remarked aloud that **"Mademoiselle Barbara"** was like the empress Anna Ioannovna with her famous statue of a little black boy, and the cornet, uncowed by the correspondent's fearsome reputation, demanded immediate satisfaction from him. Since the scene took place in Varya's presence, no shots were ever fired. She ordered Gridnev to be silent and Paladin to take back what he had said. The correspondent immediately repented, acknowledging that the comparison had been an unhappy one and that **"monsieur sous-lieutenant"** bore a closer resemblance to Hercules capturing the hind of Arcadia. On that basis they had made up.

At times it seemed to Varya that Paladin was casting glances at her for which there could be only one possible interpretation, and yet outwardly the Frenchman behaved like a genuine

Bayard. Like the other journalists, he would spend days at a time away at the front line, and they saw each other less often than in the camp near Plevna. But one day the two of them had a private conversation that Varya subsequently called and noted down word for word in her diary (after Erast Petrovich's departure, she had felt the urge to keep a diary, no doubt for lack of anything to occupy her time).

They were sitting in a roadside **korchma** in a mountain pass, warming themselves at the fire and drinking hot wine, and after the frost the journalist seemed to get a little tipsy.

"Ah, **Mademoiselle Barbara,** if only I were not who I am," Paladin said with a bitter laugh, unaware that he was repeating Varya's beloved Pierre Bezukhov almost word for word. "If only my circumstances were different, if my character were different, and my fate . . ." He looked at Varya in a way that made her heart leap in her breast as if it were skipping a rope. "Then I would certainly vie in the lists with the brilliant Michel. Tell me, would I have at least some small chance against him?"

"Of course you would," Varya answered honestly, and then realized that her words sounded as if she were inviting him to flirt. "By which I mean, Charles, that you would have the same chance as Mikhail Dmitrievich, no more and no less. That is, no chance at all. Almost."

She had added that "almost." Oh that hateful, ineradicable womanly weakness!

Since Paladin seemed more relaxed than he had ever been, Varya asked him the question that had been on her mind for a long time.

"Charles, do you have a family?"

"What really interests you, I suppose, is whether I have a wife?" the journalist said with a smile.

Varya was embarrassed.

"Well, not only that. Parents, brothers, sisters . . ."

But actually, why be hypocritical, she reproached herself. It was a perfectly normal question. She continued resolutely: "I would like to know if you have a wife as well, of course. Sobolev, for instance, does not hide the fact that he is married."

"Alas, **Mademoiselle Barbara.** No wife. No fiancée. I have never had either one or the other. I lead the wrong kind of life. There have been a few affairs, of course—I tell you that quite openly, because you are a modern woman free of foolish affectation." (Varya smiled, flattered). "As for a family . . . only a father, whom I love dearly and miss greatly. He is in France at present. Someday I will tell you about him. After the war, perhaps? **C'est toute une histoire.**"

And so it had turned out that he wasn't indifferent, but didn't wish to set himself up as a rival to Sobolev. Out of pride, no doubt.

This circumstance, however, had not prevented the Frenchman from remaining on friendly terms with Michel. Most of the time when Paladin disappeared he was with the White General's unit, since Michel was always in the very vanguard of the advancing army, where the pickings were good for correspondents.

AT MIDDAY ON the eighth of January Sobolev sent a captured carriage and a Cossack escort for Varya—he had invited her to visit the newly conquered city of Adrianople. There was an armful of hothouse roses lying on the soft leather seat. Mitya Gridnev became very upset because he tore his brand-new gloves as he was gathering the flowers into a bouquet. Varya tried to console him as they rode along and mischievously promised to give him her own gloves (the ensign had small hands, almost like a girl's). Mitya frowned, knitting his white eyebrows, sniffed offendedly, and sulked for about half an hour, fluttering his long, fluffy eyelashes. Those eyelashes were perhaps the only point of his appearance in which nature had been kind to him, thought Varya. Just like Erast Petrovich's, only lighter. Her thoughts moved on in a perfectly natural manner to Fandorin, and she wondered where his wanderings had taken him. If only he would come back soon! When he was there things were . . . calmer? More interesting? She couldn't quite put her finger on the right word, but she definitely felt better when he was there.

It was already getting dark when they arrived. The town was quiet, with not a soul out on the streets, only the echoing clip-clop of horses' hooves as mounted patrols rode by and the rumbling of artillery being moved up along the highway.

The temporary headquarters was located in the railway station building. Varya heard the bravura music from a distance—a brass band playing the anthem "Rejoice." All the windows in the new, European-style station building were lit up, and in the square in front of it there were bonfires burning and field kitchens with their chimneys smoking efficiently. What surprised Varya most of all was the perfectly ordinary passenger train standing at the platform—neat little carriages and a gently panting locomotive—as if there were no war going on at all.

In the waiting room they were celebrating, of course. A number of tables of various sizes had been hastily pushed together and the officers were sitting around them banqueting on simple fare augmented by a substantial number of bottles. Just as Varya and Gridnev entered, they all roared out "Hurrah," raised their tankards, and turned toward the table at which their commander was sitting. The general's famous white tunic contrasted sharply with the black army and gray Cossack uniforms. Sitting with Sobolev at the table of honor were the senior officers (the only one Varya recognized was Perepyolkin) and Paladin. They all had red, happy faces—they must have been celebrating for some time already.

"Varvara Andreevna," Achilles shouted, jumping to his feet. "I'm so glad you decided to come! 'Hurrah,' gentlemen, in honor of our only lady!"

Everybody stood up and roared so deafeningly that Varya felt frightened. She had never been greeted in such an energetic manner before. Perhaps she ought not to have accepted the invitation after all? She recalled the good advice given by Baroness Vreiskaya, the head of the field infirmary (with whose employees Varya was quartered), to her female wards:

"**Mesdames,** keep well away from men when

they are excited by battle or, even worse, by victory. It rouses an atavistic savagery in them, and any man, even an alumnus of the Corps of Pages, is temporarily transformed into a barbarian. Leave them in their male company to cool off, and afterward they will return to civilized manners and become manageable once again."

In fact, apart from the exaggerated gallantry and excessively loud voices, Varya noticed nothing particularly wild about her neighbors at the table. They seated her in the place of honor, on Sobolev's right. Paladin was on his left.

After she had drunk some champagne and calmed down a little, she asked, "Tell me, Michel, what's that train doing here? I can't remember the last time I saw a locomotive standing on the tracks and not lying at the bottom of an embankment."

"So you haven't heard!" exclaimed a young colonel sitting at the side of the table. "The war's over! The truce envoys arrived from Constantinople today! By railway, just like in peacetime!"

"And exactly how many of these envoys are there?" Varya asked in surprise. "A whole trainload?"

"No, Varya," Sobolev explained. "There are only two envoys. But after the fall of Adrianople the Turks were afraid to waste any more time, so they simply hitched their staff carriage onto an ordinary train. Only without any passengers, of course."

"Then where are the envoys now?"

"I sent them off to the grand duke in carriages. There's a break in the track further up."

"Oh, it's ages since I had a ride in a train," she sighed dreamily. "Lie back on your soft seat, open a book, drink some hot tea. The telegraph posts flicking past the window, the wheels hammering . . ."

"I would take you for a ride," said Sobolev, "but unfortunately the route is rather limited. The only place you can go to from here is Constantinople."

"Gentlemen, gentlemen!" exclaimed Paladin in his French accent. "An excellent idea! **La guerre est en fait finie,** the Turks aren't shooting anymore! And anyway, the train is flying the Turkish flag! Why don't we take a ride to San Stefano and back? **Aller et retour,** eh, Michel?" He switched completely into French as his enthusiasm mounted ever higher. "**Mademoiselle Barbara** will ride in a first-class carriage, I'll write a splendid article about it, and someone from headquarters staff will ride along with us and take a look at the Turks' rear lines. My God, Michel, it will all go off without a hitch! They'll never suspect a thing! And, even if they do, they won't dare fire a single shot—you've got their envoys! And then, Michel, from San Stefano it's only a stone's throw to the bright lights of Constantinople! The Turkish viziers have their country villas at San Stefano! Ah, what an opportunity!"

"Irresponsible adventurism," snapped Lieutenant Colonel Pere-pyolkin. "I trust, Mikhail Dmitrievich, that you will have the good sense not to be tempted."

Eremei Perepyolkin was so annoying—such a stick-in-the-mud. In fact, during the last few months Varya had developed quite an active dislike for the man, even though she accepted on trust the superlative administrative abilities of Sobolev's chief of staff. If only he wouldn't be so serious about everything! It was less than six months since he had leap-frogged from captain to lieutenant colonel and picked up a St. George medal, not to mention a sword of St. Anne for being wounded in action. And all thanks to Michel. And still he glared at Varya as if he thought she'd stolen something that was his by right. But then she could understand him; he was simply jealous; he wanted Achilles to belong to him and nobody else. Perhaps Eremei Ionovich was tainted with Kazanzaki's old sin? One day she had even tried hinting at it when she was talking to Sobolev, but the idea had made him laugh so hard that he almost choked.

This time, however, the repugnant Perepyolkin was absolutely right. Varya thought Charles's "excellent idea" was absolutely lunacy. But the carousing officers were all fully in favor of the project: One Cossack colonel even slapped the Frenchman on the back and called him a "crazy fool." Sobolev smiled but didn't say anything.

"Permit me to go, Mikhail Dmitrievich," one dashing cavalry general suggested (Varya seemed to remember that his name was Strukov). "I'll fill up the carriages with my Cossack lads and we'll ride down the line like the wind. Who knows—we might even capture ourselves another pasha or two. We still have the right, don't we? We haven't received any orders to cease military operations yet."

Sobolev glanced at Varya and she noticed an unusual glint in his eyes.

"Oh, no, Strukov. Adrianople was enough for you." Achilles smiled rapaciously and raised his voice. "Gentlemen, listen to my orders!" The room fell silent immediately. "I am transferring my field headquarters to San Stefano. The third battalion of chasseurs is to board the train. I want every last one of them in those carriages, even if they have to squeeze in like sardines. I'll travel in the staff carriage. The train will then immediately return to Adrianople for reinforcements and go back and forth continuously. By midday tomorrow I shall have an entire regiment. You, Strukov, are to arrive with your cavalry no later than tomorrow evening. In the meantime, one battalion will be all I need. According to reconnaissance reports, there are no battle-worthy Turkish forces ahead of us— only the sultan's guards in Constantinople itself, and they're busy guarding Abdul-Hamid."

"It's not the Turks we need to be afraid of, your excellency," Pere-pyolkin said in his squeaky voice. "We may assume that the Turks will not touch you—they've run out of steam. But the commander in chief will not be pleased at all."

"Ah, but that's not quite true, Eremei Ionovich," said Sobolev, squinting cunningly. "Everybody knows what a madcap yours truly, Ak Pasha, is, and we can use that as an excuse for all sorts of things. You know, it might prove very handy indeed for His Imperial Highness if news that one of the suburbs of Constantinople has been captured were to arrive just as the negotiations are in full swing. They might rebuke me in public, but they'll thank me in private. It wouldn't be the first time by any means. And kindly be so good as not to discuss matters when an order has already been issued."

"**Absolument!**" declared Paladin, shaking his head in admiration. "**Un tour de génie, Michel!** My idea wasn't the best after all. This article is going to be even better than I thought."

Sobolev got to his feet and offered Varya his arm with a grand gesture.

"What would you say to a glimpse of the lights of Constantinople, Varvara Andreevna?"

THE TRAIN HURTLED on through the darkness so fast that Varya scarcely had time to read the names of the stations: Babaeski, Luleburgaz, Chorlu. They were ordinary railway stations, just like stations somewhere in Tambov province, only they were white instead of yellow. Flickering lights, the elegant silhouettes of cypress trees, and once, through the iron lacework of a bridge, a glimpse of a moonlit swathe of river water.

The carriage was comfortable, with plush-covered divans and a large mahogany table. The escort and Sobolev's white mare, Gulnora, were riding in the accompanying retinue's compartment. Every now and again Varya heard the sound of neighing from Gulnora, who still hadn't settled down after the anxious process of boarding. The company riding in the main compartment consisted of the general, Varya, Paladin, and several officers, including Mitya Gridnev, who was sleeping peacefully in the corner. A handful of officers were smoking and crowding round Perepyolkin as he marked off the train's progress on a map, the correspondent was writing something in his notepad, and Varya and Sobolev were standing apart from everyone else by the window, making awkward conversation.

"I thought it was love," Michel confessed in a soft voice, seeming to stare out into the darkness through the window, but Varya knew he was looking at her reflection in the glass. "But I won't try to lie to you. I never actually thought about love. My true passion is my ambition, and everything else comes second. That's just the way I am. But ambition is no sin if it is directed to an exalted goal. I believe in my star and my fate, Varvara Andreevna. My star shines brightly, and my fate is special. I feel it in my heart. When I was still a young cadet—"

"You were telling me about your wife," said Varya, gently guiding him back to the more interesting subject.

"Ah, yes. I married out of ambition, I admit it. I made a mistake. Ambition may be a good reason to face a hail of bullets, but not to get married, not under any circumstances. How did it all happen? I came back from Turkestan to the first glimmerings of fame and glory, but I was still a parvenu, an upstart, a peasant made good. My grandfather served his way up all the way from the lower ranks. And suddenly there was Princess Titova, with a line going all the way back to Rurik. I could move straight from the garrison into high society. How could I not be tempted?"

Sobolev spoke haltingly, in a bitter voice, and he seemed sincere. Varya valued sincerity. And, of course, she had guessed where all this was leading. She could have put a stop to it then and there, turned the conversation in another direc-tion, but she wasn't strong enough. Who would have been?

"But very soon I realized that high society was no place for the likes of me. The air doesn't suit me. I was away on campaigns and she was back in St. Petersburg. And that was our life. When the war's over, I'll demand a divorce. I can afford to, I've earned it. And no one will rebuke me—after all, I am a hero." Sobolev grinned cunningly. "So, what do you say, Varya?"

"About what?" she asked with an innocent expression—her abominably flirtatious character leading her into trouble again. She knew this declaration was not what she really wanted, it would only cause complications, but it still felt wonderful.

"Should I get divorced or not?"

"That's for you to decide." This was the moment; now he would say those words.

Sobolev sighed heavily and plunged headfirst into the whirlpool.

"I've had my eye on you for a long time. You're intelligent, sincere, bold, strong-willed. Just the kind of companion I need. With you, I'd be even stronger. And you'd never regret it, I swear. And so, Varvara Andreevna, you may consider this an official—"

"Your excellency!" shouted Perepyolkin (damn him, why can't he just disappear!). "San Stefano! Shall we disembark?"

THE OPERATION WENT OFF without a hitch. They disarmed the dumb-founded guards at the station (it was a joke—only six sleepy soldiers) and spread out through the little town by platoons.

Sobolev waited at the station while the occasional shooting continued in the streets. It was all over in half an hour. Their only casualty was one man wounded, and he had apparently been shot by mistake by their own men.

The general made a cursory inspection of the center of the town with its gas streetlamps. Further on there was a dark labyrinth of crooked little alleys—it made no sense to go poking his nose in there. For his residence and defensive stronghold (in the case of any unpleasantness) Sobolev chose the local branch of the Osman-Osman Bank. One company of men was stationed in the bank and immediately outside it, another was left at the station, and a third was divided into teams to patrol the surrounding streets. The train immediately set off again to bring reinforcements.

They were unable to inform the commander in chief's headquarters by telegram that San Stefano had been taken, because the line was dead. Obviously the Turks' doing.

"The second battalion will be here by midday at the latest," said Sobolev. "Nothing very interesting is likely to happen in the meantime. We can admire the lights of Constantinople and pass the time in pleasant conversation."

The temporary staff office was established on the second floor, in the director's office. First, because from the windows you really could see the lights of the Turkish capital twinkling in the distance, and second because there was a steel door in the office that led directly into the bank's strong room. There were little sacks with wax seals lying in neat rows on the room's cast-iron shelves. Paladin read the Arabic script and said that each bag contained a hundred thousand lire.

"And they say Turkey's bankrupt," said Mitya in amazement. "There are millions here!"

"That's why we're going to use this office as our base," Sobolev said firmly. "To keep it all safe. I've been accused once of making off with the khan's treasury. Never again."

The door to the strong room was left half-open, and everyone forgot about the millions of lire. They brought a telegraph apparatus from the station to the waiting room and ran a wire straight out across the square. Every fifteen minutes Varya tried to contact at least Adrianople, but the apparatus betrayed no signs of life.

A deputation arrived from the local merchants and clergy to ask them not to loot homes or destroy mosques, but specify the sum of a contribution instead, perhaps fifty thousand—the poor citizens of San Stefano would not be able to raise any more than that. However, when the head of the delegation, a fat, hook-nosed Turk in a tail coat and fez, realized that he was facing the legendary Ak Pasha himself, the sum of the proposed contribution immediately doubled.

Sobolev assured the natives that he was not empowered to levy any contribution. The hook-nosed gentleman shot a sideways glance at the half-open door of the strong room and rolled his eyes respectfully.

"I understand, **effendi.** For such a great man a hundred thousand is a mere trifle."

News traveled quickly in these parts. No more than two hours after San Stefano's petitioners had left, a deputation of Greek traders from Constantinople arrived to see Ak Pasha. They did not offer any contributions, but they had brought sweets and wine "for the brave Christian warriors." They said that there were many Orthodox Christians in the city, asked the Russians not to fire their cannons, and if they really had to, not to train them on the Pera quarter, where there were shops and warehouses full of goods, but at the Galata quarter, or— even better—the Armenian and European quarters. When they tried to present Sobolev with a golden sword set with precious stones, they were shown out but apparently left feeling reassured.

"Constantinople!" said Sobolev, his voice trembling with feeling as he gazed out through the window at the glittering lights of the great city. "The eternal, unattainable dream of the Russian tsars. The very roots of our faith and civilization are here. This is the key to the whole of the Mediterranean. So close! Just reach out and grasp it. Are we really going to go away empty-handed again?"

"Impossible, your excellency!" Gridnev exclaimed. "His Majesty will never allow it!"

"Ah, Mitya. You can be sure that the big brains in the rear, the Korchakovs and the Gnatievs, are already horse-trading and fawning to the English. They won't have the courage to take what belongs to Russia by ancient right. In twenty-nine Dibich stopped at Adrianople, and now we've got as far as San Stefano. So near and yet so far. I see a great and powerful Russia uniting the Slavs from Archangel to Constantinople and from Trieste to Vladivostok! Only then will the Romanovs fulfil their historical destiny and finally be able to leave these eternal wars behind them and devote themselves to the improvement of their own long-suffering dominion. But if we pull back, then our sons and grandsons will once again spill their own blood and the blood of others along the road to the walls of Constantinople. Such is the cross the Russian people must bear!"

"I can just picture what's going on in Constantinople now," Paladin said absentmindedly, also gazing out the window. "Ak Pasha in San Stefano! There is panic in the palace, the harem is being evacuated, the eunuchs are running around with their fat backsides wobbling. I wonder if Abdul-Hamid has already crossed to the Asiatic side yet? And it will not even occur to anyone, Michel, that you have come here with only a single battalion. If this were a game of poker it would make a fine bluff, with the opponent absolutely guaranteed to throw in his hand and pass."

"This is getting worse and worse," Perepyolkin cried in alarm. "Mikhail Dmitrievich, your excellency, don't listen to him! It would be the end of you! You've already put your head in the wolf's mouth! Forget about Abdul-Hamid!"

Sobolev and the correspondent looked each other in the eye.

"What have I got to lose?" said the general, cracking his knuckles. "If the sultan's guard doesn't panic and opens fire, I'll just pull back and that's it. Tell me, Charles, is the sultan's guard very strong?"

"The guard is a fine force, but Abdul-Hamid will never allow it to leave his side."

"That means they won't pursue us. We could enter the city in a column, flags flying and drums beating. I'd be riding at the front on Gulnora," said Sobolev, warming to his theme as he strode round the room. "Before it gets light, so they can't see how few of us there are. And then to the palace. Without a single shot being fired! Would they bring me out the keys of Constantinople?"

"Of course they would!" Paladin exclaimed passionately. "And that would be total capitulation!"

"Present the English with a fait accompli!" said the general, sawing the air with his hand. "Before they know what's happening, the city is already in Russian hands and the Turks have surrendered. And if anything goes wrong, I might as well be hung for a sheep as for a lamb. No one authorized me to take San Stefano, either!"

"It would be an absolutely glorious finale! And to think that I would be an eyewitness to it!" the journalist said excitedly.

"Not a witness, one of the actors," said Sobolev, slapping him on the shoulder.

"I won't let you go!" said Perepyolkin, blocking the doorway. He looked absolutely desperate, with his brown eyes goggling insanely and his forehead covered with beads of sweat. "As the chief of staff, I protest! Think, your excellency! You are a general of His Imperial Highness's retinue, not some wild Bashi-Bashouk! I implore you!"

"Out of the way, Perepyolkin, I'm sick of

you!" the fearsome Olympian shouted at the rationalist pygmy. "When Osman Pasha tried to break out of Plevna, you implored me then not to act without orders, too. You went down on your knees! But who was right that time? You'll see—I shall have the keys to Constantinople!"

"How marvelous!" exclaimed Mitya. "Isn't it wonderful, Varvara Andreevna?"

Varya said nothing because she wasn't sure whether it **was** wonderful or not. Sobolev's impetuous derring-do had set her head spinning. And there was the little question of what she was supposed to do. Was she to march to the sound of drums with the chasseurs, holding Gulnora's reins?

"Gridnev, I'm leaving you my escort. You'll guard the bank or the locals will loot it and then blame Sobolev," said the general.

"But your excellency! Mikhail Dmitrievich!" the ensign howled. "I want to go to Constantinople, too!"

"Then who would protect Varvara Andreevna?" Paladin asked reproachfully, throating his r's.

Sobolev took a gold watch out of his pocket and the lid rang as he flicked it open.

"Half-past five. In two or two and a half hours it will start to get light. Hey there, Gukmasov!"

"Yes, your excellency," said the handsome cornet as he dashed into the office.

"Assemble the companies! Call the battalion to marching order! Banners and drums to the fore. Let's march in style! Saddle up Gulnora! Look lively! We depart at six hundred hours!"

The orderly dashed out. Sobolev stretched sweetly and said: "Well now, Varvara Andreevna, I shall either be a greater hero than Bonaparte or finally lose my foolish head at last."

"You won't lose it," she replied, gazing at the general in sincere admiration—he looked so wonderfully fine just at that moment, the Russian Achilles.

"Touch wood," said Sobolev superstitiously, reaching for the table.

"It's not too late to change your mind!" Perepyolkin piped up. "With your permission, Mikhail Dmitrievich, I can call Gukmasov back!"

He took a step toward the door, but just at that very moment . . .


AT THAT MOMENT there was a loud clattering of numerous pairs of boots on the staircase, the door swung open, and two men entered the room—Lavrenty Arkadievich Mizinov and Fandorin.

"Erast Petrovich!" Varya squealed and almost flung herself on his neck, but she stopped herself just in time.

Mizinov rumbled: "Aha, here he is! Excellent!"

"Your excellency!" Sobelev said with a frown, spotting the gendarmes in blue uniforms behind the first two men. "Why are you here? Of course, I'm guilty of acting on my own initiative, but arresting me is really going rather too far."

"Arrest you?" Mizinov was amazed. "What on earth for? We barely managed to get through to you on handcars with half a company of gendarmes. The telegraph isn't working and the railway line has been cut. We came under fire three times and lost seven men. I've got a bullet hole here in my greatcoat." He showed Sobolev his sleeve.

Erast Petrovich stepped forward. He hadn't changed at all while he had been away, but he looked a real dandy in his civilian clothes: a top hat, a cape, a starched collar.

"Hello, Varvara Andreevna," the titular counselor said cordially. "How well your hair has grown. I think perhaps it is better like that."

He bowed briefly to Sobolev.

"My congratulations on the diamond-studded sword, your excellency. That is a great honor."

He nodded quickly to Perepyolkin and finally turned toward the French correspondent. **"Salaam aleichem,** Anwar-**effendi."**

# CHAPTER THIRTEEN

—ᵐ—

## In which Fandorin
## makes a long speech

## DIE WIENER ZEITUNG (Vienna)
## 21 (9) January 1878

The balance of power between the combatants in the final stage of the war is such that we can no longer disregard the danger of pan-Slavic expansion that threatens the southern borders of the dual monarchy. Tsar Alexander and his satellites of Romania, Serbia and Montenegro have amassed a concentrated force of 700,000 men, equipped with one and a half thousand cannon. Against whom is it directed, one might ask? Against a demoralized Turkish army which, even according to the most optimistic estimates, can at present number no more than 120,000 hungry, frightened soldiers?

This is no joke, gentlemen. One would have to be an ostrich with one's head buried in the sand not to see the danger hanging over the whole of enlightened Europe. To procrastinate is to perish. If we simply sit back and do nothing, watching the Scythian hordes . . .

FANDORIN THREW HIS CAPE BACK off his shoulder and the burnished steel of a small, handsome revolver glinted dully in his right hand. The very same instant, Mizinov clicked his fingers and three gendarmes entered the room and trained their carbines on the correspondent.

"What sort of tomfoolery is this?" barked Sobolev. "What's all this 'salaam-aleichem' and 'effendi' nonsense?"

Varya glanced around at Charles. He was standing by the wall with his arms crossed on his chest, watching the titular counselor with a wary, sarcastic smile.

"Erast Petrovich!" Varya babbled. "Surely you went to get McLaughlin!"

"Varvara Andreevna, I went to England, but not for McLaughlin. It was quite c-clear to me that he was not and could not be there."

"But you didn't say a word when His

Majesty . . ." Varya bit her tongue before she could blurt out a state secret.

"My arguments would have been m-mere speculation. And I had to go to Europe in any case."

"And what did you discover there?"

"As was to be expected, the machinations of the British cabinet have nothing to do with the case. That is one. Yes, they do not like us in London. Yes, they are preparing for a great war. But murdering messengers and organizing sabotage—that would not do at all. It would contra-dict the British sense of fair play. And Count Shuvalov told me the same thing.

"I visited the offices of the **Daily Post** and was convinced of McLaughlin's absolute innocence. That is t-two. His friends and colleagues describe Seamus as a straightforward and forthright man who is hostile to British policy and who may, indeed, have connections with the Irish nationalist movement. There is absolutely no way he could be represented as an agent of the perfidious Disraeli.

"On the return journey, since it lay on my route, I stopped off in Paris, where I was delayed for some time. I called into the offices of the **Revue Parisienne.**"

Paladin made a slight movement and the gendarmes raised their carbines to their shoulders, ready to shoot. The journalist shook his head emphatically and put his hands back under the tails of his riding coat.

"And there it became clear," Erast Petrovich continued as though nothing had happened, "that the illustrious Charles Paladin had never been seen in the offices of his own publication. That is three. He sent in his brilliant articles, essays, and sketches by post or telegraph."

"Well, what of it?" Sobolev objected in exasperation. "Charles is no effete socialite; he's a man of adventure."

"And to an even greater d-degree than your excellency supposes. I rummaged through the files of the **Revue Parisienne,** and some very curious coincidences came to light. Monsieur Paladin's first published articles were submitted from Bulgaria ten years ago, at the very time when the Danubian Vilajet was governed by Midhat Pasha, whose secretary was the young official Anwar. In eighteen sixty-eight, Paladin submits a number of brilliant articles on the mores of the sultan's court from Constantinople. This is during Midhat Pasha's first period of ascendancy, when he is invited to the capital to lead the council of state. A year later, the reformer is dispatched into honorable exile to distant Mesopotamia, and, as though bewitched, the fluent pen of the talented journalist also moves from Constantinople to Baghdad. For three years (the precise period for which Midhat Pasha governed Iraq), Paladin writes about excavations of Assyrian cities, Arab sheikhs, and the Suez Canal."

"You're stacking the deck!" Sobolev interrupted angrily. "Charles traveled all over the Near East. He also wrote from other places that you don't mention, because they don't fit your hypothesis. In seventy-three, for instance, he was with me in Khiva. We survived raging thirst and searing heat together. And there was no Midhat there, Mister Investigator!"

"And from where did he travel to Central Asia?" Fandorin asked the general.

"From Iran, I think."

"I believe it was not from Iran, but from Iraq. In late eighteen seventy-three, the newspaper publishes his lyrical sketches about Greece. Why Greece all of a sudden? Why, because at that time our Anwar-effendi's patron was moved to Salonika. By the way, Varvara Andreevna, do you recall the marvelous feuilleton about the old boots?"

Varya nodded, gazing at Fandorin as if she were spellbound. What he was saying was so obviously absurd, but how confidently, how elegantly and masterfully he said it! And he had completely stopped stammering.

314 • *Boris Akunin*

"It mentioned a shipwreck that took place in the Gulf of Therma in November eighteen seventy-three. The city of Salonika happens to lie on the shore of the gulf. From the same article, I learned that in eighteen sixty-seven the author had been in Sofia, and in eighteen seventy-one in Mesopotamia, for that was precisely when the Arab nomads slaughtered Sir Andrew Wayard's British archaeological expedition. It was after the 'Old Boots' that I first began to suspect Monsieur Paladin seriously, but he threw me off the track more than once with his cunning maneuvers. And now"—Fandorin put his revolver away and turned toward Mizinov—"let us summarize the damage inflicted on us by the activities of Mr. Anwar. Monsieur Paladin joined the war correspondents' corps in late June last year. At that time our armies were advancing victoriously. The barrier of the Danube had been crossed, the Turkish army was demoralized, the road lay open to Sofia, and from there to Constantinople. General Gurko's forces had already taken the Shipka Pass, the key to the Great Balkan Range. We had, in effect, already won the war. But what happens after that? Due to a fatal confusion in the coding of a message, our army occupies the irrelevant city of Nikopol, and meanwhile Osman Pasha's army corps enters the empty Plevna unhindered, completely cutting off our advance. Let us recall the circumstances of that mysterious story. Cryptographer Yablokov commits a serious offence by leaving a secret message unattended on his table. Why did Yablokov do this? Because he was overwhelmed by news of the unexpected arrival of his fiancée, Miss Suvorova."

Everyone looked at Varya, making her feel as though she were an item of material evidence.

"But who informed Yablokov of his fiancée's arrival? The journalist Paladin. When the cryptographer went dashing off, insane with joy, all that had to be done was to rewrite the coded message, replacing the word 'Plevna' with the word 'Nikopol.' Our military code is not exactly complicated, to put it mildly. Paladin knew about the Russian army's forthcoming maneuver, because he was there when I told you, Mikhail Dmitrievich, about Osman Pasha. Do you recall the first time we met?"

Sobolev nodded morosely.

"Well, then, to continue, let us recall the story of the mythical Ali-bei, whom Paladin supposedly interviewed. That 'interview' has cost us two thousand dead, and now the Russian army is bogged down at Plevna with no end in sight. It was a risky ploy—Anwar inevitably attracted suspicion to himself, but he had no alternative. If it came to it, the Russians could have simply left a covering force to contain Osman and pushed their main forces further south. However, the failure of the first assault created an exaggerated idea of the danger of Plevna in the mind of our command, and the full might of the army was turned against a little Bulgarian town."

"Wait, Erast Petrovich, Ali-bei really did exist after all!" Varya exclaimed. "Our scouts saw him in Plevna!"

"We shall come back to that a little later. But for now let us recall the circumstances of the second battle of Plevna, the blame for which we laid on the treacherous Romanian Colonel Lukan, who had apparently betrayed our plan of battle to the Turks. You were right, Lavrenty Arkadievich—the 'J' in Lukan's notebook does stand for 'journalist.' But it does not mean McLaughlin, it stands for Paladin. He was able to recruit the Romanian dandy with no great difficulty—his gambling debts and inordinate vanity made the colonel easy prey. And in Bucharest, Paladin cunningly exploited Miss Suvorova in order to rid himself of an agent who was no longer useful and had actually begun to be dangerous. And in addition, I assume, Anwar needed to meet with Osman Pasha.

Banishment from the army—purely temporary, and with his rehabilitation planned beforehand—gave him the opportunity to do so. The French correspondent was absent for a month. And it was precisely during that period that our intelligence service reported that the Turkish commander had a mysterious adviser called Ali-bei. This same Ali-bei deliberately made fleeting appearances in crowded public places, sporting his conspicuous beard. You must have had a great laugh at our expense, Mister Spy."

Paladin did not respond. He was watching the titular counselor carefully, as if he were waiting for something.

"Ali-bei's appearance in Plevna was necessary in order to clear the journalist Paladin of the suspicion caused by that ill-starred interview. I have no doubt, indeed, that Anwar used that month to great advantage to himself. No doubt he reached an agreement with Osman Pasha on joint plans of action for the future and acquired some reliable contacts. After all, our counter-intelligence operations did not prevent correspondents from having their own informants in the besieged town. If he wished, Anwar-effendi could even have visited Constantinople for a few days, since Plevna's lines of communication were still open. It would have been very simple—once he reached Sofia, he could have caught a train and the next day he would have been in Istanbul.

"The third assault was especially dangerous for Osman Pasha, above all because of Mikhail Dmitrievich's surprise attack. But luck was with Anwar and not with us. We were confounded by a fatal coincidence—on his way to headquarters, Zurov galloped past the correspondents and shouted out to them that you were in Plevna. Naturally Anwar realized the significance of this statement perfectly well, and also the reason why Zurov had been dispatched to command headquarters. Somehow he had to gain time, give Osman Pasha a chance to regroup and dislodge Mikhail Dmitrievich and his small detachment from Plevna before reinforcements arrived. And yet again Anwar took a risk and improvised. Boldly, brilliantly, creatively—and, as always, mercilessly.

"When the journalists heard about the successful incursion on the southern flank, they all went dashing to their telegraph apparatuses, but Anwar set off in pursuit of Zurov and Kazanzaki. On his famous mount, Yataghan, he overhauled them with no difficulty. Once they reached a deserted spot, he shot them both. Evidently when he made his move he was galloping along between Zurov and Kazanzaki, with the captain on his right and the gendarme on his left. Anwar shoots the hussar in the left temple, at point-blank range, and a moment later dispatches a bullet into the forehead of the lieutenant colonel, who has turned toward him at the sound of the shot. The whole thing took no more than a second. There were troops moving all around, but the horsemen were riding along a depression. No one could see them, and the shots could hardly have attracted attention in the middle of an artillery barrage. The killer left Zurov's body lying where it was, but thrust the gendarme's dagger into his shoulder. In other words, first he shot him, and then he stabbed him when he was already dead, and not, as we initially believed, the other way round. Anwar's intent is clear—to cast suspicion on Kazanzaki. For the same reason, he moved the lieutenant colonel's body to the nearest bushes and staged a suicide."

"But what about the letter?" Varya reminded him. "From that—what was his name—Shalunishka?"

"A magnificent ploy," Fandorin acknowledged. "Turkish intelligence had evidently been aware of Kazanzaki's unnatural inclinations since his old days in Tiflis. I presume that Anwar-effendi kept an eye on the lieutenant colonel, bearing in mind the possibility of resorting to blackmail at some time in the future. When events took an unexpected turn, he used the information to good effect to throw us off the scent. Anwar simply took a blank sheet of paper and dashed off a caricature of a letter from a homosexual lover. But he somewhat overdid it; even at the time I thought the letter seemed suspicious. In the first place, it is hard to believe that a Georgian prince could write such abominable Russian—he ought at least to have had a grammar-school education. And, in the second place, perhaps you recall my asking Lavrenty Arkadievich about the envelope and learning that the letter had been lying in the dead man's pocket unprotected? But in that case, how could it have remained so clean and crisp? Kazanzaki must have been carrying it around with him for an entire year."

"This is all very fine," Mizinov said impatiently, "and this is the second time in the last twenty-four hours that you've expounded your ideas on this matter to me. But I ask you once again: Why were you so secretive? Why didn't you share your doubts earlier?"

"If one rejects one explanation, one must propose another, and I simply could not make all the pieces fit together," replied Erast Petrovich. "My opponent employed far too wide a range of devices. I am ashamed to admit it, but for a time my main suspect was Mr. Perepyolkin."

"Eremei?" Sobolev exclaimed in astonishment, throwing his hands up in disbelief. "Come now, gentlemen, this is sheer paranoia."

Perepyolkin himself blinked several times and nervously unbuttoned his tight collar.

"Yes, it is stupid," Fandorin agreed. "But in whatever direction we went, we kept tripping over the lieutenant colonel. Even the way he made his first appearance seemed rather suspicious—the miraculous liberation from captivity, the failed shot at point-blank range; Bashi-Bazouks usually shoot better than that. And then the business with the coded message—it was Perepyolkin who delivered the telegram with the order to attack Nikopol to General Kriedener. And who was it that egged on the credulous journalist Paladin to sneak into Plevna under the very noses of the Turks? And the mysterious letter 'J.' Thanks to Zurov's easy wit, everyone had begun to call Eremei Ionovich 'Jerome.' That is on the one hand. On the other hand, you must admit that Anwar-effendi's cover was ideal. I could construct any number of logical hypotheses, but the moment I looked at Charles Paladin, all my arguments crumbled to dust. Just take a look at this man."

Fandorin pointed to the journalist. Everybody

looked at Paladin, who bowed with exaggerated humility. "How is it possible to believe that this charming, witty, thoroughly European gentleman and the perfidious, cruel head of the Turkish secret service are one and the same person?"

"Never, not for the world!" declared Sobolev. "And even now I don't believe it!"

Erast Petrovich nodded in satisfaction.

"And now for the business with McLaughlin and the failed breakout. In this case everything was very simple, with no risk. It was not difficult to interest the gullible Seamus in a piece of sensational news. No doubt the informer he concealed from us, and of whom he was so proud, was working for you, Effendi."

Varya shuddered at hearing that form of address used to Charles. No, there must be something wrong here. What kind of "effendi" was he?

"The way you exploited McLaughlin's trusting nature, as well as his vanity, was very clever. How envious he was of the brilliant Charles Paladin, how he dreamed of outshining him! So far he had only managed to beat him at chess, and then not every time, but now he had this fantastic stroke of luck! Exclusive information from most reliable sources! And what incredible information it was! Any reporter would sell his very soul to the devil for information like that.

If McLaughlin had not happened to meet Varvara Andreevna on his way and blurted out his secret to her, Osman would have swept aside the corps of grenadiers, broken out of the blockade, and fallen back to Shipka. And then the situation on the front would have been a stalemate."

"But if McLaughlin isn't a spy, what has become of him?" asked Varya.

"Do you recall Ganetsky's story of how the Bashi-Bazouks attacked his command headquarters and the aging general barely managed to escape with his life? I think it was not Ganetsky the saboteurs wanted, but McLaughlin. He had to be eliminated, and he disappeared. Without a trace. Very probably the deceived and much-maligned Irishman is lying somewhere at the bottom of the river Vid with a stone round his neck. Or possibly the Bashi-Bazouks, following their endearing custom, hacked him to pieces."

Varya shuddered, recalling how the round-faced correspondent had wolfed down her jam pies during their final meeting. When he had only an hour or two left to live . . .

"Did you not feel sorry for poor McLaughlin?" Fandorin inquired, but Paladin (or was he really Anwar-effendi after all?) merely invited him to continue with an elegant gesture before concealing his hands behind his back again.

Varya remembered that, according to the science of psychology, hands concealed behind the back indicate secretiveness and a reluctance to speak the truth. Was it really possible? She moved closer to the journalist, gazing inquisitively into his face in an attempt to discover something alien and fearsome in those familiar features. The face was the same as ever, except perhaps a little paler. Paladin did not look at Varya.

"The attempted breakout failed, but you emerged unscathed yet again. I rushed back to the theater of military operations from Paris as fast as I could. I already knew for certain who you are, and I realized just how dangerous you are."

"You could have sent a telegram," Mizinov growled.

"Saying what, your excellency? 'The journalist Paladin is Anwar-effendi'? You would have thought that Fandorin had lost his mind. Remember how long it took me to present my proof to you—you flatly refused to abandon the idea of British machinations. And General Sobolev, as you can see, is still not convinced, even after my rather extensive explanation."

Sobolev shook his head stubbornly.

"We'll hear you out, Fandorin, and then we'll give Charles his chance to speak. A court hearing cannot consist of nothing but the prosecutor's address."

"Merci, Michel," said Paladin with a smile, and proceeded to speak in a mixture of French and Russian. "**Comme dit l'autre,** a friend in need is a friend indeed. One question for **monsieur le procureur.** When were your doubts finally laid to rest? Pray satisfy my curiosity."

"In Paris, at the **Revue** offices," said Fandorin. "You committed one act of serious carelessness. It is not good to be so ostentatious and underestimate one's opponent so badly! All I had to do was look through your early articles, when you signed yourself 'Paladin d'Hevrais.' I immediately remembered that, according to some sources, our primary foe, Anwar-effendi, was born in the small Bosnian town of Hef-Rais. Paladin d'Hevrais: the 'Champion of Hef-Rais.' You must agree that as a pseudonym it is far too transparent. Of course, it could have been a coincidence, but in any event it looked suspicious. No doubt when you began your journalistic career you still had no idea that your mask as a journalist would be required for activities of a rather different nature. I am sure that you began writing for a Parisian newspaper out of entirely innocent considerations: in order find an outlet for your exceptional literary talent while at the same time stimulating European interest in the problems of the Turkish empire and especially in the figure of the great reformer Midhat Pasha. In fact you were rather successful in those aims. The name of the wise Midhat appears at least fifty times in your published articles. You were effectively responsible for making the pasha a popular and respected personality throughout Europe, and especially in France, where he happens to be at the present moment."

Varya started, recalling how Paladin had spoken of the father he loved so dearly, who lived in France. Could it really all be true, then? She glanced at the journalist in horror. He was still as calm as ever, but Varya thought his smile seemed forced.

"And, by the way," the titular counselor continued, "I do not believe you betrayed Midhat Pasha. That was some kind of subtle ploy. Now that Turkey has been defeated, he will return, crowned with the laurels of a martyr, and take up the reins of government once again. From Europe's point of view, he is an absolutely ideal figure. In Paris they positively idolize him." Fandorin touched a hand to his temple, and Varya suddenly noticed how pale and tired he looked. "I was in a great hurry to get back, but the three hundred versts from Sofia to Germanly took me longer to cover than the fifteen hundred versts from Paris to Sofia. The roads in the rear defy all description. Thank God Lavrenty Arkadievich and I arrived in time. As soon as General Strukov informed me that his excellency had set out for San Stefano accompanied by the journalist Paladin, I realized that this was Anwar-effendi's final, deadly move. It was no accident that the telegraph wires were cut. I was very much afraid, Mikhail Dmitrievich, that this man would exploit your valiant spirit and ambition to persuade you to enter Constantinople."

"And what exactly was it that made you so afraid, Mister Prosecutor?" Sobolev inquired ironically. "What matter if Russian soldiers had entered the Turkish capital?"

"What matter?" Mizinov exclaimed apoplectically. "Are you out of your mind? It would have been the end of everything!"

"What 'everything'?" the bold Achilles asked with a shrug, but Varya spotted a glint of alarm in his eyes.

"Our army, our conquests, Russia!" the chief of gendarmes thundered. "Our ambassador in England, Count Shuvalov, has forwarded a

328 · *Boris Akunin*

coded message. He has seen a secret memorandum of the British Cabinet with his own eyes. Under the terms of a secret agreement between the British and Austro-Hungarian empires, if even a single Russian soldier should appear in Constantinople, Admiral Hornby's squadron of ironclads will immediately open fire and the Austro-Hungarian army will cross the Serbian and Russian borders. You see the difficulty, Mikhail Dmitrievich? In that case we would have suffered a rout far more terrible than the Crimea. The country is exhausted by the epic struggle at Plevna, we have no fleet in the Black Sea, the treasury is empty. It would have been a total and utter disaster."

Sobolev could think of nothing to say.

"But your excellency had the wisdom and forbearance not to proceed beyond San Stefano," Fandorin said deferentially. "Lavrenty Arkadievich and I need not have been in quite such a great hurry."

Varya saw the White General's face turn red. Sobolev cleared his throat and nodded with a serious air as he surveyed the marble floor.

And then who should squeeze in through the door at that very moment but the cornet Gukmasov. He peered hostilely at the blue uniforms and barked, "By your leave I beg to report, your excellency!"

Varya suddenly felt sorry for poor Achilles and she looked away, but that oaf carried on and reported stentoriously: "Six o'clock precisely! According to orders, the battalion is drawn up and Gulnora is saddled and ready! We are only waiting for your excellency in order to advance on the gates of Constantinople!"

"Stop there, you blockhead!" mumbled the crimson-face hero. "To hell with the damned gates!"

Gukmasov backed disconcertedly out of the door. It had barely closed behind him when something unexpected happened.

**"Et maintenant, mesdames et messieurs, la parole est à la défence,"** Paladin declared in a loud voice.

He pulled his right hand out from behind his back. It was holding a pistol. Twice the pistol belched thunder and lightning.

Varya saw the uniform jackets of both gendarmes torn open on the left side of the chest, as though by some mutual agreement. Their carbines clattered to the floor, and the gendarmes collapsed with hardly a sound.

Varya's ears were ringing from the shots. She had no time to cry out or feel frightened before Paladin had reached out his left hand, grasped her tightly by the elbow, and pulled her toward him, protecting himself with her like a shield.

Gogol's play **The Government Inspector,** the tableau without words, Varya thought stupidly as she saw a strapping gendarme appear in the doorway and freeze motionless. Erast Petrovich and Mizinov were holding their revolvers out in front of them. The general's expression was angry, the titular counselor's sad. Sobolev was frozen, his arms spread wide in astonishment. Mitya Gridnev's jaw dropped and his wonderful eyelashes fluttered. Perepyolkin forgot to lower the hand he had raised to rebutton his collar.

"Charles, you must be insane!" shouted Sobolev, taking a step forward. "Hiding behind a lady!"

"But **Monsieur Fandorine** has proved that I am a Turk," Paladin replied sarcastically; Varya could feel his hot breath on the back of her head. "And in Turkey no one stands on ceremony with ladies."

"Ooh-ooh-ooh!" Mitya howled, then he lowered his head like a calf and rushed forward.

Paladin's pistol thundered once again and the young lieutenant fell facedown with a grunt.

Everyone froze again.

Paladin was pulling Varya now—backward and off to one side.

"If anyone moves, I'll kill them," he warned them all in a soft voice.

The wall behind Varya seemed to part, and suddenly she and Paladin were in a different room.

Oh, yes, the strong room!

Paladin slammed the steel door shut and slid the bolt home.

The two of them were alone.

# CHAPTER FOURTEEN

—*m*—

## In which Russia is decried and the language of Dante is heard

## THE GOVERNMENT HERALD
### (St. Petersburg)
### 9 (21) January 1878

...**P**rovokes gloomy reflections. Here are the essential points from a speech given by the minister of finance, State Secretary M. H. Reitern, last Thursday at a conference of the All-Russian Banking Union. In 1874, for the first time in many years, we achieved a positive balance of payments, with revenue exceeding expenditure, said the minister. The balance of the budget for 1876 had been calculated by the State Treasury at a net surplus of 40 million rubles. How-ever, the cost to the treasury of somewhat less than a year of military action had been one billion, twenty million rubles, and there were no resources left to fund continued hostilities. Due to the cutback of expenditures on civil construction projects in 1877, not a single verst of railway line had been laid anywhere in the territory of the Empire. The sum total of the state's domestic and foreign debts had risen to an unprecedented level, amounting to . . .

PALADIN RELEASED HIS GRIP on Varvara, and she darted away from him in horror.

She heard the muted sound of voices behind the massive door.

"Name your terms, Anwar!" It was Erast Petrovich.

"No terms!" (That was Mizinov.) "Open the door immediately or I'll have it blown open with dynamite!"

"Save your orders for the gendarme corps!" (That was Sobolev.) "Use dynamite and she'll be killed!"

"Gentlemen," shouted Paladin, who was not really Paladin at all, in French. "This is hardly polite! You are preventing me from discussing the situation with the lady!"

334 • *Boris Akunin*

"Charles! Or whatever your name is!" Sobolev roared in a booming general's bass. "If a single hair of Varvara Andreevna's head is harmed, I'll have you strung up without benefit of trial!"

"One more word and I'll shoot her first, then myself!" Paladin declared, raising his voice dramatically, then suddenly winked at Varya, as though he had cracked a slightly improper but terribly funny joke.

There was silence behind the door.

"Don't look at me like that, as though I have suddenly sprouted horns and grown fangs, **Mademoiselle Barbara,**" Paladin said in a low voice, speaking normally now. "Of course I'm not going to kill you; I would not wish to place your life in danger for the world."

"Indeed?" she asked acidly. "Then what is the point of this farce? Why did you kill three entirely innocent people? What are you hoping to achieve?"

Anwar-effendi (it was time to forget Paladin) took out his watch.

"Five minutes past six. I needed this farce in order to gain time. And by the way, you needn't be concerned about the junior lieutenant. Knowing your fondness for him, I merely put a hole in his thigh—nothing too serious. Afterward he will boast of his war wound. And as for the gendarmes, that is the nature of their job."

Varya asked warily, "To gain time? What for?"

"Well, **Mademoiselle Barbara,** according to the plan, a regiment of Anatolian infantry is due to enter San Stefano in one hour and twenty-five minutes, that is, at half-past seven. They are one of the finest units in the entire Turkish guards. The assumption was that, by then, Sobolev's detachment would already have reached the outskirts of Istanbul, come under fire from the English fleet, and pulled back. The riflemen would have struck the Russians from the rear as they withdrew in disorder. An elegant plan and everything was going without a hitch until the very last minute."

"What plan do you mean?"

"As I said, it was an elegant one. First, gently prompt Michel to start thinking about that temptingly abandoned passenger train. You were very helpful to me in that, for which I thank you. 'Open a book and drink some hot tea'—that was magnificent. After that it was simple—the vaulting ambition of our peerless Achilles, his indomitable mettle and belief in his star, would have carried things to their conclusion. Oh, Sobolev would not have been killed. I would not have allowed it. In the first place, I'm genuinely obligated to him; in the second, the capture of the great Ak Pasha would have made a spectacular start to the second stage of the Balkan war." Anwar sighed. "It's a shame the plan miscarried. Your youthful old man is to be congratulated. As the Eastern sages say, it is karma."

"What is it they say?" Varya asked in astonishment.

"There now, you see, **Mademoiselle Barbara,** you are an educated, cultured young lady, but there are elementary things that you do not know," her bizarre companion said reproachfully. "Karma is one of the fundamental concepts of Hindu and Buddhist philosophy. Something akin to the Christian Providence, but far more interesting. After all, the East is far more ancient, wise, and complex. My country, Turkey, happens to be situated precisely at the crossroads of the East and the West. It is a country that could have a great future."

"No more lectures, if you please," said Varya, cutting short his deliberations. "What do you intend to do?"

"Why, what can I do?" Anwar asked in astonishment. "Naturally, I shall wait until half-past seven. The original plan has failed, but the Anatolian infantry will arrive nonetheless. There will be a battle. If our guardsmen prevail—and they have the advantage of numbers, and the training, and the factor of surprise—then I am saved. However, if Sobolev's men hold out . . . But let us not attempt to guess the future. By the way," he said, looking Varya in the eye earnestly, "I know how determined you can be, but don't imagine you can warn your friends about the attack. The moment you open your mouth to shout, I shall be obliged to stop it with a gag. And I will do it, despite the sincere respect and sympathy that I feel for you."

So saying, he unfastened his necktie, rolled it into a tight ball, and put it in his pocket.

"A gag for a lady?" Varya laughed. "I liked you much better as a Frenchman."

"I assure you that a French spy would behave in exactly the same way, if so much depended on his actions. I am used to taking no thought for my own life; I have gambled it many times for the sake of the cause. And that gives me the right to take no thought for the lives of others. In this game, **Mademoiselle Barbara,** the rules are the same for all. It is a cruel game, but then life is a cruel business. Do you imagine I felt no pity for the brave-hearted Zurov or the good-hearted McLaughlin? Why, of course I did, but there are higher values than personal sentiment."

"And exactly what values might those be?"

338 • *Boris Akunin*

Varya exclaimed. "Pray explain to me, **monsieur intriguant,** what exalted ideas can justify killing a man who regards you as his friend?"

"An excellent subject for discussion," said Anwar, moving up a chair. "Please, take a seat, **Mademoiselle Barbara,** we need some way to while away the time. And don't scowl at me in that way. I am no ogre; I am merely an enemy of your country. I do not wish you to regard me as the heartless monster depicted by the preternaturally perceptive **Monsieur Fandorine.** He was the one who should have been neutralized in good time.

"Yes, I am a killer. But then, all of us here are killers—your Fandorin, and the deceased Zurov, and Mizinov. But Sobolev is a superkiller; he's simply awash in blood. In these men's games of ours, there are only two possible roles: the killer or the victim. Do not cherish any illusions, mademoiselle—we all live in the jungle. Try to regard me without prejudice: Forget that you are Russian and I am a Turk. I am a man who has chosen a very difficult path in life. And, moreover, a man to whom you are not indifferent. I am even a little in love with you."

Varya frowned, stung by the words "a little."

"I am most exceedingly grateful."

"There now, I have expressed myself clumsily," said Anwar with a shrug. "I cannot possibly allow myself to fall in love in earnest; it would be an unforgivable and dangerous indulgence. Let us not talk of that. Let me rather answer your question. It is distressing to deceive or kill a friend, but that is a price that must sometimes be paid." He twitched the corner of his mouth nervously. "I have had to do things . . . However, if one commits oneself absolutely to a great idea, one is obliged to sacrifice one's personal attachments. One hardly needs to go far to seek examples. I have no doubt that as a progressive young woman you are inclined to view revolutionary ideas sympathetically. Am I not right? I've noticed that, in your Russia, the revolutionaries have already started shooting occasionally. But soon a genuine clandestine war will begin—you can take the word of a professional on that. Idealistic young men and women will start blowing up palaces, trains, and carriages. And, inevitably, in addition to the reactionary minister or the villainous governor they will contain innocent people—relatives, assistants, servants. But that's all right if it's for the sake of the idea. Give them time and your idealists will worm their way into positions of trust, and spy, and deceive, and kill apostates— and all for the sake of an idea."

"And just what is your idea?" Vera asked sharply.

340 • *Boris Akunin*

"I will tell you, by all means." Anwar leaned his elbow against the shelves full of bags of money. "I see salvation not in revolution, but in evolution. But evolution needs to be set on the right path; it has to be given a helping hand. This nineteenth century of ours is a decisive period for the fate of humanity, of that I am profoundly convinced. The forces of reason and tolerance must be helped to prevail. Otherwise, serious and needless convulsions await the Earth in the very near future."

"And where do reason and tolerance dwell? In the realms of your Abdul-Hamid?"

"No, of course not. I am thinking of those countries where a man learns to respect himself and others a little, not to bludgeon others into agreement, but to convince them through argument, to support the weak and tolerate those who think differently than him. Ah, what promising processes are in train in Western Europe and the United States of North America! Naturally, I do not idealize them—far from it. They have a lot of filth of their own, much crime, and a lot of stupidity. But they are heading in the right general direction. The world has to follow the same course, otherwise mankind will founder, sink into an abyss of chaos and tyranny. As yet, the bright spot on the map of the world is still very small, but it is expanding rapidly. It needs to be protected against the onslaught of darkness and ignorance. A great game of chess is being played out, and I am playing for the white pieces."

"And I suppose Russia is playing for the black?"

"Yes. Today, your immensely powerful state constitutes the main danger to civilization. With its vast expanses, its multitudinous, ignorant population, its cumbersome and aggressive state apparatus. I have taken a keen interest in Russia for a long time, I learned the language, I traveled a lot, I read historical works, I studied your state apparatus, became acquainted with your leaders. Try listening to our own dear Michel, with his aspirations to be the new Bonaparte! The mission of the Russian people is to take Constantinople and unite the Slavs? To what end? So that the Romanovs might once again impose their will on Europe? A nightmarish prospect indeed! It is not pleasant for you to hear this, **Mademoiselle Barbara,** but lurking within Russia is a terrible threat to civilization. There are savage, destructive forces fermenting within her, forces that will break out sooner or later, and then the world will be in a bad way. It is an unstable, ridiculous country that has absorbed all the worst features of the West and the East. Russia has to be put back in its place; its reach has to be shortened. It will be good for you, and it will give Europe a chance to continue developing in the right direction. You know, **Mademoiselle Barbara**"—Anwar's voice trembled unexpectedly—"I love my poor unfortunate Turkey very much. It is a country of great missed opportunities. But I am prepared deliberately to sacrifice the Ottoman state in order to deflect the Russian threat to mankind. To put it in chess terms, do you know the meaning of the term 'gambit'? No? In Italian, **'gambetto'** means a trip, as in 'to trip someone up'—**dare il gambetto.** A gambit is an opening in a game of chess in which a piece is sacrificed to the opponent in order to secure a strategic advantage. I myself devised the sequence of play in this particular game, and I opened by offering Russia fat, appetizing, weak Turkey. The Ottoman Empire will perish, but Tsar Alexander will not win the game. Indeed, the war has gone so well that all may not yet be lost for Turkey. She still has Midhat Pasha. He is a quite remarkable man, **Mademoiselle Barbara;** I deliberately left him out of the action for a while, but now I shall reintroduce him. Provided, of course, that I am allowed the chance. Midhat Pasha will return to Istanbul unsullied and take power into his own hands. Perhaps then even Turkey will move from the zone of darkness into the zone of light."

Mizinov's voice spoke from behind the door.

"Mr. Anwar, what is the point of dragging this business out? This is mere cowardice! Come out and I promise you the status of a prisoner of war."

"And the gallows for Kazanzaki and Zurov?" whispered Anwar.

Varya filled her lungs with air, but the Turk was on the alert—he took the gag out of his pocket and shook his head expressively. Then he shouted: "I shall need to think about that, **monsieur général**! I'll give you my answer at half-past seven."

After that he said nothing for a long time, striding agitatedly around the strong room and looking at his watch several times.

"If only I could get out of here!" this strange man eventually murmured, striking a cast-iron shelf with his fist. "Without me, Abdul-Hamid will devour the noble Midhat!"

He glanced apologetically at Varya with his clear blue eyes and explained: "Forgive me, **Mademoiselle Barbara**—my nerves are under strain. My life is of some considerable consequence in this game. My life is also a chess piece, but I value it more highly than the

Ottoman Empire. We might say that the empire is a bishop, while I am a queen. Although, for the sake of victory, even a queen may be sacrificed . . . In any case, I haven't yet lost the game, and a draw is guaranteed!" He laughed excitedly. "I managed to delay your army at Plevna for much longer than I had hoped. You have squandered your forces and wasted precious time. England has had time to prepare herself for the confrontation; Austria has recovered its courage. Even if there is no second stage of the war, Russia will still be left out on the sidelines. It took her twenty years to recover from the Crimean campaign, and she'll be licking her wounds for another twenty after this war. And that is now, at the end of the nineteenth century, when every year is so important. In twenty years, Europe will move on far ahead. Henceforth, Russia is destined to play the role of a second-class power. She will be devoured by the canker of corruption and nihilism, she will no longer pose a threat to progress."

At this point Varya's patience gave out.

"Just who are you to judge who is the bringer of good to civilization and who is the bringer of destruction? He studied the state apparatus, became acquainted with the leaders! And have you made the acquaintance of Count Tolstoy and Fyodor Dostoevsky? Have you read Russian literature? I suppose you had no time for that? Two times two is always four and three times three is always nine, isn't it? And two parallel lines never intersect? In your Euclid, they don't intersect, but for our Lobachevsky they have!"

"I don't follow your logic," Anwar said with a shrug. "But of course I have read Russian literature. It is good literature, no worse than English or French. But literature is a toy; in a normal country it cannot have any great importance. I am myself something of a literary man, in a sense. But one must do something serious, and not just compose sentimental fairy tales. Look at Switzerland. It has no great literature, but life there is incomparably more dignified than in your Russia. I spent almost my entire childhood and adolescence in Switzerland, so you may take my word for it that—"

Before he could finish, there was a crackle of gunfire in the distance.

"It has begun! They have attacked ahead of time!"

Anwar pressed his ear against the door, his eyes glittering feverishly.

"Curses, what infernal bad luck that this room doesn't have a single window!"

Varya struggled in vain to calm her pounding heart. The thunderous noise of shooting was drawing nearer. She could hear Sobolev issuing orders, but she couldn't make out the words. From somewhere there came a cry of "Allah!" and a rapid volley of shots.

Anwar murmured as he spun the chamber of his revolver.

"I could try to break out, but I have only three bullets left—how I detest inaction!"

He started at the sudden sound of shots inside the building.

"If our men win, I shall send you to Adrianople," Anwar said rapidly. "Clearly, the war will end now. There will be no second stage. That's unfortunate. Not everything turns out the way you plan it. Perhaps you and I will meet again. At this moment, of course, you hate me, but time will pass and you will realize that I was right."

"I feel no hatred toward you," said Varya. "But I do bitterly regret that such a talented man as you is engaged in such dirty goings-on. I remember Mizinov relating the story of your life . . ."

"Indeed?" Anwar put in absentmindedly, still listening to the shooting.

"Yes. All those intrigues and all those people

who died! Wasn't that Circassian who sang an aria before his execution a friend of yours? Did you sacrifice him as well?"

"I don't care to recall that story," he said severely. "Do you know who I am? I am the midwife; I help the child to enter the world, and my arms are covered up to the elbows in blood and mucus . . ."

A volley of shots rang out very close by.

"I'm going to open the door now and help my own side. You stay in here, and for God's sake don't stick your head out. It will all be over soon."

He pulled back the bolt and suddenly froze—there was no more shooting in the bank. A voice was saying something, but it was not clear whether it was speaking Russian or Turkish. Varya held her breath.

"I'll rip your ugly face off! Sitting it out in the corner, you blankety-blank-blank," a sergeant major's deep bass roared, and the sweet sounds of her native speech set her heart singing.

They had held out! They had beaten them off!

The sound of shooting was moving further and further away, and there was a quite distinct, long, drawn-out cry of "hurrah!"

Anwar stood there with his eyes closed. His expression was calm and sad. When the firing stopped completely, he pulled back the bolt and opened the door a little.

"It is over, **mademoiselle.** Your captivity is at an end. Go now."

"What about you?" whispered Varya.

"The queen has been sacrificed without any particular gain. Regrettable. But everything else remains unchanged. Go, and I wish you happiness."

"No!" she cried, dodging away from his hands. "I won't leave you here. Give yourself up and I'll testify on your behalf at the trial."

"So they can stitch up my throat and then hang me anyway?" laughed Anwar. "Thank you kindly, but no. There are two things I detest more than anything else on earth—humiliation and capitulation. Farewell—I need to be alone for a moment."

He managed to grab hold of Varya's sleeve and with a gentle push he sent her out through the doorway. The massive slab of steel immediately slammed shut.

Varya found herself facing a pale-faced Fandorin. General Mizinov was standing by a shattered window and yelling at the gendarmes who were sweeping up the shards of glass. It was already light outside.

"Where is Michel?" Varya asked in fright. "Is he dead? Wounded?"

"Alive and well," replied Erast Petrovich, looking at her closely. "He is in his natural element—pursuing the enemy. But poor Perepyolkin has been wounded again—a **yataghan** took off half his ear. He will obviously be awarded another medal. And have no fear for Ensign Gridnev; he is alive, too."

"I know," she said, and Fandorin's eyes narrowed slightly.

Mizinov came over to them and complained: "Another hole in my greatcoat. What a day. So, he let you out? Excellent! Now we can use the dynamite."

He cautiously approached the door of the strong room and ran his hand over the steel surface.

"I'd say two charges ought to be just enough to do it. Or perhaps that's too much? It would be good to take the villain alive."

A carefree and highly melodic whistling suddenly started up behind the door.

"And now he's whistling!" Mizinov exclaimed indignantly. "Some nerve, eh? Well, I'll soon whistle you out of there. Novgorodtsev! Send to the sappers' platoon for some dynamite!"

"No d-dynamite will be necessary," Erast

Petrovich said in a soft voice as he listened carefully to the whistling.

"You've started stammering again," Varya said to him. "Does that mean everything is all over?"

Sobolev strode into the room with a loud clattering of boots, his white greatcoat with the scarlet cuffs hanging open.

"They've fallen back!" he announced in a voice hoarse after the battle. "Our losses are appalling, but never mind—there should be a troop train here soon. Who's whistling that tune so marvelously? It's **Lucia di Lammermoor,** I adore it!" And the general began singing along in his pleasant, husky baritone.

**Del ciel clemente un riso
la vita a noi sara!**

He sang the final stanza with feeling, and at the very moment he reached the end there was the sound of a shot from behind the door.

# EPILOGUE

―᷎᷎᷎᷎᷎᷎᷎ᨒ᷎᷎᷎᷎᷎―

## MOSCOW PROVINCIAL GAZETTE
### 19 FEBRUARY (3 MARCH) 1878

### PEACE IS SIGNED!

Today, on the joyous anniversary of His Imperial Majesty's magnanimous act of charity to the peasantry 17 years ago, a joyous new page has been written in the annals of the glorious reign of the Tsar-Liberator. In San Stefano, Russian and Turkish plenipotentiaries have signed a peace bringing to a conclusion the glorious war for the liberation of the Christian nations from Turkish overlordship. The terms of the treaty grant Romania and Serbia complete independence, establish an extensive Principality of Bulgaria and grant Russia the sum of one billion, four hundred and ten million rubles in reparation for her war costs, the greater part of this sum to be paid in territorial concessions, including Bessarabia and Dobrudja, as well as Ardagan, Kars, Batoumi, Bajazet . . .

"YOU SEE, A PEACE **HAS** BEEN SIGNED, and a very good one—despite your gloomy predictions, Mister Pessimist," said Varya, failing yet again to find the words she really wanted to say.

The titular counselor had already said good-bye to yesterday's suspect and today's free man, Petya, who had got into the carriage to settle into a compartment and lay out their things. In honor of the victorious conclusion of the war, Pyotr Yablokov had been granted a complete pardon and even a medal for diligent service.

They could have left two weeks earlier, but although Petya had tried to hurry her, Varya had kept putting it off, as if she were waiting for something that she couldn't explain.

It was a shame that her parting with Sobolev hadn't gone well; in fact, Sobolev had been bitter about it. To hell with him, anyway. A hero like that would find someone to console him soon enough.

And now the day had arrived when she had to say farewell to Erast Petrovich. Varya's nerves had been on edge since early that morning; she'd thrown a fit of hysterics because of some lost brooch and blamed Petya for it, then burst into tears.

Fandorin was staying on in San Stefano—the diplomatic hustle and bustle was by no means all over simply because the peace had been signed. He had come straight to the station from some reception, in a tailcoat, top hat, and white silk tie. He gave Varya a bunch of Parma violets, sighed a little, and shifted from one foot to the other, but his sparkling eloquence had deserted him today.

"The peace is f-far too good," he replied. "Europe will not recognize it. Anwar executed his gambit p-perfectly, and I lost the game. They have given me a medal, but they ought to have put me on trial."

"How unfair you are to yourself. Terribly unfair!" Varya exclaimed passionately, afraid that any moment her tears would start to flow. "Why are you always so hard on yourself? If not for you, I don't know what would have become of us all."

354 • Boris Akunin

"Lavrenty Arkadievich told me much the same thing," said Fandorin with a smile. "And he p-promised me any reward in his power."

Varya was delighted.

"Really? Well, that's wonderful! And what did you wish for?"

"For a posting somewhere on the far side of the world, as far away as possible from all this." He waved his hand vaguely in the air.

"What nonsense! What did Mizinov say?"

"He was furious. But a promise is a promise. When the negotiations are c-completed, I shall travel from Constantinople to Port Said, and from there by steamship to Japan. I have been appointed second secretary at the embassy in Tokyo. There is nowhere further away than that."

"To Japan . . ." The tears broke through after all, and Varya furiously wiped them away with her glove.

The bell rang and the locomotive sounded its whistle. Petya stuck his head out the window of the carriage.

"Varya, it's time. We're leaving."

Erast Petrovich hesitated and lowered his eyes.

"G-good-bye, Varvara Andreevna. I was very glad—" He did not finish the phrase.

Varya clutched hold of his hand impetuously and began blinking rapidly, shaking the teardrops off her eyelashes.

"Erast," she began in sudden haste, but the words stuck in her throat and would not come out.

Fandorin jerked his chin and said nothing.

The wheels clanked and the carriage swayed.

"Varya, they'll take me away without you!" Petya shouted despairingly. "Quick!"

She glanced around, hesitated for just one more second, and leapt onto the step as it glided along the edge of the platform.

"FIRST OF ALL, a hot bath. Then Filippov's bakery and some of that apricot pastille you're so fond of. And then the bookshop for all the new publications, and then the university. Can you imagine all the questions everyone will ask, all the—"

Varya stood at the window, nodding in time to Petya's contented babbling. She wanted to keep the black figure left behind on the platform in sight for as long as possible, but the figure was acting strangely, blurring like that . . . Or could there perhaps be something wrong with her eyes?

## THE TIMES (London)
## 10 March (26 February) 1878

### HER MAJESTY'S
### GOVERNMENT SAYS "NO"

Today, Lord Derby announced that the British government, supported by the governments of the majority of European states, categorically refuses to recognize the exorbitant peace terms imposed on Turkey by the rapacious appetites of Tsar Alexander. The Treaty of San Stefano is contrary to the interests of European security and must be reviewed at a special congress in which all the great powers will take part.

# About the Author

Boris Akunin is the pen name of Grigory Chkhartishvili, who was born in the republic of Georgia in 1956. A philologist, critic, essayist, and translator of Japanese, Akunin published his first detective stories in 1998 and has already become one of the most widely read authors in Russia. He has written eleven Erast Fandorin novels to date, and is the author of two other series as well. He lives in Moscow.

# About the Translator

Andrew Bromfield was born in Hull in Yorkshire, England, and is the acclaimed translator of the stories and novels of Victor Pelevin. He also translated into English Boris Akunin's first two Erast Fandorin mysteries, **The Winter Queen** and **Murder on the Leviathan**.